MASTER OF MASTERTON

by
Kay Stephens

Dales Large Print Books
Long Preston, North Yorkshire,
England.

British Library Cataloguing in Publication Data.

Stephens, Kay
   Master of Masterton.

   A catalogue record for this book is
   available from the British Library

   ISBN 1-85389-631-4 pbk

First published in Great Britain by William Collins Sons &
Co. Ltd., 1977

Published in Large Print January, 1996 by arrangement with
Doreen Stephens.

Dales Large Print is an imprint of
Library Magna Books Ltd.
Printed and bound in Great Britain by
T.J. Press (Padstow) Ltd., Cornwall, PL28 8RW.

ONE

'Can't take you any nearer, Miss, you'll have to walk the rest.'

The driver of Katherine's hired carriage, stopping outside large iron gates, had alighted then rapped on the window beside her. She frowned, looking towards the great stone house over half a mile away. She'd hoped to impress by being driven up to the door.

'I'll pay you well...' she began.

The man shook his head. '*He* wouldn't like it—Mr Rushton—can't abide strangers inside the park, must be nearly three years since...'

'But you are bringing me,' she protested, 'and there's my trunk and...'

'Old John at the lodge will take care of that, and show you the way, like as not. I'm sorry, Miss, but it's as much as my job's worth.'

Sighing irritably, Katherine took hold of her skirts and stepped down on to the wet road. 'Please be careful with that box,' she directed the coachman, as he unloaded her belongings. Whatever would she do if anything befell that precious machine!

Hearing the door of the nearby lodge open, she turned thankfully. A small woman, grey-haired and smiling, looked out. 'Miss Sutcliffe?' she enquired.

Katherine nodded, returning the smile; the woman seemed so ordinary—dispelling that swiftly aroused foreboding. How foolish she had been, letting the man's words disturb her. She found the necessary coins, and dismissed him.

'If you'll just step inside, Miss Sutcliffe, I'll give my John a call, he'll see to your luggage.'

Katherine lowered her head to go through the small doorway, noticing at once the welcoming fire in the grate, the smell of freshly-baked bread, the sparkle of well-polished brasses.

'This is nice,' she remarked approvingly, when the woman returned to the room. 'So cosy.'

'Thank you, Miss, very kind I'm sure. John won't be long, he's putting your things round the back—safe like, till he's taken you up to the house.'

Katherine had only just thanked her, and

taken the proffered seat, when she heard a door slam and the sound of boots crossing the flagged kitchen. The parlour door burst open. A large, robust, elderly man, with white hair springing out all round his moon of a face, John dusted down his palms either side of grimy trousers, then shyly offered a hand.

'I'm John, ma'am—keeps the lodge for the master, and I look after the grounds and stables—with help, of course, from the village.'

'How do you do, John?' Katherine took the rough hand in her gloved one. He was too much like her own grandfather to be treated as less than an equal.

'Sarah, my wife,' he went on, 'used to keep house for Mr Rushton, till...' Katherine intercepted a covert glance between the two. He shifted uneasily on his feet, '...some while ago. Shall I be showing you the way now?'

Katherine needed no help in finding the house, set as it was on the crest of a hill, visible over the tree-tops of a copse. But she was glad, all the same, to have somebody beside her.

The drive was rough-surfaced; water, from the recent rain, lay in ruts made by carriage wheels. 'Someone must be permitted to ride right up to the house,' she reflected, before realizing that might be only Mr Rushton himself.

John had fallen silent, despite her attempts to make him talk; he seemed on edge—and, outside his own home, less self-assured.

Perhaps this enormous estate, surmounted by the imposing house, inhibited him. Drawing nearer, Katherine found her awe increasing.

Until that afternoon, she had given scarcely a thought to her future employer's residence. She had imagined it vaguely as large, maybe the size of the Rectory near her own home, but nothing—nothing on this scale.

It looked, indeed, from this angle very like a castle—its corner towers, complete with battlements, lending strength to the whole. They appeared ancient, possibly older than the rest of the building.

But a hundred yards from the entrance, Katherine paused to study the impressive façade. Rising to a shaped gable, ornamented by crests, this section was higher than those by which it was flanked, although half a storey lower than the towers. The windows here were mullioned, the double doors of oak would need, she thought, two men to open each of them.

She smiled to herself, wishing her parents could see her embarking on something that augured of even more distinction than she'd intended.

Soon they were mounting the steps and Katherine found she was breathless—regrettably, from a sudden nervousness, rather than exertion.

In answer to the jangling bell, a man-servant opened one of the massive doors. Katherine turned to John, thanking him for escorting her. She saw him redden, as though unused to courtesy; beneath shaggy eyebrows, wary eyes went to the other man's impassive face.

' 'Tis only my job, ma'am,' John demurred hastily, turning on his heel, 'I'll see to that trunk of yours now.'

Katherine followed the disdainful, frock-coated figure into the hall, feeling the chill, despite being enraptured by its beauty. The sun, electing to show a glimmer, caught exquisite linen-fold panelling; a beam going beyond drew her eyes to the first steps of an elegant staircase.

The balustrade was of delicately wrought-iron, above the staircase hung a cut-glass chandelier...

But Katherine was permitted no time to assess or admire her surroundings. Going to high double doors, the man flung them open, awaiting her attention with some impatience. He nodded to her to enter. 'I will tell Mr Rushton of your arrival,' he informed her—with immense dignity.

It was cool, too, in this room; Katherine noticed the fire, recently kindled, trying to establish itself. This was obviously the drawing-room, but was (to her mind) too spacious for true comfort. And yet—the two chairs beside the fire looked inviting; one of them appeared well used, though the other, once its twin, still seemed new. The furnishings were beautiful, with no sign of the slightest need for economy. She smiled, anticipating sharing this luxury; contemplating the effort required on her part to live up to it, her smile faded.

Katherine crossed to sit on the edge of a high-backed, velvet-upholstered chair. Then she took a deep breath, dismissing thoughts of inadequacy, and settled more comfortably.

She was about to prove herself a

woman of some importance. Hadn't she had considerable, intensive training—with tutors justly delighted with her? Wasn't she one of the few women who had mastered the intricacies of that new invention, the typewriter? Hadn't she thus ensured that she'd avoid the alternative—going into service?

She smiled again, finding, and scanning through, her future employer's letter.

> *Masterton Hall,*
> *Near Maidstone,*
> *Kent.*
> *23rd October, 1875*
>
> *Dear Miss Sutcliffe,*
> *You will please present yourself at the above address before four in the afternoon, on Tuesday of next week, for the purpose of commencing your employment as my secretary.*

The signature was a scrawl, but she knew it to be Lawrence Rushton's. And she could scarcely believe, even now, that she was here, in the house of this great writer, about to start working with him.

'Refreshing your memory?' Rapped out from three yards away, the words startled her; Katherine sprang to her feet, dropping gloves, muff, and the letter.

He watched from what seemed a great height, tall and slender as he was, his brown, almost black, eyes noting her discomfiture, while she retrieved her possessions.

'How do you do?' Katherine murmured, her face suffused with a glow as she thrust her things on to a chair, so she might offer him her hand.

He sniffed, made no move to take the hand. She withdrew it slowly. He came nearer then, and she saw that on his right arm there was no hand—it ended somewhere in the folds of his cuff.

'Well?' he demanded.

'I am Katherine Sutcliffe.'

'Of course you are—who else would you be?' The man lowered his eyelids momentarily, then returned to scrutiny of her. 'I sensed you were about to make some comment!'

Katherine forced her eyes to keep away from that incomplete arm, raised them to *his* eyes, and found them challenging. She managed a smile. 'Indeed, sir, I was going to say I am happy to have arrived here.'

'Happy?' His tone was mocking. 'A strange place to seek happiness... Well, since you've come, we'll waste no time over tiresome pleasantries. We work from eight-thirty till six, with half an hour at mid-day for luncheon. Today, however, seeing your arrival has interrupted my concentration, I will return to my desk after dinner; you will please join me in the study at—' he considered for a moment—'eight o'clock.'

Katherine nodded, disconcerted by his insistence on an immediate start. She'd travelled for two days, staying one night with an aunt because of the distance involved. Briefly, she contemplated protesting on account of tiredness, but something in Lawrence Rushton's expression warned he'd not take kindly to opposition.

'Very well, sir.'

'Do I observe a hint of reluctance? You're here to be of use, remember: if you fear you will lack sufficient time to unpack, there are fully three hours before dinner. Unless you have a remarkable collection of clothing and impedimenta for a working woman, that ought to be enough!'

Katherine swallowed back a retort.

The wretched man was still studying her minutely; embarrassed, she longed to tell him to look to his manners. His way of addressing her inferred that he considered

13

her his inferior, but his courtesy was sadly lacking!

'And the machine...?' he enquired, 'this...er...typewriter, you have it safely?'

'At the lodge, Mr Rushton, with the rest of my things. John will attend to them, I believe.'

'Saunders—yes.' He crossed the room briskly, and reached for the bell-pull. 'Mrs Hawkins will show you your room. I'll get Rivers...'

The haughty-expressioned Rivers came in. 'Yes, sir?'

'Mrs Hawkins was in the dining-room, tell her to leave what she is doing and show this...Miss er...'

'Sutcliffe,' Katherine prompted.

Mr Rushton's glance implied she had spoken out of turn, '...to her room,' he finished, then turned his back on them.

Katherine followed Rivers across the hall, and waited, gazing into the dining-room. It was exquisite, dominated by a long mahogany table, with an elegant sideboard in the Regency style, the matching chairs upholstered in gold brocade.

Whatever else, Lawrence Rushton was a man of taste; she would enjoy living in such pleasant surroundings. Her own

14

home (which suddenly seemed very far away) was comfortable and bright, but she'd never before even visited a house of this grandeur.

'This way...' Mrs Hawkins, tall and stately, although too heavily built for pretensions towards beauty, sailed round the door and swept to the staircase. She hesitated not at all for Katherine to gather her skirts in readiness for mounting the stairway. Thus it seemed as if she were some mighty flagship and Katherine an unimportant tug in her wake, chugging uncomfortably to keep up.

The stairs appeared endless, winding as they climbed, and Katherine's hand went to the wrought-iron balustrade for help. They were, too, she observed, beyond the first storey, uncarpeted. After they had reached these bare steps Mrs Hawkins at last led the way along a corridor. Dark and stale-smelling it was, without windows, and illuminated by a single gas mantle.

Disappointment descended on Katherine's spirits, bowing them a little. The door flung open by the housekeeper, revealing a stark little room, was the door opening on to the awful truth of her situation. She looked to Mrs Hawkins, wishing to complain that she was not some menial to be banished to servants' attics—but the woman was regarding her with a sombre pretence of a smile. 'Mr Rushton is sure you will be comfortable here...'

'Comfortable!' Katherine thought, remembering regretfully the beautiful furnishings in the master's rooms. What kind of man was he—so obviously admiring delightful surroundings, yet readily consigning the woman who would work with him to such dreariness?

She sighed when Mrs Hawkins had gone, and went to unfasten her trunk which had been brought to the room. Slowly she went round, setting out her treasured possessions. The silver-backed hairbrush, a gift from her grandmother on her twenty-first birthday, looked strangely incongruous on the old marble wash-stand, its neighbours a chipped jug and basin.

Dressing-table there was none, merely a heavy chest of drawers—peeling paint announcing its mockery of walnut.

Carefully, she laid her undergarments in the drawers—which were, if nothing else, clean and dust-free.

The door of the wardrobe creaked, as though the merest touch would tear it from its hinges, belying its great bulk. A bulk threatening to overwhelm Katherine as well as the room's meagre contents. She steeled herself against weeping as she started hanging dresses in the monstrosity.

This wasn't how she'd pictured her first job—after the meticulous preparation. The setting should have been bright and airy to do justice to the clothes she had brought. Katherine thought wryly of the hours spent with her needle, transforming yards and yards of silks and satins, fine woollens and lace, into the gowns she was now unpacking. Greens and blues vied with pinks and purples, bows with frills, for attention.

What had she imagined...?

Sitting, after the day's work, in the drawing-room—talking intelligently with the man who had chosen her for her skills, and with his wife, and matching their elegance. Mingling with his guests when he was entertaining, as surely he—a successful author—must entertain. Listening while he introduced her as his secretary and as more—one who held the distinction of mastering a most ingenious invention.

Remembering the box and its precious contents, she glanced round, frowning.

And then her face cleared—of course, it would have been taken to Mr Rushton's study.

Katherine looked at the tiny gilded clock which she had set on the chest of drawers, thoughts of the evening ahead reminding her how time was passing. Swiftly, she unpacked the rest of her things, pushing them uncaringly into the available spaces in drawers or wardrobe—since all was so unsightly here, there seemed little point in her normal neatness.

Her task completed, Katherine went at last to the window; small and drably-curtained, it could in no way diminish the magnificence of what it revealed. She gasped delightfully.

Hills rolled gently into the distance, green fields, and brown where the plough-man had been busy; sheep grazing lazily, and a flock of lapwings, wheeling then slowly descending. The evening sky, slashed with blue now the rain clouds were vanishing, sat on far, purple-hazed hills; and somewhere in the middle distance through misty trees, russet in their autumnal beauty, was a glimpse of a lake. In the mist surrounding the lake something moved, startling her; there it was again—a pale brown shape, and another. Deer. She looked more intently and spotted several among the trees.

Katherine smiled and turned from the window. So there would be an escape, she could walk as far as the lake; wander, maybe, through the copse just below the house, get away from the harsh reality of this abominable cell.

She breathed deeply; it would take more than this slight on her position here to crush her. Having summoned courage to come, she must show Lawrence Rushton she was no mere girl to be deterred by his treatment; and she'd begin right now. The gown she'd worn for travelling was crumpled, its hem mud-bespattered; she would change before dinner, then, she hoped, make those incredibly hard eyes widen, those forbidding brows arch towards his hair. She may never have had a superfluity of money, but she'd learned to use what there was to some effect, and had no false modesty about her prowess as a needlewoman.

Katherine selected emerald green—in fine wool, because of the ominous chill of the place. She had to steady her fingers, fastening the tiny buttons of her bodice, and her reflection showed apprehensive eyes. They were arresting, though—she was aware they frequently drew glances. Green, they gazed back from the old, tarnished mirror, and she practised lowering their dark lashes. 'My one good feature,' she thought; 'if only I were a beauty, that arrogant master of the house might take more account of me.'

But where was the use of wishing and hoping? She'd spent long hours perfecting her skill with the typewriter, to secure a position above the commonplace—would she permit misgivings about her appearance to ruin that already?

No...she must, instead, concentrate on concealing that everything since her arrival had conspired to destroy her happiness, her self-assurance.

Forcing a confident smile, Katherine went along that dreary corridor to descend the stairs. Once her feet touched carpet, her step was lighter—more positive. Behind her she'd left all suggestion of poverty, bordering on squalor—that must symbolize her attitude here. Away from that room, she would be a woman of some consequence— her bright, alert, self—Lawrence Rushton's equal. She must, somehow, achieve that.

20

Outside the dining-room door she paused, took a deep breath before reaching for the handle. She raised her chin, smiling, sure she was looking poised, composed, the perfect companion. What was there, after all, to scare her?

He was sitting, alone, at the farthest end of the long table. A book was propped against a crystal decanter and, frowning, he glanced from it and stopped eating.

'Yes?' He appeared astonished to see her.

'It is time for dinner?' she began.

Lawrence Rushton's lip curled unpleasantly. 'You seem to have missed your way—ring the bell, Rivers will show you where to go...' He returned to his book.

Katherine blinked, 'You mean...?'

He glanced up again, impatiently: 'Well, go along then...'

Ignoring his suggestion to summon Rivers, she made for the door; as it closed behind her she discovered she was trembling. He must never learn, she vowed, how easily he had reduced her almost to tears, making her feel small...and unwanted.

Following the aroma of cooking, finding the kitchen was simple enough, but how

Katherine hated having to enter! Mrs Hawkins presided over the table—one side being occupied by several girls, whom Katherine took to be maids and domestics.

A young man, whose apparel proclaimed him the coachman, sat opposite, with a girl in a dark dress next to him. Rivers was supervising another maid as she prepared a silver tray at a side table.

'Good evening,' Katherine greeted them. Nobody answered. Mrs Hawkins nodded, reluctantly, pointing to a vacant seat beside the coachman.

He alone spoke to her during the meal, confirming her guess as to his occupation. Introductions, it seemed, were not the order of the day and, aware that they would all know who she was, Katherine felt at a disadvantage. She was also somewhat out of her element, and not at all sure how best to rise above the situation. She chose silence as her ally in regaining her composure, her doubts about the wisdom of coming here increasing.

A little before eight o'clock she rose to her feet.

'What about Grace?' Mrs Hawkins demanded. 'Aren't you accustomed to it?'

Katherine apologized, explaining she

believed Mr Rushton would be awaiting her, then stood, head bowed, while Rivers rectified the omission.

★ ★ ★ ★

Crossing the hall she met Lawrence Rushton and was at once on guard, following their unfortunate encounter. He appeared, however, disposed to be courteous.

'Ah, you're punctual. This way...'

He held open the study door so she might precede him. Her eyes went immediately to the typewriter, set on a heavy desk, and she crossed to it.

'Your precious toy!' Mr Rushton exclaimed, and she observed a hint of amusement in his eyes.

'It's not a plaything!' she retorted, and was surprised to hear him laugh before coming towards her.

'Of course not—vital equipment!'

Despite her instinctive dislike for the man, she could not avoid noticing the magnetism of him, whilst standing thus close to her. She saw how slender his fingers were as his left hand struck the keys.

23

He sighed, after a moment's dallying, 'Vital, indeed—for me, indispensable.'

She realized then the importance of her role; how otherwise could an author with no right hand pursue his career?

'Well, to work now...' Without further delay, he seated himself behind a grand desk facing her own. 'Are you acquainted with my books?'

Katherine avoided his gaze; there hadn't been time, not with so many things to prepare.

'I see—not sufficiently interested!'

'I was busy.' For some reason she did not wish him to sound so harsh.

'Of course.' He cut her short, then went to one of the many bookshelves. Selecting a volume, he gave it to her.

'Read that at your leisure. Meanwhile, we must begin—it's long enough since I touched this. Some of my work is for the journals; they accept that my "copper plate" is no longer all it should be...' His voice had dropped, was showing the first genuine emotion since Katherine's arrival. 'It's slow, Miss Sutcliffe, too damned slow for my liking. There's no flow—the words seem halting by the time I've...' He stopped, seemed to collect himself.

24

'A novel, this is; I've been examining my notes again, knowing you were coming. How quick are you, Miss Sutcliffe, can you take down the work from my reading of it?'

'I can try.' Katherine smiled at him, warming to his frankness about the disability.

Starting to read, his voice took on a different tone, caring, concerned, loving the phrases.

Katherine concentrated on the actual words, rather than their meaning, until accustomed to his methods. Once familiar with transcribing it on to the paper in her machine, though, its spell captured her. Out of nowhere, or so it seemed, into the quiet room, came beauty and understanding—even humour. From this cool, enigmatic man people were emerging —people he loved, whom she might love, good people, bad, weak and strong and all of them real human beings.

Around them scenes sprang up, vibrant with colour; bustling streets, enveloping homes, wide stretches of magnificent countryside. This man could see it all, was making her see it. He had all the imagination of Katherine's favourite,

Charlotte Brontë, yet less of her gloom. Carried along by a tide of wonder, she worked on, enraptured, fingers flashing over the keys.

The grandfather clock in the hall chimed ten, and Lawrence Rushton's laugh startled her.

'I thought earlier it'd be interesting noting your reaction; a novelist rarely experiences, face to face, the honest estimation of his labours. Friends flatter... But you, Miss Sutcliffe—I rate your absorption with this book higher than flattery...' He paused, she felt his eyes questioning her. 'Or were you reducing it to words, letters, mere tools of the trade?'

'How could I?' Her shining eyes were raised slowly from the paper, to meet his, in something close to admiration.

He smiled across at her, all cynicism, at last, missing.

'You, I believe, will work well for me. I find I'm actually looking forward to continuing.'

★ ★ ★ ★

Getting into bed half an hour later in

26

that cold little room at the top of the house, Katherine's thoughts were muddled beyond her comprehension. This strange man who was her employer had, after only minutes in his home, antagonized her past belief, increasing that by his subsequent behaviour in the dining-room—only to later reveal an aspect which she could only find endearing. She had wanted to hate him for his indifferent reception of her, for banishing her to this attic room and the servants' quarters, but now she could feel no hate for him. She had determined to dismiss him as wholly bad, inconsiderate, a boor of a man; but someone who wrote as he wrote, who felt as he must feel—for people, could not be so. And in his honesty about the deprivation of the missing hand, her heart had gone out to him, as to any wounded creature.

Perplexed, disturbed from confidence in her opinion, it was hours before Katherine slept.

In the night she wakened, suddenly, hearing a scream followed by sobbing. The crying continued—from the room beneath her own, she thought—precluding sleep until she decided something or somebody must stop it.

Sighing, Katherine got out of bed, lit the candle, shivered, and slipped a robe over her nightgown. Somebody in this great house was alone and afraid, and nobody cared—but she would not let that continue. The crying sounded like a child's, making urgency imperative. She recalled her sister Clare's nightmares and how, sharing a room as they had, the younger child had clung to her for comfort. Katherine could not bear to think of anyone awakening thus disturbed.

The house creaked eerily when she stepped on to the landing, as if it too were uneasy and restless. It was no difficult task to follow down the stairs and locate the room which must be beneath her own. At the door she hesitated, listening; still the sobbing went on.

Katherine eased the door open, her candle softly illuminating the area immediately inside the door. The bed, curtained with velvet draperies, stood several feet away. She crept towards it, and drew aside the velvet. Dark eyes, startlingly familiar, regarded her warily from beneath wet lashes. Near-black hair clung damply to the pale forehead—a forehead also familiar, the miniature of one she'd studied but a few hours ago.

Katherine smiled, 'Hallo—what's your name?'

'Simon Rushton.'

'And you wakened in the night, alone...'

He nodded. 'I was dreaming. I'm frightened. Where's Janet? Who are you... why isn't she here?'

The face crumpled, tears threatening again. Katherine sat on the edge of the bed, gathered the small body to her.

'I'm Katherine—but you may call me Katy. Who's Janet?'

'Nanny, of course, only Father won't let her sleep in the next room any more. He says I'm not to behave like a silly infant.'

Katherine could imagine Lawrence Rushton's hard voice saying that! The man hadn't a morsel of tenderness.

In the night stillness she remembered the book he was writing, his insight into its characters, his sympathy towards them. She hugged the child closer. Why had this man feeling only for the people his pen created? Why was he so unyielding towards those he encountered daily—towards this child, one person who surely needed his affection and understanding?

She stroked the soft, dark hair, but the child wriggled, trying to free himself.

'You may go away. I only want Janet.'

'But are you going to sleep now, like a good boy...?'

A wail set up, Simon thrashing his arms wildly, trying to be rid of her. 'Janet!' the boy yelled, 'I want you, Janet!'

Slippered feet came running towards the room, a young woman burst through the door. 'Master Simon, what is all this nonsense?'

She stopped on seeing Katherine. It was the girl who had been sitting beside the coachman in the kitchen.

'Did Simon disturb you?' she asked, seeming embarrassed.

Katherine smiled, nodding. 'I had to discover what was wrong.' She crossed towards the door.

At the bed, Janet was rocking the boy in her arms. Her eyes met Katherine's over his head. 'Poor mite—no wonder he has nightmares in this place, with the likes of the master for a...'

Katherine glanced pointedly at Simon, who couldn't avoid hearing this criticism of his parent. Janet nodded, sighing. 'Best

30

keep quiet, you're right—but my heart aches for the child, it does really.'

Since she could fulfil no useful purpose there, Katherine returned to her room; but not to sleep. Having spoken with Simon, she was convinced that the scream she had heard before the sobbing was an adult's. And what manner of man was Lawrence Rushton to deny his son the comfort of a nurse at hand, when the little boy was prone to waking scared of everything?

★ ★ ★ ★

Katherine's perplexity increased daily, for she saw nothing further of Simon—and there was no sign of Mrs Rushton. Without a mistress of the house in evidence, how could she, a single young woman, remain here? In accepting the position, she had imagined Lawrence Rushton married, and yet some aloofness about him suggested anything but a family man. And he dined, didn't he, in splendid isolation?

On Saturday morning, Katherine rose early and, since Mr Rushton intended working without her help on an essay for a London journal, she decided to explore the park.

She headed towards the lake, enjoying the sunshine now tempering the autumn chill and rejoicing in her newly-acquired walking skirt for, hitched up on cords as it was, it afforded so much freedom.

Reared in the picturesque Yorkshire Dales, Katherine was happy to find herself in beautiful countryside. She had known little about Kent before making her home in this mansion and was surprised to find it, not flat as she'd been led to believe, but enhanced by hills. These were less awe-inspiring than her Northern ones, agreed—but they were hills nevertheless.

As for the lake, which she was now nearing, it was but small in comparison with the tarn beyond her own home, but still attractive.

The deer she'd noticed from the window that first day aroused her interest most of all; previously she had seen them only in paintings.

Silently, she stole through the trees, trying to get closer to them. She was nearing a placid fawn with its attendant doe when, a peal of laughter startling them, the pair darted away.

'Oh, they've gone!' Katherine exclaimed,

as Janet, with Simon, came towards her. 'You've scared them!' But she smiled to see the boy's happy face.

Simon laughed again, seeming—away from the house—a different child. 'They won't go right away, they'll come back,' he told her. 'They belong to Father.'

'Does everything here belong to your father?' Katherine asked, going down on her knees beside him.

Janet laughed, answering for him, 'Every blade of grass, every stick, stone...you, me...'

Katherine frowned. 'Is that what you really think?'

She shrugged. 'Does that worry you? Being owned by him—or near enough?'

'But I am not,' Katherine asserted. 'I am in possession of myself—my own mistress.'

'He pays your wages, doesn't he? And well for the 1870's.'

'That's as may be, but I am not tied to him.'

'You're fortunate.' Janet paused, wistfully. 'Have you folks of your own then?'

'In Yorkshire—my mother and father, and a sister.'

'There's the difference—I've nobody. It'd have been the workhouse for me, if I hadn't picked up a few things about being a nanny.'

Katherine felt sudden compassion for the girl. She hid her problems behind a cheerful face, and obviously had great affection for her young charge.

Katherine touched the other woman's arm. 'But you've made friends here...'

'What—with that lot? The servants in some of these places think they're a cut above their masters!'

Katherine smiled. 'Oh—I thought they just resented me!'

Janet laughed. 'They give everyone that treatment when they arrive—and later on, if you don't sweeten them up.'

'And do you—sweeten them up?'

Janet shook her head. 'Me—no. So long as Mr Rushton fills my purse when he should that's all I care—and for that young master...' She nodded to Simon romping in the grass and suddenly darted off in chase of him.

The boy's delighted laughter rang out, and as Janet ran this way and that, over the springy turf, Katherine envied them. Her life here promised to be staid, to a degree; it would be good to share the fun of a lively child's company.

'Come...' Janet called. 'He'll love it with another one...'

They ran and laughed, dodging between the trees, till Simon himself called a halt by falling breathless to the damp ground.

Janet scooped him up. 'Come along—time for your milk, young sir.' She turned to Katherine and smiled. 'See you at the kitchen table, this evening...' She hesitated. 'Tell you what—if you've a mind, come to my room this afternoon. It's the last one past Simon's. We could sit and talk, get to know one another.'

Katherine agreed, thinking she would need some friend in this hostile household.

Deep in consideration of the girl's suggestion, still glowing from the exercise, she continued across the park. Turning aside from the lake, she struck out for a church that nestled amid a cluster of trees.

Absorbed as she was, Katherine didn't hear the sound of hooves until the horse was almost upon her. She swung round, about to admonish whoever was riding with so little regard for her safety.

Sitting high in the saddle, Lawrence Rushton seemed a slender giant as he reined in his mare and laughed down at her.

'I've frightened you!' He sounded triumphant.

'You need not appear pleased: you gave me quite a turn, sir!'

He laughed again. 'Madam, your sparkling eyes and flushed cheeks belie your professed alarm—and, indeed, become you!'

Surprised by his compliment, Katherine put a hand to cheeks that were now more flushed than they had been.

Her employer smiled, leaning from his horse to say quietly, 'And besides I was fully aware of you—would I harm the woman who is so useful to me?' His eyes sought hers, half-mocking, half-serious. 'Now tell me—what occasioned that glow of colour—the breathless vitality that's so bewitching?'

'Playing with your son.'

He frowned. 'My...?'

'Simon.' She smiled up at him. 'He's an enchanting child.'

He sniffed. 'Enchantment is dangerous!' he flung over his shoulder, turning his steed and riding off without a backward glance.

Katherine, bewildered by her employer's extraordinary reaction to her intended compliment, stared after him until he'd galloped into the distance, towards the rear of the house.

She continued to the tiny church, and pushed open its oaken door. Cold and ugly, the building's one redeeming feature was a beautifully carved choir screen; a plaque told her this screen had been donated by Lawrence Rushton, in memory of his father.

She smiled, pleased by this hint of affection in him, and of this proof of this patronage of the church. Maybe he wasn't, after all, so self-contained as he appeared.

It was almost time for luncheon now and so Katherine walked back to the mansion.

Crossing the hall, she encountered Lawrence Rushton, still dressed for riding, coming through a side door.

'Enjoyed your walk,' he enquired, 'despite its hazards?'

Katherine smiled, thankful he was inclined to be pleasant.

'Thank you, yes—very much. I stopped to see the church but couldn't find a notice board. At what time does the household attend morning service?'

He seemed to pale, and scowled. 'Eleven o'clock is the time, I believe, Miss Sutcliffe,' he replied, his voice cool. 'You're at liberty to go, of course, but you will never find me there.' Once more he turned from her, leaving her to gaze after him.

* * * *

Janet was always absent from the somewhat frugal mid-day meal in the kitchen, taking luncheon and tea in the nursery with Master Simon. Katherine almost envied her. The boy would chatter on, she was sure, while here the servants still took pains to avoid conversation.

The meal over, she went to her room and sat at the window. This was becoming her favourite place indoors; looking out over this part of the Weald, she could ignore the drab box of a room allocated to her.

At two-thirty she made her way to the next floor, deciding to see Janet that afternoon while Simon was resting. She knocked on Janet's door, but there was no response so she waited and knocked again. About to move away, Katherine heard voices coming up the stairs. Mr Rushton's was one of them, and he was patently very angry. The other was Janet's, sounding close to tears.

Katherine had no wish to remain as witness to an embarrassing scene; she glanced round for an escape, noticing another door to her right at the end of the corridor.

The handle turned, though with difficulty, as if unused for some long time. But the room afforded her sanctuary and in a flurry of skirts, Katherine hastened inside.

Looking about her, she took a quick, astonished breath. She stood in a gallery some sixty feet long. Its sparse furniture stood shrouded in dust sheets, and cobwebs hung from ceiling and curtains. On opposite walls hung oil paintings, landscapes and portraits. With mounting interest, she progressed from one picture to the next. Some landscapes she recognized as being of the park or surrounding countryside; one showed the front of the house as it must have appeared some years ago, for she observed certain changes. The next puzzled her; again it was of the house but painted from another angle—possibly from the rear. It revealed even more spaciousness than she had imagined. Reflecting on the undoubted wealth necessary to maintain such an edifice, Katherine frowned wonderingly.

Many of the portraits looked antiquated and proved to be dated during the last and the preceding century. She was intrigued; knowing little of Mr Rushton's family, she would like to learn something of his antecedents.

Katherine explored, working her way first along one wall and then returning to scrutinize the pictures along the other.

Nearing the door, there were several blank spaces. The wallcovering showed darker where frames had been removed. She hesitated, wondering why, till her attention was captured by another portrait. It showed a seated woman, young, of most pleasing countenance, with a man standing at her side. He was unmistakable, without the inscription at the base of the frame, its date revealing the portrait as being four years old. Lawrence Rushton's eyes were as today, dark, brilliant, challenging; also the forehead, high, proclaiming the knowledge and wisdom stored within—only then it appeared to have been unfurrowed.

The head was neat, the dark hair rather longer than at present, the face without the current whiskers. But how the mouth differed! Katherine narrowed her eyes and stared afresh. The lips, here, curved into a slight smile, generous; not the taut, thin, line she knew—tightly clamped till they sprang apart to spit out cruel phrases.

She sighed; he was handsome, more handsome than she'd realized—maybe the present hardness of the mouth detracted from the splendour of his features.

Her eyes strayed again to the woman, noting the coffee-coloured lace of her gown, the low décolletée revealing neck and bosom in so lifelike a manner one could almost imagine its rise and fall in breathing. Katherine's eyes travelled to the face, framed by corn-coloured curls. A lovely face—high cheek-boned, with enormous blue eyes and the prettiest mouth, which seemed strangely familiar. But, of course, it was Simon's mouth. What a handsome couple they made...

Katherine mused on the curious way she had neither seen, nor heard mention of, the mistress of the house, and as she stepped back for another view of the portrait, something caught her attention.

41

Lawrence Rushton rested one hand on his wife's shoulder, and the other at his side.

Saddened, Katherine again studied his face; perhaps his terrible injury had changed the set of his mouth. This could be the reason why his lips curled no longer in humour, but in...?

'You should close the door behind you if you wish to remain undetected!'

The voice at her elbow startled her and set her heart thumping. She did not need to turn to identify the speaker.

'Prying, Miss Sutcliffe?'

She turned now, to look into those dark, demanding eyes, and trembled before them.

'I was...interested,' she responded.

A half-smile played on his mouth, fleetingly, and vanished.

Katherine looked once more at the picture. 'Your wife is very beautiful.'

'Wife? I have no wife.'

Confused, she glanced at him again. The dark brows were drawn together, lines etched from nose to turned-down mouth. At a loss for words, she swallowed, opened her mouth to speak, and closed it again.

Lawrence Rushton turned towards the

door. 'Rivers must attend to the lock. I will not have this door open.'

'That would be very wise, Mr Rushton. There must be great value in these paintings,' Katherine said carefully, as they moved into the corridor.

She glanced up in time to see his eyes return to the woman in the portrait, then he closed the door silently and stood looking down at her. 'For me, Miss Sutcliffe, nothing in there holds the slightest value!'

TWO

'He's so hard, Katherine, you wouldn't believe how hard, with his son,' Janet began, her grey eyes ablaze with hatred. 'Simon's not wicked, he's a little angel compared to some I've known, but the way Mr Rushton treats him!'

Katherine forced her attention on to what the other girl was saying, as they sat either side of the window in Janet's room.

'He rarely visits the nursery, but when he

does...my, there's always a regular squall! This time Master Simon had left a tiny piece of cabbage, that was all, only such a bit...'

'Children must be made to eat properly,' Katherine heard herself say in defence of this man who, she was sure, needed no one's words in his defence.

Janet would have none of it, anyway. 'I had to say something, couldn't keep the words back, with little Simon shaking and quivering before the father he adores so. Told Mr Rushton straight I did—how I thought he was being too firm with the little fellow.' She smiled ruefully. 'He turned on me then—rather have that, I would; he don't scare me, Mr High-and-Mighty Rushton.'

Katherine wished she had Janet's assurance: she was positive that in many ways and for some long while, Mr Rushton would continue to scare *her.* Except...well, there had been moments, brief ones admittedly, when he was the one who had seemed afraid.

'Maybe there's a reason for his behaviour,' Katherine suggested, wanting to be fair in her appraisal of him, reluctant to believe all that Janet was saying, and

44

surprised by this reluctance.

The other girl snorted. 'What, when he makes poor Simon stay in two rooms, in a great house the like of this! As if he can't bear to set eyes on the boy. Now tell me that's not harsh, and him his own father!'

Katherine sighed; Lawrence Rushton did, indeed, appear unduly unkind—but she'd no wish to dwell on that. And so much had mystified her since the arrival, she felt impelled to learn more from Janet.

Choosing her words carefully, she began, 'I haven't seen Mr Rushton's wife about thc house; is she away? Does Simon never see her?'

Head on one side, Janet considered Katherine pityingly before saying, 'You mean you don't know there's some...secret about her?'

'No—tell me...'

'It's only what George—the coachman, you know—says. It seems the master will not have her name mentioned, nobody knows why, or if they do they're not saying. Like you, I was curious when I first came here, and began asking. None of the others have seen her—unless it's

45

Mr Rivers—he's been here a long time. Mrs Hawkins shut up, tight as a drum, when I asked her; told me to mind my own business. I think she knows more than she's prepared to tell though, and I believe old John...do you know John...?'

'At the lodge?'

Janet nodded. 'I suspect he knows the whole story, but he's afraid of losing his job, and his home; he won't talk—ever.'

Katherine made a mental note to discover if, with her, John would prove equally uncommunicative.

'What do you suppose then?' Katherine asked. 'Has Mrs Rushton left him—run off with someone else, maybe?'

'If you ask me,' Janet replied, her voice hushed, 'he's got her locked away.'

'Here?'

'He comes close to that with young Master Simon! And there's this room that's never opened—in the West tower. Isobel and the other maids swear it's haunted, but it was voices I heard. And I saw a woman in grey, in the attic corridor. It was when I asked Mrs Hawkins about her they moved me down to this room, told me not to be so curious.'

Janet's suspicions made Katherine even

more uneasy, and this disturbed her. But why should it? It didn't affect her employer's treatment of her in any way—and if some mystery surrounded his matrimonial state that was scarcely her concern.

Next morning in church, Katherine found her eyes focused on that beautifully-carved screen during most of the service—a service which she found uninspiring and the sermon long and unspeakably tedious. The handsome columns of timber, surmounted by a life-size crucifix, however, seemed to have some messages for her...

It was as though they were set there to remind her that, despite what people said, and despite his perplexing temperament, there was another, more appealing, side to Lawrence Rushton.

Glad to be out in the air after the dank building, Katherine walked towards the house, recalling the pictures she had seen in the long gallery. From this direction it appeared larger than she'd first thought, and what she'd taken for the rear of the house in one of the paintings had been this East side. Thus its construction was unusual, the great main doors being set at one end of the building.

It was not yet mid-day, so, coming closer, Katherine allowed curiosity to lead her on to the terrace adjoining the East Wall.

A wind swept across the rolling parkland from the north, buffeting her, and she drew her cloak more tightly around her. Footsteps ringing on the hard ground, she walked quickly, pausing only now and again to glance up at the high, arched windows to her left. There was nothing very extraordinary about them—nor, she was thinking, about the house itself...

She lowered her head, briefly, against a particularly strong gust of wind.

When she raised it, looking sideways again, she gasped.

The building here was but a shell—its windows, devoid of glass, stone outlines of their former beauty. Katherine tiptoed across the grass towards the wall to peer inside. This part of the house was open to the sky, with nothing separating the storeys. She saw a crumbling fireplace and a door, hanging half off its hinges.

The floor was made up of slabs of stone, covered with dust and bird droppings. Something scurried into a corner: she shuddered, imagining mice...even a rat.

The place fascinated her, nonetheless, and trying to see farther over to the right where this empty room gave on to another, she turned slightly.

Too late, she heard the thud of hooves, then a horse's breath behind her—as Lawrence Rushton halted his mount.

'Miss Sutcliffe!'

Katherine swung round to meet his gaze, poised for flight should he admonish her. Slowly he dismounted, checked that the mare would nibble the grass contentedly, patted the animal's side, then ambled towards Katherine. His eyes glinted with a touch of humour.

'And who but you, my dear young lady, would be so inquisitive?'

She met his eyes once more, unflinchingly now, encouraged by the sudden warmth enlivening them. Her mouth twitched but she stilled the smile. 'Would you, sir, with your trained, inquisitive mind, which notes every detail, storing it for possible use in your novels—would you, with your interest in people and their surroundings, deny me my piece of curiosity?'

He opened his mouth to speak, then

closed it, seeming nonplussed. He scrutinized her, through half-closed lids, as though narrowing his gaze to direct it the more keenly. And then, astonishing her, threw back his head and roared with laughter.

'You're a piece of curiosity yourself! With a clever tongue, Miss Sutcliffe, and courage to use it. You and I will have a new respect for each other...' He paused, smiling still. 'I admire your spirit—how sick I am of mumbling, fearful women! Only remember, my Kate, that *my* curiosity is professional.'

'And do you think mine couldn't be, sir?' she went on, her colour rising as she observed how easily he'd used her Christian name. 'Do you then reserve for yourself the right to express every observation in words...?'

Lawrence Rushton was clearly taken aback by her claim to similar literary aspirations, as—so she might confess—was Katherine herself. She knew not what demon had prompted her to pretend this interest. But he was the very man to ensure she did not evade it.

'Prove it then,' he challenged, eyes lighting with the thrill of battle. 'I'll give you a month to place your manuscript on my desk, then I will believe you!'

Katherine was on the point of admitting that she'd been teasing, that she really had no such intention, when it occurred to her that this could serve her well. If, just supposing...*if* she succeeded in putting pen to paper in a manner to attract his attention, he might see her anew. It could make him cease treating her like one of the servants.

She took a deep breath and nodded. 'I will do my best, sir—just as I intend always to try and please you...'

Lawrence Rushton shook his head, eyes mocking. 'That's the wrong answer, Miss Kate—altogether too demure and submissive...!'

With that, he remounted and was gone, leaving Katherine feeling bereft, as if she would have lingered with him, while he was being so provocative, so...human.

With a sigh she went indoors and tidied her windswept hair, then went reluctantly to the kitchen.

Stimulated by the encounter with her employer, she was more than ever irked by the uncommunicative company in the servants' quarters.

That evening Katherine wandered rest-lessly round her tiny room, read a few chapters of her bible, wishing Sunday didn't preclude anything livelier. She longed to be stirred, as she had when Lawrence Rushton's mind confronted hers. Reading these well-worn, though dearly-loved words, wasn't now a sufficient palliative.

She went to the volume loaned by Mr Rushton, and as yet unread. 'Tomorrow,' she promised herself, 'tomorrow I will begin that.'

But there was no time until late evening, when the candlelight tried her eyes. Unsatisfied after only a few pages, she had to lay aside the book. It had been a difficult day. All trace of humour vanished, Mr Rushton had made her work, and that unceasingly. And, much as she loved his words, flowing through her machine on to the paper, there was never time to dwell on them. Noting a sentence here, a phrase there, was no way to appreciate his undoubted talent. Katherine had, indeed, once bade him stop. Thus arrested in mid-sentence, he'd regarded her coldly.

'Is something wrong then?' he'd de-manded.

Smiling slightly, she'd replied, 'Only that I want to savour this phrase,' and had expected him to be flattered.

'Savour,' he'd grunted. 'What next! You are here, Miss Sutcliffe, not for your enjoyment, but to achieve the work I require of you!'

She smiled ruefully now, remembering. From one moment to the next she was never sure if he'd be some great bear, making her tremble—or the man with smiling eyes, calling her his Kate, for all the world as though he'd known her for years.

At odd minutes, during that week, Katherine reflected on the absent Mrs Rushton, on the closed gallery, on the ruined East wing, wondering how they all fitted into the picture of life there. Were they linked—or was each a separate mystery? And was any one of them to be unravelled? Given her way, she wouldn't delay finding the solution. Who to ask was the problem—if, as Janet said, the staff were so unforthcoming.

It was strange, too, that most of the servants had been employed here for only two years or so. It seemed Mr Rushton had rid himself of the entire staff in one fell swoop—had that been an attempt to conceal something...? Whatever his reason, it made extracting an answer more difficult. The gallery appeared to have been neglected for at least that length of time, and the ruins left to crumble for a similar period.

Katherine decided John and Sarah Saunders were the people to approach; certainly one could not contemplate questioning the unbending Rivers.

Visiting the lodge must be deferred until the week-end; the daylight failed long before she'd had her evening meal each day, she could not walk through the park in darkness. And from finishing breakfast of a morning, Lawrence Rushton claimed her every second.

She was happy, though, in his study; shut off from the rest of the world, sharing his creative mind—his world. Katherine acknowledged that whatever she might think of him the rest of the time, whilst they were working together he had her admiration.

One evening, coming away from dinner, Janet drew Katherine aside in the hall.

'How are you spending this evening?'

Katherine shrugged. 'Reading for a while, and then...well, nothing important—why?'

'So the master doesn't expect you to keep him company?'

Katherine laughed at the notion. 'Indeed not, I'm sure he is convinced I'm not a fit companion for him!'

'I see.' Janet appeared thoughtful.

'What, Janet?'

'It was only—well, we did notice the time you spend with him, behind closed doors...'

'He's a busy man, and enjoys working—I help him.'

Janet shrugged, rather awkwardly. 'Oh, well—you know how people talk...'

Katherine smiled. 'I'm learning!'

Janet hesitated. 'I wonder if I dare ask you now, about tonight, it's a favour, really...'

'Yes?'

The girl's voice dropped to a whisper. 'George and I are...walking out. We don't get much time to ourselves and I wondered... You see, he's got permission to use the brougham and go into Maidstone to visit his mother, and he wanted to take me, only...'

'Somebody must remain here for Master Simon.'

She nodded. 'I know it's my job, but he hardly ever wakens, and I'd make it up to you...pay you...'

'Nonsense,' Katherine insisted. 'If you and George are walking out you must start saving. I don't want payment, I'll sit with the boy gladly.'

'Oh, not sit with him—just be in my room—in case he calls out, you'll hear him.'

Remembering Simon's cries the other night, Katherine could believe that.

Taking the book Lawrence had entrusted to her, she went along to Janet's room and settled to while away the hours. Larger than her own, the room was more comfortable and—more important to Katherine—lit by a gas mantle. At almost nine-thirty her reading was interrupted by a high-pitched scream—not from Simon's room, but some distant corner of the house. Silence followed, and heart-beats steadying, Katherine returned to her book, from then Simon's lusty voice disturbed her. She hurried to his room.

'Katy!' he exclaimed, when she drew aside the velvet bed-hangings, and her heart warmed to his pleasure.

'Where is Janet?' he asked.

'I've come instead—will I do?'

The child held his head on one side, his eyes—so like his father's—weighing her, then nodded, grinning. 'Tell me a story...'

Perplexed, Katherine searched for something to amuse him, but recollected only one thing, her own childhood. She began narrating how a little girl was born in a farm worker's cottage far away in the Yorkshire Dales. She related the fun of playing with the animals, of watching her father milk the cows, or feed their one goat—of riding atop the big shire-horse when he was ploughing. The boy listened, fascinated by this way of life so unlike his own, until eyelids lowered on softly-rounded cheeks and he turned over, rolling into a ball, his breathing slow and even.

Katherine smiled, looking down at the sleeping boy before leaving him. Then, with a stab of pain, wondered how any man could treat him harshly. A great sadness came over her—and she realized joltingly, it was not solely for the boy, but for the man who had thus shut himself off from tenderness.

She had been back in Janet's room but half an hour when the girl returned, and Katherine prepared to leave. They talked for a few minutes, just inside the door, then Katherine bade Janet good night, and picked up her candle.

Something metallic, shining in the gloomy corridor, caught her eye. Holding the candle aloft, she glanced round. It was a bunch of keys, hanging from the lock of the gallery door.

Katherine felt impelled to re-examine the portrait of her employer and the wife whose existence he denied. Silently, she opened the door and, seeing no light proclaimed another's presence, advanced a few steps into the gallery. In candlelight, Lawrence Rushton's face softened further, smiling out from the picture. Turning to his lady, Katherine herself smiled, noting anew the likeness to that child of whom she was growing fond.

A breeze along the gallery disturbed the curtains, fluttered the ghostly dust-covers and, from a shrouded table, whisked a sheet of paper, dancing it in the draught along the floor. Katherine retrieved it, feeling its dustiness on her fingers. The wind blew again the length of the gallery and she guessed that a door was ajar at the far end in the shadows. She hurried lightly towards it, seeing a curtain partly obscuring a half-open door. She put out a hand...

'Katherine!'

The voice, echoing round the gallery, startled her beyond all reason. She grasped the door handle, and was about to escape to whatever was on the other side.

'For God's sake—I forbid you to open that door!'

But it was yielding already, in seconds she would be through it and away—away from that commanding voice, from this high-handed, dictatorial man, who resented any exploration of his property.

A hand descended on her left shoulder, the nails digging in, an arm—yes, without its hand—found her waist.

'Now will you obey me!'

He held her till her struggling ceased, then a foot came round her skirts, kicking the door to. Still he did not release her, but held her to him. Katherine felt his breath, quick and sharp, stirring the hair on top of her head.

'Leave me be!' she cried. 'Why arc you so afraid that I might see anything of your precious, unfriendly mansion?'

He let her go at that, but only to catch her hand in his, to draw her close to his side.

'Open the door then,' he ordered, 'let us satisfy your overworked curiosity.'

She raised questioning eyes to Lawrence Rushton's—so black and anxious in the candelight. He nodded. 'Yes, Kate, open it...'

The door creaked as she swung it open. She moved forward but the hand on hers tightened, restraining her. 'Raise your candle then,' he ordered, 'so you can take in every detail...'

Before it fluttered and died in the draught, the flame revealed a void—bare walls, space where her feet would have trod; bats swooping in and out through empty window-frames and, in place of a ceiling, clouds scudding across the moon.

Katherine shuddered and swayed; she would have fallen if strong arms had not held her.

'How could I lose you,' he murmured into her hair, crushing her against him, 'and you only recently come to me?'

He led her to sit on one of the chairs, briefly letting her go to whisk the cover from it. He busied himself with the gas light on the wall above their heads, then spoke once more.

'After all, you're proving useful.'

Katherine looked up at him—recovering from the shock of a fall that so easily might *not* have been averted and receiving now a new shock—finding concern in those normally cold eyes. There was something else there, it appeared almost like...apprehension.

Lawrence Rushton smiled, then sighed deeply, running a hand through his hair. He laughed a little. 'How you scared me!'

Katherine closed her eyes against threatening tears. 'How do I ever begin to thank you?' she asked in a whisper. Then glanced up, astonished, at hearing him chuckle.

Mischief now lit those dark eyes, the very last thing she would have anticipated. 'Are you not afraid then, that I—with my fertile imagination, might think of a way?' he demanded.

Katherine was forced to smile, this was so unlike him.

'You're not alarmed?' he mocked. 'Don't I frighten you?'

'Frequently,' she replied, with a candour

which set him laughing—only to stop abruptly, sweeping his eyes over her face, as though searching for something. 'But not frighten away—not from this house, Kate, from my...as you said "unfriendly" home?'

She smiled at his anxiety, pleased by it; feeling, for the first time there, needed. 'Not away from you,' she answered softly, meeting his eyes. 'Not yet...'

'Come...' he extended a hand to help her rise, 'this is no place for lingering—full of ghosts...'

'If you believe in them...'

'Aren't we all, my dear Miss Sutcliffe, haunted by something?' Lawrence Rushton asked, with a sigh. About to walk away, he stopped suddenly, remembering the light to be extinguished. Unthinking, he raised his right arm, then made an impatient sound and let go her hand to attend to the light with his left one. Before it died, Katherine saw his expression had changed, as if that too had returned to gloom.

The dim candlelight remaining, casting deep shadows, isolating them in its pool of flickering radiance, made her bold, and compassionate. Gently, her hand went to his incomplete arm as she glanced quickly up at him. 'How...?' she began, before her voice faltered and her glance slid away.

Silence hung between them—a barrier; he sighed again; she observed from the corner of her eye his look towards that door. 'An accident,' he told her. 'Now will you stop your questions?'

Before leaving the gallery, Katherine took a deep breath. 'I didn't speak, Mr Rushton, from mere curiosity.'

He stood gazing at her, then his hand went to her shoulder. 'I know, Kate,' he murmured, 'I know.'

At the stairs he said good night, but she felt his eyes following her ascent to the next floor. Reaching a bend in the stairs, she turned. He was frowning.

★ ★ ★ ★

Katherine, at her desk when Lawrence Rushton entered the study next morning, smiled when he greeted her. Without preamble, he began, though she wasn't sure she believed him, 'I had no idea Mrs Hawkins had accommodated you so unsuitably. I must rectify the situation.'

She smiled again. 'Thank you, Mr

Rushton, I would appreciate a more pleasant room.'

He nodded. 'I'm sure you would.'

By mid-morning Katherine had a pile of typewritten pages beside her machine. Pausing for a moment, she put a hand to the pocket of her dress and discovered a folded piece of paper. Remembering retrieving it from the gallery floor, she smoothed out the creases.

A sketch, beautifully executed, it was of something she recognized—the choir screen in the tiny church.

'What have you there?'

Katherine jumped at Mr Rushton's voice.

'I'm afraid it is not mine, sir, I...' she stopped awkwardly; he had risen, was coming to stand beside her, setting her pulses racing. Only then did she see the sketch was signed—Lawrence Rushton. She gasped, just as he spoke.

'So I see! And that you now know whose it is. And where, might I ask, did you acquire that?'

'In the gallery, sir—it fluttered to the floor. I retrieved it, thinking it might be important.'

He reached for it. 'Whereas it is of no

consequence.' He made as if to crumple it.

'Oh, don't do that,' Katherine protested, and he tossed it back on to her desk.

'What a child you are,' he remarked, 'despite your self-possession. What use is the thing now?'

'It's exquisitely drawn.'

He snorted. 'And of what use is that now?' He sighed. 'May we turn our minds to a little work, Miss Sutcliffe?'

★ ★ ★ ★

Katherine, first to arrive in the kitchen at mid-day, couldn't avoid overhearing Mrs Hawkins addressing somebody in the pantry.

'It's as true as I stand here, Mr Rivers: those were his very words, "I have changed my mind. Miss Sutcliffe must not be pushed away at the top of the house. You will give her the green room, next to mine." Next to his, mark you! We shall have to watch Madam there—before we know it she'll have taken the mistress's place, and where will you be then, I ask you? Back where you started, Mr Rivers, with as many threats as before to your master.'

Katherine frowned; what on earth could the woman mean? How could her presence threaten Lawrence Rushton—she only wanted to help him...?

Isobel, the parlour maid, hurried in to announce that Mr Rushton was demanding luncheon, so there the conversation ended, leaving Katherine mystified, and uneasy.

★ ★ ★ ★

Once settled into her new room, Katherine began to enjoy life at Masterton. Her only grievance was that she still ate her meals in the servants' hall, but her growing friendship with Simon's nanny compensated for this small humiliation, although the prevailing silence made more than the occasional whispered exchange difficult.

And Katherine's love of her work increased; Mr Rushton's eloquence in part compensated for the long hours and rapid pace she was expected to maintain.

She spent a deal of her leisure reading his books and he seemed pleased by her interest. But since their meeting in the gallery she shared with him only the working hours: away from the study, they scarcely met.

Of late, the weather had been unkind, days of fog and rain alternating with high winds, affording her no opportunity for further exploration of the extensive grounds. She had, however, to her delight, made a staunch friend of Master Simon. Janet, after that first occasion, readily accepted Katherine's offer to listen for the boy during an evening.

Simon, remembering the story of her childhood, had pressed her for more episodes. Katherine complied happily, her only anxiety Mr Rushton's possible annoyance if he discovered her frequent visits to his son. She reckoned, anyway, the little good she was doing Simon outweighed his father's probable displeasure.

Katherine, losing count of the weeks since her arrival at Masterton Hall, was surprised one morning when Lawrence Rushton asked if she was aware of the date.

She told him and he raised an eyebrow.

'So you do know. I was sure you must have forgotten...'

'Forgotten?'

Katherine's heart sank—what sin of

omission had she committed?

'You made me a promise, Kate,' he responded, using her Christian name for the only time in weeks. 'And I'd have said you'd be the last person to break it...'

'What promise?' she asked, raising bewildered eyes to inscrutable brown ones.

He rapped his desk, without the flicker of a smile. 'It was to be here within the month, you said...'

She sighed; he was tiresomely obtuse! 'Mr Rushton, would you please explain to what you are referring.'

'Your manuscript, of course.'

'Oh, that...' She started smiling.

'Yes, that! I might have known you couldn't produce one.'

'As you say,' she agreed, meekly, resolving to write something, somehow, and surprise him.

That evening she took pen and paper to the table in the room she already loved. She sat for an hour, trying to think of some story, some essay even, but nothing came.

So, he was right after all—she hadn't an ounce of creative talent. But she hated admitting defeat, hated the prospect of confessing to him that her tongue had run away with her.

'It's so easy just telling a story,' she sighed, 'as with young Simon, but this is...impossible.'

All next day, Katherine apprehensively awaited the opportune moment to admit she'd been wrong, but each time she would have opened her mouth to speak, she was deterred by the prospect of Lawrence's probable mockery.

As he went off to dinner, her spirits sank even farther: so, she also lacked the courage to be honest with him. Once he'd commended her for speaking out—what would he think of her now?

At the kitchen table, she pushed food around her plate, her appetite vanished, feeling ridiculously miserable at so trifling a matter. Somehow, she must rectify things and, she decided as she left the kitchen, before another day ended.

In the hall she encountered Rivers and approached him, her voice unnaturally loud in her nervousness.

'Is...is Mr Rushton in the drawing-room?'

'Yes.' His scowl demanded, though he did not, the reason for her enquiry.

'I...I wish to speak to him, if he can give me a little of his time.'

Rivers subjected her to a long scrutiny, as if to deflect her from her purpose, but the matter broached she would not draw back.

'If you please,' she insisted, wishing the interview over and done with, 'or shall *I* see if...?'

Hastening as much as dignity permitted, he reached the door ahead of her, knocked, opened it, then closed it in her face.

He spoke no word on reappearing, but—holding the door ajar just sufficiently for her entry—indicated she might go inside.

Katherine was thankful for long skirts that concealed the unwarranted shaking of her legs. In this room, she had first made acquaintance with her employer: she suspected this occasion would prove equally inauspicious. She did not at once see him, sitting as he was beside the log fire, his back towards her.

Lawrence Rushton didn't look up, but asked her to be seated. Katherine perched on the edge of one of the hard chairs, as she had at that previous interview, and waited...

He was studying a stiffly-bound ledger, his lips moving silently, as he totalled columns of figures. He was frowning.

Taking this as an ill-omen, Katherine allowed a sigh to escape.

He glanced round for her. 'Oh, Kate! Katherine—really!' he exclaimed, sending her heart plummeting to her feet.

How could she have offended him, already? She'd only...

And then he smiled.

'Could you not—just this once, unbend sufficiently to sit on a more comfortable chair in this "unfriendly" mansion of mine?'

She blinked at his words, rose, then hesitated. Smiling still, he beckoned and inclined his head towards the arm-chair across from his own.

'Will this do?' she enquired, the laughter unrestrained in her eyes, as she seated herself, happy to learn she need have no fear of him. For the moment.

A smile flickered at his mouth. 'Admirably!'

But still he seemed in no haste to pursue the reason for her presence. Instead, he had turned from perusal of his accounts to contemplation of her. She dropped her eyes to the hands clasped in her lap.

'Well?' he prompted her, at length. Then, when she sat there, speechlessly fumbling for a beginning, 'I cannot imagine why you seek me out after a whole day of my company!'

Despite herself, Katherine laughed. 'Sir, you jest...'

'And why not—it pleases me to bring merriment to those beautiful green eyes, which all too often regard me with great solemnity!'

She felt colour flooding her cheeks and tried foolishly to excuse it, turning a little from the fire. 'Your logs burn hotly, do they not?'

The sound emitting from his lips might have been a laugh, but his face was impassive when she ventured a look.

'What is it, Katherine?'

She rose, moved away from his watchful eyes. 'You...assumed correctly—I am totally incapable of writing even one word of a manuscript!'

There—she'd blurted out the truth, let him laugh at her.

But Rushton was so long silent that she turned from the window, at which she'd found herself.

He only shrugged, without speaking.

'So—you're not surprised, but you could, at least...'

'I asked you to sit, Kate—won't you?' he interrupted, smiling; when she had complied, he continued, 'Beware of that tongue of yours, even when provoked— don't let it trap you into rash statements! As for your being unable to put pen to paper...I confess to relief! Had you proved competent, I'd have felt compelled to prove *my* ability with *your* typewriter...and so on—*ad infinitum,* and to extreme tedium!' He came to stand before her. 'Life is not so obvious a competition.' He put on a severe expression, though she suspected he was not entirely serious. 'Permit me to reprimand you...'

He made her wait until her earlier relief was giving way to trepidation. 'You have let me down,' he went on. 'A woman pioneering in using business skills to win herself respect, shouldn't be overheard speaking so timorously to a servant!'

Katherine recalled how this very man had frequently put her in her place. She must protest.

But he forestalled her. 'Did you expect then to have your path smoothed here, your life made easy...?'

She shook her head. 'I knew not what to expect.'

His smile surprised her. 'Nor I. I, too, am unaccustomed to...this situation.'

Smiling, Katherine rose to go. 'Then that must be our common ground.'

Lawrence's arm went about her shoulders as he escorted her to the door. 'And if, Kate, interest in your surroundings makes your life here the more pleasant, we must do all we can to further it.'

Astonished by this, and no less so by the familiarity with which he used her Christian name, and placed his arm (which she could still feel) about her, Katherine found difficulty in settling her mind towards sleep that night.

★ ★ ★ ★

On the following Friday, Lawrence Rushton departed for London, taking Katherine into his confidence as he issued instructions for the work to be completed in his absence.

'I have urgent business with my publishers—and with the fellow who has charge of my finances.'

Something about his ready explanation made her wonder, fleetingly, if it had been offered simply to allay curiosity.

Freed, for a time, from his surveillance, Katherine intended learning everything possible about Lawrence Rushton—and his eerie home. She'd still have no opportunity to discover his wife's fate (for she deemed Janet's theory unlikely) nor why screams were heard at night; nor, indeed, why part of the house remained a ruin.

Now, she decided, John and Sarah Saunders would enlighten her.

The Saturday was dry and frosty, and Katherine was happy to be outdoors after the long inclement spell. Happy, too, to escape her awareness of the unusual quietness of that room next to her own.

Sarah, after initial surprise, seemed pleased to see her and soon had the kettle on the hob. Chatting in the snug parlour, Katherine led the conversation round to the years Sarah had worked at the Hall.

'I understand Mr Rushton's wife was very beautiful,' she began. 'What became of her?'

Anxiously, the elderly woman regarded her, and shaking her head said, 'No,

Miss, don't ask questions about her, I beg you...'

'Why not? Surely no mystery surrounds her?' Katherine made her query sound matter-of-fact, but this failed to reassure.

'Please, Miss Sutcliffe, forget all about Mrs Rushton, forget you asked the question —as I will. No good will come of prying...'

'What nonsense you talk, Sarah—Mr Rushton and the boy are two very ordinary people,' she protested, with a conviction she wished she could feel. 'What could our employer possibly conceal?'

Sarah stood up, twisting the corner of her apron between restless fingers. 'I warmed to you that first day, Miss; you're the kind we need. But if you keep asking me things I cannot answer, you'll have to stay away.' Her worried eyes sought Katherine's. 'Don't go on like that. Good for the master you'll be—but only if you learn to trust him.'

'Trust?' Katherine frowned. 'But, Sarah, he's only the man who employs me, why should I do otherwise?'

★ ★ ★ ★

Although she'd dismissed Sarah's words

at the lodge, Katherine found it more difficult to do so at night, in her bed. How had she succeeded in implying that Katherine would play a special part in Lawrence Rushton's life—and why had this suggestion struck an answering chord within her?

She wanted to demonstrate her mastery of that splendid typing machine, and her skill as an efficient secretary—but there the matter ended, or did it?

Within the confines of her room, Katherine admitted now to a yearning for more. Any lightness of heart, springing all too infrequently from Lawrence Rushton's sombre being, called to something in herself. And found a response.

And that is wrong, she decided. He is a married man, whether or not he chooses to live as one. I will do nothing to encourage any familiarity between us.

★ ★ ★ ★

Day succeeded day, wearily, and there was little to differentiate one from the next. Katherine's attempts to discover the truth about the situation at Masterton Hall were abortive.

On Thursday evening she heard Rivers direct George to meet the master off the mid-day train at Maidstone on the following day. Katherine retired to her room with a light heart. He was coming back. She would no longer sit alone, transferring his near-illegible script on to the paper in her machine, until her eyes pricked with fatigue and her body screamed for respite. Boredom, farewell! she thought as she fell asleep.

Next morning a strange brightness reflected from the walls of her room. Curious, though sleepy, she drew back the brocade curtains. Snow, still falling, transformed the already lovely scene to a wintry magnificence.

Shivering as she washed, despite the almost boiling water brought by a maid, Katherine hoped the inclement weather wouldn't delay Lawrence Rushton's return.

Throughout the day, at her typewriter, she kept one ear alert for the sound of hooves and carriage wheels, but nothing broke the surrounding stillness. When, by late afternoon, he had not returned, Katherine was disappointed—and anxious, speculating suddenly if the ready explanation of his absence had been the true one.

Dinner over, she sighed, wondering how she would pass the evening that stretched so interminably ahead.

'Miss Sutcliffe!' The cry echoed from the hall, to be followed, seconds later, by: 'Kate!' More urgently.

Suppressing an instinctive smile, she hurried from the kitchen. *He* was home again.

He stood, stamping snow from his boots, then tossed her his cape. 'Give that to Rivers, would you? Then come with me, Kate, I want you...'

No words ever sounded more sweet, but Rivers interrupted, appearing as if from the shadows. 'Anything else, sir?' he asked, taking the cloak from Katherine.

'Yes, there is. I haven't eaten since noon—bring me something right away.'

Katherine hesitated when Rivers had gone. 'Perhaps, sir, if you would tell me when you'll need me...'

He seized her by the arm. 'Now, my Kate, this very moment...'

'But...'

'What! Would you argue with me?' His eyes laughed down into hers. He seemed in fine spirits. He strode towards the dining-room—so rapidly she was obliged to hurry beside him. He released his hold of her only when they reached the far end of the long table. Drawing out a chair next to his own, he indicated, with a flourish, that she should sit. 'Pray be seated, madam...'

Katherine's eyes narrowed as she watched him, wondering what game he was playing, but his expression revealed no more than an unaccustomed light-heartedness.

'Perhaps you wish me to take notes, Mr Rushton?'

'Perhaps.'

She started to rise. 'Then I'll go and get...'

His hand flew to her shoulder, detaining her. 'Later.'

He moved to the sideboard and poured something from one of the cut-glass decanters; then, to her surprise, set a glass before her. Next he filled a glass for himself and sat at the head of the table again.

'You haven't tasted yours,' he reproved her. 'Surely you've had sherry wine before?'

Katherine smiled a little and met his gaze. 'I thought it more polite to wait until you joined me.'

His eyes mocked her, though not

unkindly, as he raised his glass to her. 'The perfect lady.'

She smiled again. 'And your visit to London, sir—was it satisfactory?'

He frowned briefly. 'My publishers are well content with the first chapters of the book. They also complimented me on its neatness. I confess it pleased me to learn I am the first of their authors to present a typescript.'

Katherine was somewhat annoyed that he appeared to take all the credit upon himself. Where did that place her?

But she had misjudged him: she felt his eyes boring into her and he shrugged when she looked towards him. 'Dare you no longer challenge anything I say?' he demanded. 'Has my absence returned you to the docile creature I encountered on your arrival? Or are you still the woman who tries to match my words?'

Katherine's lips twitched. Soon she would laugh and all pretence of dignity would vanish. But how could she, for one moment, recognize this mischievous man as her dour employer?

'I am so pleased,' she began, 'that *you* have found favour because of *my...*'

'...skill,' he finished for her. 'And be not

anxious, I was happy to tell them how I have acquired a secretary. And now you may laugh, suppress it not!'

Katherine could, indeed, do nothing but laugh.

Lawrence was smiling. 'It is good to be home, Kate,' he began, only to be interrupted by Rivers coming in with the soup.

Lawrence Rushton nodded acknowledgement as the man-servant unfolded the linen napkin. When Rivers reached the door his master rose swiftly, calling him. Katherine noticed Lawrence's slight nod, indicating that the conversation should be out of her hearing. From beyond the door, she caught a surprised, 'Very well, sir...if you are sure,' from Rivers, among the murmuring. Then, smiling, Lawrence returned to her.

'And what, Kate, has occupied you in my absence?'

'Working on your book, of course—and loving every moment of that!'

'Indeed! Despite my infernal hand-writing, eh? I declare you're the one person who doesn't complain!'

How could she—enraptured by the excellence of his literary prowess, against which any difficulty seemed inconsequential?

She smiled at him and he returned the smile.

Encouraged, she decided to learn more of his visit to London. 'And was seeing your publishers your only business there?'

Again, he frowned. Already she regretted the question: choosing, now it was too late, to remain in ignorance. What if he should reveal some contact with Mrs Rushton?

That was something she had no wish to contemplate.

'There are...problems,' he began, then shook his head. 'No, this is not the time even to think of them. You must remind me, afterwards, that I have something for you.'

'For me...?' She was quite taken aback. 'But why?'

He did not reply at once, seeming embarrassed by the question. 'As an appreciation, we will say, of your...efficiency.'

Before Katherine could marvel at something so uncharacteristic as Lawrence Rushton bringing anything from London for her, Rivers came into the room.

Nothing was said until the man-servant had departed, leaving on the table a dish with a silver cover.

Raising that cover, her employer frowned. 'Oh—how careless, Rivers has omitted to cut up the meat. He must be reprimanded.' As he glanced from the plate, though, Katherine noticed amusement rather than annoyance in his expression.

'Shall I call him back?' she offered, half rising.

'No,' he replied calmly, 'you shall attend to it for me.'

His gaze never left her hands while she executed the task, and she talked to fill the silence. 'What is it then, that you have brought for me?'

'Ah, Katherine's famed curiosity!' he exclaimed. 'You will have to wait, will you not, to satisfy it!'

She warmed to his teasing, giving him a sidelong glance from beneath her lashes as she set the plate in front of him.

'And *I* shall learn,' he added, 'by your reaction, how well I know you—if I have it in me to in any way please you...'

'Oh, how you do,' she thought, her colour rising, 'simply by being here—by being approachable.'

But he was speaking again, of the tiresome journey endured that day; and she found herself, because she was interested, asking questions and receiving ready answers. Thus it was that, each to the other supplying a lead, their conversation lasted until he had eaten.

When Rivers appeared with coffee, Mr Rushton demanded a cup be brought for Katherine. She saw the hesitation, heard the sniff of disapproval, before Rivers complied.

The cup and saucer were placed before her, ungraciously, making them rattle. Mr Rushton called Rivers back from the door—Katherine thought, to reprimand him for the ill-temper. But it was to issue further instructions.

'Starting with tomorrow breakfast, you will ensure two places are set in here.'

'Two, sir?'

'Two, Rivers. That is all—thank you.'

He turned to her with a smile as the door closed, a smile she could not return. Something inside her was sinking. So this intimate evening was no precedent. It showed no significant warming towards her. It was but an expression of his satisfaction with life.

Mrs Rushton was taking her rightful place. Much as Katherine had known that this could happen, she had allowed herself to forget the fact. And now, a quick glance told her, her employer was ill-at-ease. He had risen and was standing at the fireplace, one foot on the brass fender, his back to her.

Abruptly, he swung round. 'You did not shrink from it, then?' he demanded, his eyes cold, and avoiding hers.

'Shrink...from what?' She was puzzled.

'Oh, Miss Sutcliffe, cease this prevarication! You know and I know...' Still he did not look at her.

'Indeed, sir, I know nothing of your meaning. Why must you talk in riddles?'

His eyes sought her face, reluctantly, fearing the pretence he might find there. Finding only honest bewilderment, he smiled. 'This helpless mortal feeding—requiring food cut up for him...'

She sprang to her feet, rushed impulsively to him. 'Don't!'

'You protest at my words, yet gave no sign of embarrassment earlier.' The dark eyes looked deeper into hers. 'You're a rare woman, Kate. You don't object then to making this a habit, to dining with me?'

'I'll look forward to it.' A smile caught at her lips. 'You were testing me?'

He continued to search her expression, then laughed somewhat ruefully. 'One of us, Katherine. I was testing one of us.'

★ ★ ★ ★

Sleep proved elusive that night—how she had longed for Lawrence Rushton's return, never guessing a changed man would confront her. For gone was the hasty dismissal, the glance reducing her to the level of his menials. The man returned to her was wary, perhaps, but treating her as an equal.

Katherine longed to prove herself worthy of his revised opinion. But, more important, to show him that (disregarding appearances indicating he was harsh) she would keep an open mind. A mind ready to admit his own to it.

She had tried to ignore that notion, to tell herself, yet again, that—tied to another—he must be given no special place in her affections. He must not be sought out, she must not...

How could she deny her instincts so utterly, how withhold the understanding springing unbidden towards him? How turn aside from this man who'd confessed himself inhibited by that disability? Some-body must convince him it detracted from his personality not one whit.

And he had requested her company. Albeit purely during meals, but he had requested it.

And so now it was beginning, as she had dreamed. She had found her place here. That he was a lonely man had been obvious from her arrival; that she had been chosen to help ease his loneliness was something to be cherished.

Still unable to sleep, Katherine heard the clock in the hall strike the hour. She counted with it...nine, ten, eleven. A loud knock sounded on the door next to her own, startling her to acute awareness.

'Yes, Rivers, what is it?' Mr Rushton's voice sounded irritable.

She heard the door open and close, then raised voices. She tried not to listen, nor to strain for some hint of the trouble. But she could not miss the shout of, 'You're dismissed—get away from here. I'll have no more of this!'

'Oh, yes, sir, you will!' Rivers retorted, his tone masterly, not subservient. 'You'll keep me here, and pay, Mr Rushton—to avoid the alternative.'

Was this blackmail? It sounded very like it. Distressing in itself, the thought conjured up greater distress. Nobody was ever blackmailed unless they were hiding something. And she'd no wish to believe Lawrence Rushton had anything to conceal; she wanted him as he'd been that evening with her, disarmingly honest.

Katherine sighed, wondering what was amiss now in this strange household. Then she heard its master shouting again.

'Take it then, and be done—and I warn you, and Mr Barnabas, this is the last you'll have from me!'

There was a laugh, not his, then the sound of a door opening and closing.

THREE

Eventually Katherine slept, but fitfully, as though even in sleep her ears were straining for some sound from the next room. Her body was tense, ready to spring, and to what purpose? How could she, a woman, come to the aid of Lawrence Rushton? She smiled at her own stupidity, but not at her urge to stand beside him. That disturbed her past all description. What was happening to her—what was this strange power in her employer, ever drawing her, despite her resolution, towards him?

Before going down to breakfast, Katherine reached a compromise with these somewhat alarming urges. She would channel any feeling for the man into working efficiently for him—and distracting him from his worries, whenever possible. In this lovely, but uncanny, house of numerous secrets, she would be the touch of the ordinary.

She would be the one reminding him that, in the routine, the everyday, the commonplace, could be found an escape—relaxation.

Looking up from the sideboard, where he was filling his plate from a chafing-dish of kidneys and bacon, he smiled on seeing her. 'Ah, Miss Sutcliffe, so here you are! Just in time to pour the coffee. I told Rivers I wouldn't require his services now an attractive young lady presides over my table.'

She smiled, relieved that his argument with Rivers last night had apparently caused no lasting distress.

When she had poured coffee, he led her

to the sideboard.

'I must act host till you learn where to find things in here. I can recommend the kidney, though the bacon's a trifle salty. The toast is good, as a rule—and Mrs Hawkins's preserve, but perhaps you're already familiar with that...'

After serving herself, she joined Lawrence at the table. He chuckled, nodding towards the far end.

'Would you believe it—they'd set your place right away over there! But I'd have none of it. I moved the cutlery myself—much to Rivers's disapproval.' He leaned confidentially towards her. 'They'll try to push you down, my Kate—don't let them! There's no need, you see, with my authority upholding you.'

Her heart warming to his concern, she looked her thanks.

'Do you think it doesn't please me?' he demanded. 'Do you imagine I don't long for just such a chance, when all I normally have is the opportunity to pay wages, or issue orders?'

Katherine thought back to her arrival at Masterton, to his cool demeanour—and wondered.

If what he now claimed were true, why

begin in such a manner?

'I see you have a memory.' He broke in on her thoughts. 'That you are asking why—if that *is* how I feel—why I did not show some warmth on your arrival?'

Katherine felt the colour rush to her cheeks. 'Of course I wasn't...'

'Katherine,' he warned, 'be honest with me—you always can, you know. Between friends, less than the truth is an insult.'

Friends? She held back the question, but again he read her silence. 'Friends, I said. Or am I being presumptuous?'

She smiled at the suggestion that he, master of this mansion, might ever be that. 'Friends,' she repeated, 'I think I would like that.'

'Then answer me; were you not wondering at this conflict of character?'

She squirmed a little, and meeting his gaze looked away hastily. Pityingly, he answered for her.

'I had to try you—to discover whether you were some weakling to be crushed by the first hint of difficulty or someone to rely on—as an ally.' He smiled. 'You've proved yourself.' Then he hesitated, awkwardly. 'And there I go—expecting truth, and giving only half-truths.' He sighed, nodding to his right arm. 'You'd be a fool—and you're not—if you hadn't noticed how...' and again he hesitated. She longed to tell him there was no need to say more, but, pedantic about frankness, he judged himself no more tolerantly. He sighed. 'How I nurse this "thing" as though it were some child to protect from a critical gaze.' He met her glance. 'Now rebuke me for my womanish sensitivity.'

Katherine shook her head. 'There's no reason to, although I can't for the life of me see why you're inhibited by your disability. You manage well enough with the one hand, I scarcely notice it has no fellow.'

'I'll pretend I believe you, my Kate,' he began, eyes fixed on his plate, 'because I'd like to.' And then as he swung their near-hypnotic brilliance on her—'Life can be devilish hard, pray God I don't involve you in my problems. I count myself lucky, nonetheless; I'll never again feel so entirely misunderstood.' He smiled. 'And now no more of this—before you're convinced it's an introspective neurotic who has wished his company on you!'

He indicated the morning paper, discarded when she joined him. 'And so

Disraeli has acquired us the Khedive's shares in the Suez Canal, eh? Tell me, what do you think to that?' And so he led her into a discussion which continued until, with an arm about her shoulders, he walked with her to the study.

That evening the tranquillity engendered by her employer's changed attitude was shattered by now-familiar screams. Katherine stilled her racing pulse, glancing across her room to the clock. It wanted ten minutes to nine.

Resolutely, she moved to the door. Exploration, unthinkable during the night, might be attempted at this hour.

Swiftly, silently, on slippered feet, she found the corridor above her own, and headed towards the West Tower. Confirming Janet's words, the screams—coming again—were louder here. She hastened her steps.

The candle she held aloft flickered in a sudden draught and she fancied somebody followed. Shivering with fright she concealed herself in a shadowy doorway.

Something brushed her hand. She stifled a cry as her candle sputtered out. Away in the darkness, light flooded from a doorway. A grey figure whisked through, and vanished.

Trembling, in total blackness, Katherine steadied herself against the wall. She could not remain here—but how, unseeing, could she do otherwise?

Feeling her way along the wall, she retreated slowly. Whatever, or whoever, occupied that tower she wished no knowledge of the matter—escape alone she desired.

As she reached the safety of her own room Katherine paused, knowing she could not endure its solitude. Anyone, Rivers even, would be welcome company.

Down the rest of the stairs she ran, breathlessly. Before her hand left the balustrade, another closed over it.

'Katherine!'

'Mr Rushton!'

'I see I've startled you—forgive me.'

She would, readily—and for finding excuse for her agitation.

'Where have you been?' he enquired, smiling. 'I've looked for you everywhere.' Not waiting for a reply, he continued. 'I told you on my return from London that I'd something for you. You haven't pressed me for it. Have you no interest in my gift?'

Fortunately, he could not guess that his homecoming, and other preoccupations, had driven the matter from her mind. She was still seeking the correct response when he indicated the drawing-room, opening the door to usher her in.

The room was welcoming, its firelight flickering over glass domes covering stuffed birds, waxed flowers, and a skeleton clock. Katherine stood admiring this, while Lawrence Rushton turned up the gas lights. Observing her interest, he came to her side. 'My mother chose that—when they became so popular, after the Great Exhibition.'

His hand went to her elbow. 'Shall we sit near the fire?'

Katherine chose the chair opposite his, and waited...

Holding something behind his back, her employer came to her. 'You seemed, I thought, interested in my pictures of the house and countryside, perhaps this will further that interest...'

He gave her a book. Katherine glanced from its gilt-tooled leather binding to its donor.

'Thank you very much, Mr Rushton.'

But why...? What had prompted him to do this?

Katherine opened the volume and gasped. It was a book of engravings, hundreds of them it seemed, and each apparently of a Kentish scene. 'Beautiful,' she murmured.

'I thought so, too. The engravings are from the work of George Shepherd, a fine artist, with a feeling for atmosphere.'

Katherine nodded, but didn't respond: already she was turning page after page, eagerly. It wasn't until she reached the last one that she found her employer, from his own chair, watching her. Their eyes met and she stood up, hastily, clutching the book to her.

'I'm sorry, I was so enthralled. I quite forgot where I was. I must not take up more of your time. I...thank you once again for being so...kind to me.'

He appeared, she observed, somewhat taken aback, unsure of his next move. At the door she hesitated; had her thanks been insufficient, her enthusiasm inadequate?

'I see...' He sounded...resigned, deflated.

She turned surprised eyes to him. 'Was there something else, sir?'

He shrugged. 'No—be off with you, if that's what you wish.'

'What I...?' Katherine didn't understand.

Sighing, he reached for a heavy tome.

'What is it, Mr Rushton?' she persisted.

'Nothing, Miss Sutcliffe.' His tone inferred she had done him some injury. He spoke again, his eyes never straying from his book, 'I only...fondly hoped I might deserve company—as a reward, say, for my..."kindness"?'

'Company, sir? My company?' Whatever next?

He made an elaborate show of looking round the room. 'So far as I'm aware, there's no one else here whom I might be addressing!'

Katherine laughed. 'But how was I to know you wished me to remain?'

Mr Rushton laid aside his tome and came to her. 'Miss Sutcliffe, could I persuade you to sit with me, despite the minute measure of light conversation I may offer? I assure you, I will try...'

Again, she laughed, but he preserved a grave expression.

'I had intended showing you—see, I have the map ready—each place in your book. And if that failed to amuse you, well—I should try even harder...'

Seated now at the table, the map spread before her, Katherine observed he could no longer restrain his smile.

One by one, he indicated the situation of each scene, adding further information to interest her. So absorbed was she that she exclaimed, astonished, when the hall clock struck a half hour past ten o'clock. 'You must excuse me now, Mr Rushton—or I shall be unable to work well tomorrow.'

He rose with her. 'And is that of paramount importance?'

She met his eyes. 'Perhaps not solely—but it is why I am here.'

As he held open the door, he remarked, 'A delightful evening, Kate—for which I thank you; dare I hope there may be others?'

She smiled at his pretended humility. 'I believe that would be very pleasant. Yes, I would like—thank you, Mr Rushton.'

'And very formal occasions they're to be, by the sound of it! Oh, come, Kate—this "sir" and "Mr Rushton"—do you not, in all honesty, find formality tedious? Or is it calculated to keep me just that distance away—for your safety perhaps?'

His dark eyes, large and compelling, held her own.

Katherine felt obliged to smile at him, though she couldn't help wondering if the familiarity he implied was in fact permissible between employer and employee.

He raised an eyebrow. 'So you might, with practise, accustom yourself to saying, "Lawrence"!' He gave a mock bow, then she felt him watching her as far as the bend in the staircase.

★ ★ ★ ★

She responded to Lawrence Rushton's manner, half-serious, half-teasing, and noticed he became less morose.

His conversation was mainly of books and literary friends, like Charles Kingsley, whose untimely death last January had been a sad loss. Katherine was thinking that soon she also would have the one consuming preoccupation, when they discovered a mutual delight in music.

One dull, dank Saturday, when one could only stay indoors, they were discussing a biography of Chopin when Katherine remarked, 'I so used to love playing a polonaise by Chopin.'

'Playing? The piano? I didn't know you could.'

'Yes, but not well, I'm afraid. We couldn't afford lessons, nor a piano; but an aunt with whom I used to stay taught music. Indeed, my sister, Clare, is about to follow in her footsteps. Teaching English, as well—at the local school.'

But Lawrence was paying no heed, having sprung to his feet. 'Come with me...' He led the way upstairs, along the corridor past their bedrooms, and then paused to unlock a door.

He grimaced at the dimness of the room, swiftly drew the blue velvet curtains, and lit candles set on a grand piano. He raised the lid, nodding towards her. 'Try it...'

Nervously, Katherine ran her fingers over the keys. The tone was magnificent—if only she could do it justice. Lawrence handed her a sheet of music, listened while she played, found her another. Leaning against the piano, he wasn't watching her, and he seemed far away. At the end of the piece, Katherine frowned.

'Not very good, am I?'

'Have I criticized?' He was staring across the room, beyond her line of vision. 'Do you play anything else?'

Katherine made a face. 'Isn't this enough? I expected you to thank heaven that I don't!'

He shook his head. Then, a hand on

101

her shoulder, turned her to follow his gaze. Against the wall was an organ.

'Like to try it?'

'But I couldn't...'

'How do you know, before attempting it? It isn't very different...'

'So, that's what you used to play,' Katherine commented, as she crossed the room with him.

Lawrence sighed, about to say something, changed his mind, then nodded.

When Katherine hesitated, looking down at the double keyboard, he slid on to the long seat and bade her join him. Shyly, though unable to refuse, she sat beside him, to listen while he explained the various stops and demonstrated the effect they had. Then he showed her the foot pedals, coming last to the keyboards, or manuals, as she learned to call them. The upper was the Swell, he told her, the lower the Great. With his left hand, Lawrence traced a simple melody, then turned to her. 'Your turn now...'

Katherine blessed the aunt who had taught her to read music, but, nevertheless, found the organ somewhat intimidating. She was so fascinated, watching Lawrence manipulating the various steps, that she lost her place in the score. She laughed, a little anxiously, and found kind, smiling, eyes resting on her.

'Interested?' he enquired.

'Of course—it's most intriguing.'

'Like to learn to play it?'

Katherine laughed. 'I'm afraid it's quite beyond me.'

Lawrence shook his head. 'I think not. You've the necessary clean fingering...'

'But...'

'I'd find a lot of happiness in teaching you—if you'd let me.'

She swallowed hard, scarcely able to believe her good fortune. She smiled, 'Thank you—I'd love to learn.'

Lawrence seemed delighted. 'We'll begin right away. Start you off on easy pieces, gradually work up to the interesting ones.'

He went straight into a more detailed explanation, guiding her hand over the stops. He frowned suddenly. 'You're getting cold—I should have thought of that earlier, this room hasn't been used in years. Here...' He stood up, slipping off his own coat and putting it round her shoulders.

Katherine made as if to protest, but he insisted. 'Just whilst I send for some logs for the fire. Unless you would rather leave this till another day...'

'I'm happy here.'

'And so am I—though we run the risk of freezing to death!' He went to the bell-pull, then returned to stand behind her. 'That's it, you're doing well...' he commended, leaning over her shoulder to reach a stop. Smiling up at him, Katherine was surprised by the animation in his dark eyes.

Rivers appeared in the doorway and looked briefly astonished to find them there. Lawrence gave orders that one of the maids bring kindling and logs. When the girl arrived he told her to set them in the hearth: he would attend to the fire himself.

He observed Katherine's amazement and laughed. 'I'm not entirely useless! And you can come to the piano—to keep me amused by playing whilst I am busy.'

Once the fire was crackling into life Lawrence interrupted her, bidding her warm herself at the fire. Katherine went to the hearth and extended her hands to the blaze.

'It's warmer here...' Lawrence leaned back against his heels and, when she made no move to kneel beside him, held out his hand. 'Come along, now...'

Then: 'You see...' he said, as she settled her voluminous skirts around her on the hearthrug and a smile tugged at his lips.

'This reminds me of nursery tea in winter; kneeling before the fire, while Nanny toasted muffins.'

Lawrence gave a sidelong glance when she vainly stifled a laugh. 'Yes, Kate—even I was once a child—many, many years ago!'

'I—I beg your pardon.' She was embarrassed to have such a thought detected.

He smiled. 'It doesn't matter. If you only knew how old I feel—sometimes. Not only today...I feel ridiculously young, almost irresponsible, ready to dismiss all problems.' He blew a fleck of soot from his white cuff, inspected his fingers; 'I must wash—stay where you are, I won't be long.'

On returning, Lawrence stood, momentarily, in the doorway, regarding her. 'This is very good, you know,' he began, then crossed to the fireplace, gazing at her; 'Very good for me.'

He offered a hand to help her rise, but didn't immediately release her fingers. He examined them as they lay in his.

Katherine thought for a moment he was about to raise them to his lips, they were half-way there when he let them go. She heard him sigh, he nodded towards the organ, 'Ready then...?'

Before going to it, she removed his coat from her shoulders and handed it to him.

'Thank you,' she murmured, smiling.

Putting it on, Lawrence grinned. 'I'm only surprised you needed it—you, the one who's brought warmth into this place.'

Unable to meet his eyes, Katherine gave attention to arranging her dress as she seated herself.

Lawrence immediately sat beside her and, she noticed, closer than earlier. Startlingly aware of him, she feared concentration would be difficult, but could not move away lest that be obvious. She must, therefore, summon control over her racing pulse, and heed his teaching.

For some long while they sat thus; with Lawrence's coaching, Katherine began playing the right-hand melody whilst he contributed the left, supervising control of the stops. Not satisfied with that, he suggested she take over the manuals. But he remained seated. She glimpsed his smile and, confused, wondered at it. She sat there, not commencing to play, then his right arm encircled her waist.

'There,' he said, 'you can reach all the keys now.'

'That's all very well,' she thought, 'but you have taken away all chance of my giving mind to the matter!'

Perhaps sensing this, Lawrence moved away during the piece, and was standing, back to the fire, when she had stumbled to the end.

'Yes,' he remarked, 'a good beginning; we'll leave it there for today.' He chuckled, mischievously. 'We mustn't teach you too much too soon—where would our excuse for this be?'

Excuses or not, that afternoon set a precedent for many happy hours in the music room, adding another facet to what, for Katherine, was developing into an all-absorbing relationship.

She was, indeed, having difficulty finding time for becoming better acquainted with Janet and Master Simon. She slipped into the nursery at odd moments, hoping that growing closer to the boy would bestow a deeper understanding of his enigmatic father.

For this, above all, Katherine desired.

She had come to love this house as her own home, despite its eeriness. She had grown to be contented here. This was (she admitted to herself) Lawrence's doing. Doubts there were yet concerning him, but whenever they were together she could give him no less than her whole attention, and in so doing felt satisfied.

There were still, nevertheless, strange comings and goings about the mansion; nocturnal footsteps echoing along corridors—and frequently those high-pitched screams, startling her awake to lie with palpitating heart.

Katherine, despite the shadowy grey figure she'd encountered, dismissed any theory of a Masterton ghost. She determined to seek the explanation, praying this would not necessitate a return to that upstairs corridor. Her determination increased when she found Lawrence was perturbed by those screams.

In gathering dusk they were together at the organ; suddenly the scarcely-human cries penetrated the music. She saw him stiffen, then frown. He strode from the room without a word, and she saw nothing further of him until the following morning.

After breakfast, Katherine would have

questioned Lawrence had she not been disturbed. Opening her door to a stentorian knocking, she found Mrs Hawkins, nostrils flaring, hands firmly clasped across her well-upholstered front.

'If I might have a word, Miss Sutcliffe...'

'What is it?'

The housekeeper nodded towards the room. 'I think, Miss, you'll prefer what I have to say be said in private.'

Katherine stood aside to admit her, but didn't offer a seat.

Mrs Hawkins scanned the room as if she'd never seen it before. 'Very nice—I'm sure you consider you've done well for yourself.'

'It is pleasant. I am happy here.'

A sinister smile twisted the older woman's face. 'Oh, we're fully aware, Miss Sutcliffe, what pains have gone into securing your position.' She paused, though through no uncertainty. 'Have you reflected what you're relinquishing for your...friendship with the master?'

'Relinquishing? Surely I'm the one to gain from it?'

'That's just it, isn't it, Miss? Well, let me tell you that tongues are wagging—already. Yes, made you start, didn't it! We know why you came here! Why you've ingratiated yourself with Mr Rushton, till he—fool that he is—is besotted. Yes, Miss, you need look at me! You should look to your own behaviour, before it's too late. He could never wed you—you understand that, don't you? So what else would be the outcome, eh? You think of that—while there's still time.' At the door, she turned. 'I speak only as one who cares—for you, and for the master. Avoid shutting yourself away with him—alone, hour after hour. It's dangerous. Mark my words, there'll be a scandal at Masterton—and you out on your ear, without even a reputation to take with you!'

Katherine stilled her trembling limbs and opened the door. 'Would you leave, Mrs Hawkins; I have nothing to say to you.'

'Remember what I've said, Miss, stop making up to Mr Rushton. You young hussy, you're no better than you should be!'

Katherine closed the door on her and leaned against it, panting agitatedly. What cool effrontery! How dared Mrs Hawkins convey such tittle-tattle! And if the servants were gossiping about her relationship with Lawrence Rushton? She sighed.

Nothing would change her attitude towards him—nothing could. But it was sullied by maliciousness. And it had been so fine, so undemanding. Friendship, shared interest in literature, in music, a need for company.

Furious tears sprang to her eyes; it was so unjust. She'd never, for one moment, believed these pleasant leisure hours could lead further. She'd contemplated nothing beyond the immediate future—and the sharing by two lonely people of a warm fireside.

Or had she? Why had Mrs Hawkins's '...he could never wed you' stung so?

Weeping still, Katherine heard knocking at the door again; gentle, this time, almost hesitant.

'Katherine, are you there? Is something wrong?' Lawrence called.

She uttered a cry, then covered her mouth; he'd heard her sobbing.

'Kate, will you answer me?'

She took a deep breath. 'I am...well, thank you.'

There was a pause. 'Oh, if you say so.' And he went away.

Later, though, as they ate together, she felt him regarding her keenly, and when questioned pleaded a headache. She sensed that Lawrence didn't believe her, but he let it rest there, although for some days she felt him scrutinizing her.

On the Monday evening she excused herself from visiting the music room on the pretext of listening for Master Simon during Janet's time off.

Lawrence frowned. 'Very well—if that's what you prefer.'

'I didn't say it was, only somebody's got to keep an ear open for the boy. You ought to be pleased...'

'Pleased?' he snorted. 'Pleased, that you choose to pander to the child—why should I be?'

'But he is...' Katherine began to protest.

'A confounded nuisance!' Lawrence declared, interrupting impatiently. He nodded to the door. 'Very well then—be off with you!' And he turned his back on her.

Simon didn't waken that evening, so Katherine was alone with her thoughts—and distressed by them. Why was Lawrence so unyieldingly hard with the boy? Somehow she must unearth the reason; for reason, she was sure, there was. Meanwhile, many things about Lawrence Rushton bewildered her, but his behaviour towards

Simon left her no confusion of emotions—
only complete abhorrence.

★ ★ ★ ★

Janet, flushed and light-hearted from an
evening with her George, returned and
detained Katherine in the doorway as she
was about to go to her own room.

'You want to take a leaf out of my
book, Katy—find someone of your own
class, instead of setting your cap at...'

'Instead of what?' she demanded angrily.
'Say that again...'

Janet only shook her head. 'I'm sorry—it
just slipped out, but I don't like to see you
throwing yourself at somebody like that.'

Katherine sighed. 'So now you're jump-
ing to conclusions, judging...'

Janet seemed contrite. 'I shouldn't have
said it, only...'

'Only what?'

'It's all right for him, he's master here,
can face criticism, but it's you who'll be
left broken and disappointed when he's
had his way with you...'

'When he's done what?' Katherine
shouted. 'You owe me an apology, Janet—
and Lawrence Rushton. I can imagine what

113

insinuations slip back and forth in the kitchen. Let me inform you, they're entirely without foundation. Lawrence Rushton's a fine, honourable gentleman—and has never laid a finger on me!'

Blinded by tears, Katherine turned, dashing along the landing, almost colliding with her employer.

'Katherine!' he exclaimed, dismayed, trying to detain her—but, his right arm being the nearer to her, she evaded him.

'Kate!' He pursued her as she hastened to her room. Reaching the door ahead of him, she flew inside, and locked it.

He rapped impatiently, then rattled the handle.

'Will you open this door!'

Katherine covered her face with her hands.

'For the last time—unlock the thing, or I swear I'll break it down!'

Still she made no move.

'You will not defy me!' he roared, rattling the door again.

Slowly, she turned the key in the lock, then stood with her back turned, as far away as she could get from him.

'Now, what is it?' he asked softly, coming to stand behind her.

Katherine didn't answer.

'Come and sit down...' he suggested. She ignored him.

Finding a chair, he placed it beside her. 'Sit!' he bellowed.

Trembling, she obeyed, but refused to meet his eyes. He sighed, and went down on one knee at her side.

'Katherine, I heard what you said. Why not tell me the whole, it must be obvious I've guessed what Janet has said.'

Katherine closed her eyes, shaking her head, fingers pulling at the scrap of cambric handkerchief.

He stilled her hands with gentle fingers. 'They've upset you and it's my fault...'

'Of course it isn't,' she protested. And then looked at him. His eyes were anguished. 'It's all right,' she whispered.

'That it's not!' He rose swiftly, began pacing the room, then faced her.

'How long have they been gossiping?'

She shook her head, looking away. He went to her, raising her chin, compelling her to look at him. 'How long, Kate? I will have a reply.'

'I will tell you nothing.'

'Katherine, I am tired, I've had a busy day—and so have you. Tell me, then we can both rest—with quiet minds.'

When she remained silent still, Lawrence located a further chair and set it facing her own.

'Very well—I shall sit here until you recover your senses.'

'Oh, leave me alone!' she cried, drying her eyes. 'There is nothing wrong.'

'Nothing? I find you in tears—defending my name, and you claim that is normal. Or perhaps it is—perhaps you're accustomed to the staff maligning me—and worse, yourself?'

He sighed. 'So that is it—or near enough. Since you refuse to reveal the truth, *I* will tell *you*. These—these servants have chosen to blacken your name as well as mine—and for why? Because you, in your kindness, in your concern, your gentleness, took pity on my solitude...'

'It wasn't like that, sir.'

'Lawrence,' he corrected, firmly.

'Lawrence then.' Anxious eyes sought his. 'Don't you know I wanted this from the start—being with you, talking as we have done, exchanging ideas, just...' Lost for words, she halted.

He smiled. 'I'm pleased to learn that. But, my dear, these foul insinuations must be stopped. How long have they been hurling accusations?'

Again, she shook her head. 'It's of no consequence.'

'For some time, I'll be bound. And you, my sweet Kate, thought to endure it alone.'

'I would have endured it, if you hadn't...'

'...found out?' He smiled, shaking his head. 'Think of this, though, Kate—you declare the times we spend together valuable to you. To me, also, they are very...precious. Would you deny me the right to defend their continuance?'

He fell silent, as if reflecting, then, rose, going to the door; he hesitated, just inside it. 'Do you...want to...leave?' he began, haltingly.

'That's the last thing,' Katherine responded quickly.

She watched his slow smile spreading.

'Then you must let me handle this my way.'

★ ★ ★ ★

The following Sunday, Katherine was crossing the hall, ready for church, when

Lawrence called her.

'Have you a moment? This won't take long.'

She stood still, waiting for him to state what he wanted, but he turned aside, beckoning somebody from the drawing-room. Janet emerged, face pale and eyes reddened as if from weeping.

Katherine heard Lawrence murmur, 'Go on then, girl...'

Janet came towards her.

'I apologize,' she started, before reaching Katherine, 'I should not have said what I did—nor even contemplated it...' She glanced over her shoulder to their employer, lingering in the doorway. 'I have been told now what the position is. I hope you can forgive me and that we'll be friends once more.'

'Of course,' Katherine responded, kissing the girl's cheek, meeting the brown eyes of the man looking on, and smiling gratefully. She longed suddenly to show him thus easily that all was well, then felt hot colour flood her cheeks. How could she even have thought thus!

'Are you going to church?' Janet asked. 'For Master Simon and I would happily accompany you.'

Katherine nodded, and Janet called Simon, who rushed from the drawing-room. The boy paused, gazing up at Lawrence.

'Will you not come also, Father?'

Katherine bit her lip, observing Lawrence stiffen, then shake his head. 'Why ask a question when you already know the answer? What a stupid boy you are!'

The child's expectant face crumpled. 'Sorry, sir.' Turning swiftly, he ran from him.

Katherine glimpsed Lawrence's weary face, heard his sigh, as he watched them open the door and go outside. She herself sighed. The boy would soon recover from the curt dismissal, as children so quickly did, on having their interest diverted. An unpleasant conviction remained that Simon wasn't the one who was the more distressed by the incident.

★ ★ ★ ★

Christmas was nearing, yet Katherine saw no sign of preparations for its celebration. She asked Janet what plans were normally made.

The girl laughed, ruefully. 'It's easy to

119

tell you haven't been here long, Katy. The answer's none. We scarcely do anything special.'

'What?' She was incredulous—recalling family gatherings in the tiny parlour of a certain Yorkshire cottage—the merriment, opening presents, singing carols...

Janet sighed. 'I know—awful, isn't it? A dreary old time we had last year, and no mistake!'

'But...Simon—he must have a tree, gifts, and some fun, for once.'

'Oh, Mr Rushton always buys him something—something expensive, I can tell. But useful, not toys or frivolities.'

'Poor child,' Katherine exclaimed. 'What has he done to deserve such an existence!'

She resolved at that moment to persuade Lawrence the time had come for a little gaiety.

★ ★ ★ ★

'What festivities have you in mind, for Christmas?' she enquired, as he stood beside her as she practised the organ.

She felt eyes boring into her. 'None— why?' he demanded, coldly.

'Well, it is a time for rejoicing—and with

120

a child in the house...'

Katherine heard his sharp breath. 'Believe me, I find no cause for rejoicing in his presence!'

'You can't mean that...' she started, earnestly, before the bitter set of his lips cautioned her into silence.

'Indeed? Do you doubt my word?'

'No,' she replied, firmly, 'but, perhaps, your judgement...'

Lawrence hauled her to her feet, made her face him; rage had drained his colour.

'And since when have you been set to judge me, madam? You've been full of your own importance since the day you came—and why? Because you happen to use some new-fangled machine that everybody managed without for hundreds of years! Oh, you have certain skills—but I cannot imagine how that entitles you to criticize me!'

He strode to the door, then thought further. His tone was imperious, 'Miss Sutcliffe,' but she wouldn't look at him. He continued, nevertheless: 'If the prospect of Christmas in my miserable household so alarms you, we must arrange that you return to your native...where was it...Yorkshire? Temporarily, or otherwise...'

The door closed behind him.

Apprehensively, Katherine moved to the fire, only to recall that first day she'd come to this room with Lawrence. To discover that he needed moments of quiet, of relaxation, even gentleness.

She sighed; did this evening's exchange mean that if she continued here she would only find that aspect driven from their relationship?

Away in the copse, an owl hooted. Katherine jumped, shivered, drew even closer to the fire. This was one of the few rooms in the entire mansion where she felt at ease—was that significant? Was the melancholy air of Masterton Hall reflected from its owner? Had she been lulled, by his apparent interest in her, into overlooking the atmosphere of the place? Had his changed attitude, his friendliness, been calculated to achieve just that?

The exquisite furnishings did little to relieve the eeriness of this lovely old house, where the servants went about in ominous near-silence, and the master thwarted all attempts to alleviate its gloom.

Had—Katherine shuddered, allowing the doubts shadowing her for weeks to form an all-too-vivid picture—had Janet been near the sinister truth in suspecting that Lawrence imprisoned his wife here? Were hers the screams repeatedly heard?

FOUR

For two whole wearisome days Lawrence spoke to Katherine only when compelled. Because of this, she avoided him after dinner, retiring instead to her own room—to be surprised when the click of Lawrence's door revealed he'd retired also.

On the third morning she was first in the study, although dreading the renewal of his morose company and already wishing the time away.

Lawrence entered, sat facing her at his desk, then tossed across several gold sovereigns.

Bewildered, Katherine frowned. 'What's this for?'

'Your heart seems set on turning the place into some...pleasure palace! Take Janet and go into Maidstone—George has orders to put the carriage at your disposal. Buy what you deem needful to transform the nursery—even the servants' quarters. Only I forbid you to decorate any of my rooms!'

She gasped delightedly, feeling the weight lifted. 'You dear man! I knew you didn't intend remaining so solemn and severe—it really isn't like you.' She rushed impulsively from her chair, running round to hug him.

Lawrence seemed even more taken aback than Katherine herself by the gesture. Apparently sensing her apprehension, though, as she recognized its familiarity, he checked the instinct to free himself, and patted her hand.

'Go and sit down now, Kate, we have work to do. I trust you are satisfied!'

Eager to please, she rattled away at the keys until Lawrence stopped dictating.

'I should have asked, I suppose, if you'll manage to accomplish that before you go away for Christmas.'

Katherine smiled to herself, staring hard at the paper in her machine.

'Well? You are going, are you not?'

'I didn't say so,' she murmured—and, glancing up, caught a smile on his lips.

During dinner that evening, she ventured a further suggestion.

'Would you object if, when Janet and I go shopping, we took Master Simon with us? He'd love to see all the toys and the shop windows, brightly decorated...'

Lawrence snorted, then smiled wryly. 'Do as you please, Kate; you seem determined to have your way. I'm sure you'll only find the boy a nuisance.'

That evening, leaving the dining-room, she hesitated.

'Don't...' Lawrence said quietly, following her gaze to the stairs.

She felt his hand on her shoulder.

She turned to smile at him, and he smiled back. 'Unless we both go up—to the music room.'

★ ★ ★ ★

Surprising Katherine further, Lawrence gave her the next day off, for the shopping expedition.

It was an excited Simon who clambered on to the carriage seat to chatter the journey away. It was the first time he recalled riding in his father's brougham, so that alone was a treat.

When they arrived in Maidstone, however, and the boy espied the shops decked for

Christmas, he shouted gleefully, attracting the attention of passers-by. Momentarily, Katherine wished Lawrence could witness this delight, then frowned, realizing that, too, might fail to warm him towards Simon.

They chose a Christmas tree, then glass baubles and tinsel, before thinking of presents. Katherine, sure that George and Janet wished some time alone, took Simon with her, arranging a meeting place for the homeward journey.

Katherine enjoyed seeing things through Simon's eyes, and didn't protest when he constantly delayed her, exclaiming over some novelty. In one shop he stopped to admire a miniature farmyard.

'Look, Katy, just like in our story.'

On impulse, she turned his attention away to a musical box, requesting the shopkeeper to pack the farmyard. She would ensure that this year he had at least one gift he'd enjoy.

Completing a tour of the shops, Katherine watched Simon eyeing rows of sticky cakes in a confectioner's window, and so decided on visiting a tearoom. This he declared great fun, as they emerged, well pleased.

Further along the street, Katherine

paused, passing a jeweller's, attracted by a silver tiepin. Small and neat, she knew suddenly she must have it for Lawrence. Quickly, she checked her purse's contents; just sufficient remained from her last wages, providing she budgeted carefully.

She smiled. Her wants were always modest, and, scarcely venturing beyond the estate, she'd have little occasion for spending. Besides, she knew now she'd give Lawrence something on Christmas morning, and didn't intend being miserly.

Later, re-examining the tiepin in its velvet nest, she felt the glow of knowing she had done the right thing—the only—thing. Now she longed for Christmas, and Lawrence's surprise on opening the gift.

★ ★ ★ ★

On the following Saturday, Janet and Katherine took Simon through the park, towards the lake, in the crisp December air. Walking back they stopped in the copse to gather holly and mistletoe to add to their decorations.

Lawrence had relented further, allowing the giant tree a place on the landing. It stood, resplendent, above the hall.

Katherine, whilst trimming it, smiled to herself. Slowly but surely, Lawrence was accepting that Christmas was nearing, and that something must be done to mark the festival.

★ ★ ★ ★

On the day preceding Christmas Eve, Katherine emerged from her room to find Mrs Hawkins standing beside the landing balustrade, gazing up at the tree.

'Would you give me a hand, Miss?' the housekeeper began, more congenially than usual. 'One of the ornaments has fallen off the top and even with the step-ladder I cannot reach to replace it.'

Briefly, Katherine wondered that this woman, who was taller than herself, couldn't do so; but, recalling the housekeeper's greater age, smiled and said, 'Of course—give it to me...'

Taking the bauble, she mounted the step-ladder.

At the top, as she stretched out a hand to set the decoration in place, Katherine heard the wood cracking and splitting beneath her, and felt herself falling. She thought in horror of the enormous well of the staircase, of the steps—stone beneath the carpeting—convinced she was hurtling to her death. But her back caught the balustrade, then her head struck it, and she fell with a thud on the landing.

Katherine bit her lip, striving not to lose consciousness, and was astonished to see, when Mrs Hawkins bent over her, not shock, but disappointment. Suddenly she was terrified, more so than on feeling the ladder give way under her; but she managed to keep her senses, although only vaguely aware of what was going on around her. Doors were flying open, as occupants of the various rooms hurried to investigate. Simon came racing along from the nursery, with Janet closely following.

'It's Katy—she's hurt...' she heard the boy scream.

At that another door opened and she heard more feet speeding towards her.

'All right—stand aside, let me get to her,' commanded the voice accustomed to giving orders.

'I can stand by myself, if you just let me rest here for a second,' Katherine started to protest, as Lawrence knelt beside her.

'Can you move your legs?' he asked,

ignoring her protest.

Katherine nodded, wincing at the sharp pain from her back when she tried to do so. Without a word, he gathered her up in his arms.

'Don't stand staring like a pack of idiots,' he shouted, over his shoulder. 'Send George for the doctor.'

He carried her to his own room, kicking open the door, before laying her gently on the exquisite counterpane.

His eyes were anxious. 'Oh, Kate,' he sighed, 'what have you done?' He glanced to the open door. 'Do you want Janet—shall I fetch her?'

Katherine shook her head, trying vainly to stem her tears. Lawrence gave her another searching look then shut the door.

'Thank you,' she started, 'but you could have taken me to my own room...'

'And have all and sundry prying, disturbing you? Here, people enter only on my admission.' He sat on the edge of the bed. 'Where did you hurt yourself?'

'My back mostly—and my head. I think I hit them both.'

'But what on earth were you doing?'

'Mrs Hawkins asked me to replace an ornament on the Christmas tree; I'd almost succeeded when the step-ladder collapsed beneath me.'

Lawrence opened the door to look along the landing towards the broken ladder. He returned to her, dark eyes grave.

'You know, I suppose, that you could have gone crashing down on to those steps?' She saw him close his eyes, as though to block out the image.

Tears spilled from her eyes. 'I thought I was going to.'

'Oh, my dear!' Lawrence exclaimed, shaking his head, then taking charge of himself.

'We must discover how much damage is done—if we can without hurting you. That fool of a doctor may be ages. Can you move at all? Try sitting up...'

Katherine grimaced, attempting to lean on one elbow and force her aching back to support her.

'One moment...' He returned to the edge of the bed. 'Take my arm, Katherine. That's right...hang on to it hard. Now, prise yourself up, slowly...'

She struggled and his other arm came round to aid her. She heard his great sigh of relief.

'Thank God,' he murmured, holding

her to him, gently, but firmly. She felt his breath against her hair, but he said nothing. For some little time he held her thus, before resting her against the pillows.

'Oh, Kate...' he sighed again. When she met his eyes, she was amazed that they appeared moist.

As though conscious of her awareness of this, he moved from the bed to stand at the window, his back turned. 'Do you want anything?'

'No, thank you. I'm much better already—I could go to my room.'

'You will stay where you are—at least until Dr McLaren has been.' He smiled. 'What's the matter with you? Are you really afraid I've earned the reputation the rest of the household chooses to give me?'

Katherine laughed at that, as she was meant to, and won his smile of approval.

'You should know you can trust me, Kate.'

'I do—oh, I do...' she responded emphatically, bringing the smile to his eyes again.

When Dr McLaren at last arrived, he pronounced her bruised and badly shaken, but not seriously injured, although he warned that she would experience quite severe pain from her back for some time. With Lawrence's help the doctor saw her to her own room before departing.

Lawrence then sent for Janet to help prepare her for bed, but before he left promised to return when she was settled.

The rest of the day passed hazily for Katherine; the doctor had prescribed medicine to help her rest more easily, and she wakened only intermittently for the light meals sent up to her with Isobel. On and off throughout the day she wakened to find Lawrence in the room, and he left her only when it was time for her to settle for the night.

Katherine screamed, loudly, and again. Mrs Hawkins was bending over her; they were on the landing again, and the housekeeper was trying to force her over the balustrade. And then she wakened, shivering in the darkness, her nightgown clinging to her cold, yet perspiring, body.

With no preliminary knock, Lawrence burst in. 'It's all right, Katherine, I'm here—I'll take care of you.'

He came to the bed, helping her sit up, holding her to him. 'There's nothing to fear now,' he whispered, comfortingly, and she marvelled at his gentleness.

She could, nevertheless, still see Mrs Hawkins menacing her. She buried her head against Lawrence's shoulder, clinging to him. She knew, as certainly as if told in so many words, that the breaking ladder had been no accident. She longed to reveal her suspicions to this man, holding her so securely, but it sounded foolish. Lacking proof, she remained silent.

Presently Lawrence leaned her against the pillows and moved away to light the gas mantle. Then he seated himself in the bedside chair.

'You could go now...' Katherine began, though reluctantly.

He smiled. 'Are you dismissing me? Am I no longer permitted to move at will about my own home?'

'You know I would not say so! I—I should not keep you from your bed.'

Lawrence chuckled. 'Am I so very old and frail then, that you fear I will suffer for loss of a few hours' sleep? Is that what you think of me? Is it, Kate?'

She shook her head, smiled, and then, closing her eyes, listened whilst he talked quietly to her.

By morning Lawrence had gone, but

soon after one of the maids had brought in a tray he returned to enquire how she was.

Katherine rested until Dr McLaren, calling in the late afternoon, gave permission for her to get up for dinner. She dressed slowly, alarmed by the pale face regarding her from the mirror, then limped on to the landing. She shuddered as she passed the tree, and taking a deep breath continued towards the stairs.

Cautiously, clinging to the heavy rail, she began to descend. Every step she took was painful.

Lawrence must have heard some sound for he came out of his study.

'Katherine!' His expression was a curious mixture of joy and anxiety. 'Wait there—I'll come and assist you.'

Thus, with his help, Katherine arrived downstairs once more.

Next morning, being Christmas, she was determined to be down for breakfast. Dr McLaren had consented to this, providing that she took care and rested during that and the ensuing days.

She rose early, allowing adequate time to wash and dress, and so was in the dining-room before Lawrence. The gift she'd chosen for him, now carefully wrapped, she placed beside his napkin. After glancing about the room—and thinking how even that exquisite place would be brightened by festive decorations—she limped to the window seat.

Outside everything looked enchanting. Snow had fallen again overnight—the park was thick with it, the copse touched with a delicate frosting. Katherine looked beyond to the cluster of trees surrounding the tiny church, wondering if she would be able to walk so far.

The door opened and Lawrence came in, not immediately seeing her.

'Happy Christmas!' she exclaimed, turning to smile at him.

He stopped, appearing surprised that anyone should greet him thus, and then came to her.

'It might be—it might well be even that,' he responded quietly, 'now that you're much more like my Kate again.'

His hand went to her shoulder as, standing beside her, he contemplated the wintry landscape.

'Isn't it wonderful!' Katherine cried, and felt his eyes quizzing her.

He gave a tiny snort. 'You say that as

if you loved the place...'

'But of course I do—don't you?'

'Not any longer...' He opened his mouth as if to explain, then shut it again, firmly. He sighed and then, 'Not...not today, Katherine, don't ask me...'

He went to the table, then seeing the prettily wrapped package his eyes narrowed. 'Not for me, surely?'

'For whom then?'

'What? When there couldn't be a man further removed from the spirit of Christmas? And, my dear, sweet Kate—when I'm much too selfish to have considered buying something for you...'

'I didn't expect anything.'

'And that's the truth, I'll be bound! That's what you all think, isn't it, of Lawrence Rushton—a boorish man without an ounce of generosity in him.'

'Don't,' Katherine said firmly, going to him and laying a hand on his arm. 'You've been so kind to me, these last two days; and you've given me a lot, you know—teaching me to play the organ...and the volume of engravings...'

'That was only...' he began, then their eyes met. Suddenly, his slender fingers went to the back of her head, as he pressed

137

her face gently against him. 'Katherine,' he whispered gravely, 'what do you think of me?'

She laughed softly. 'Enough to wish to give you something—why not open it?'

Lawrence sat down. 'You'll have to help...'

Together they unwrapped the tiny parcel and she waited while he sprang the catch of the lid. For a long time he just looked at the fine silver tiepin, without speaking, then reached for her hand.

'Why, Kate—why are you so kind to me?'

She was standing beside his chair, and turning quickly, he buried his face against her. 'So kind,' he repeated, 'and so very good for me.'

Recovering a little from her astonishment, Katherine stroked the dark hair, as though he were Master Simon turning thus to her in some game, or on awakening. And then she laughed. 'I am becoming very hungry, Lawrence. Surely you are too?'

He raised his head, shaking it and smiling. 'Not in the slightest—food was the last thing occupying my mind.'

'Indeed?' she asked lightly. 'What was then?' But he only smiled.

★ ★ ★ ★

At the end of the meal Lawrence rose, enquiring if she would be attending morning service. Katherine's spirits soared, believing he intended accompanying her, but when she suggested this he frowned. 'Just as far as the door—to see you safely there. We can take the brougham.'

Katherine protested that she needed exercise, so they walked across the park, slowly, with Lawrence supporting her. When they reached the church, Katherine pleaded with him to reconsider, but he shook his head. 'You're as bad as Simon—and you also know the answer.'

But he was waiting for her after the service, and tucked her hand into the crook of his arm. They talked amiably on the way home.

She and Lawrence were in the drawing-room, reading, that afternoon when Janet rapped on the door, intent on having Katherine join the special nursery tea.

Katherine hesitated, her mind on the man who sat close by, the father who chose to ignore his son. She stood and gave a cry of pain, putting a hand to her back. She felt Lawrence glance from his book.

'Oh, dear, Janet! I've been sitting too long in one position. I'd never manage the stairs...'

'I'd give you a hand,' Janet offered. But this wasn't Katherine's intention.

'I don't think you'd be strong enough.' She turned towards Lawrence, now staring gloomily into the fire. 'Will you help me, Mr Rushton?'

Lawrence made some pretence at reluctance but rose to join them.

'Pray let me assist you, madam.' Wryly, he offered an arm.

At the nursery door he would have turned back, but Simon, full of Christmas excitement, hurled himself through the open door and clung to Lawrence's legs. 'I knew you'd come,' he shouted joyfully.

Katherine held her breath, awaiting Lawrence's reaction. He paused, as if weighing the matter—his eyes sought hers. He seemed at a loss. She inclined her head, very slightly, so Janet wouldn't notice.

'Very well, my...' he hesitated. 'Very well.'

The pleasures of nursery tea did not come readily to Lawrence Rushton. He sat uneasily, toying with a slice of cake, carefully avoiding Simon's adoring gaze.

He took no part in the childish games which followed, in which Katherine joined enthusiastically, biting her lips against the pain which shot intermittently through her.

Glancing across the nursery after almost an hour, she noticed a great sadness in Lawrence's eyes. Moments later she heard the door open as he slipped away.

'I must go now,' she whispered quickly to Janet, and followed.

He had reached the stairs, but she called after him, 'So, you're not prepared to give me your arm once more?'

He was not smiling when he swung round. 'You appeared in no need of assistance in there. It was contrived to get me there, wasn't it?'

'I won't lie to you.' She had caught him up now, and was close to flinching from those dark, penetrating eyes.

'Are you satisfied now?'

'No. You're not happy.'

Lawrence sighed, impatiently. 'Oh, leave me be—go to your room, can't you?'

Katherine smiled, undeterred. 'I've a better idea; you didn't eat much tea. I'll

141

see if Mrs Hawkins has some muffins. Then we'll lock ourselves away in the music room and toast them...'

She saw him considering the idea, wavering...

'Please, Lawrence...'

'I can't see why you seek my company.'

'But it doesn't displease you?'

He shrugged. 'Oh, have it your way.'

When she joined him in the cosy room, with its thick blue velvet curtains and blazing log fire, Lawrence was standing with his back to the hearth.

'Put those down for a moment, Kate,' he bade her, 'and come here...'

Katherine went to him, meeting the still grave eyes, which seemed to be boring into her soul. 'Yes?'

'I'm not young Simon, you know,' he said finally. 'You won't win me over so easily. There's too much, Katherine, too much that has happened in the past.'

She smiled gently; standing on tiptoe, she hastily kissed his cheek. About to back away, she was startled to find she couldn't. Lawrence was holding her, crushing her to him. His mouth sought and held her own. When he eventually released her, there was an odd light in his eyes.

'It had to happen—but you should not have allowed it...'

'Is a kiss between friends, at Christmas-time, so very unforgivable?'

Lawrence smiled slightly. 'I hope not...'

'Well then...'

He scowled suddenly. 'Nothing will develop from it. You understand? Nothing!'

'Why should it?' Katherine asked, forcing her tone to remain light. Yet, what had it meant? Lawrence surely was not the sort to snatch kisses covertly.

He was shaking his head now, though his smile returned. 'Oh, Kate—you're not so unsophisticated! And I am serious, my dear; your working for me has permitted our being together unchaperoned. I would hate it if you deemed a third party's presence necessary.'

'So—our being alone is important to you?' She had to ask—had to know.

'Haven't you observed how I have changed, how I am losing that awful tension, how—' he caught her hand to his lips—'how I find contentment in the hours we spend together—and only then?'

Katherine busied herself toasting muffins, mind and pulses agitated by Lawrence's kiss, and this admission. It was well that he restrain her; they may be almost in 1876, but there were strict conventions still.

Eating in companionable silence, beside the fire, it was easy to forget that so recently this man had caused that throbbing. Just as it was easy to believe there had been no violent threat to her life two days ago. Fleetingly, she wondered if Lawrence, by avowing dependence on their relationship, was contriving her rejection of disquieting thoughts. Was his every action a calculated reassurance—to keep her there, unquestioningly?

She shivered, then glimpsed his expression, looking across at her. How could she imagine him capable of such duplicity? All the same, no amicability would revise her opinion of his behaviour towards Simon. And that she would challenge—this evening.

Turning from the organ, where he was teaching her some of the easier Christmas carols, she began, 'Lawrence, why do you treat Simon as some stranger—and an utter nuisance?'

Immediately, his good humour evaporated. 'Questions, questions, always more questions! Confound it, Kate, why must I suffer this interminable inquisition from you!'

'Maybe—' she hesitated, and then took courage—'maybe because I care.'

He studied her minutely, then sighed. 'Can you begin to understand that all I see when I look at the child is a reminder of things I prefer to forget? Can't you see that even I, devoid of feeling as I am, can be hurt by remembering...?'

'I'm sorry,' she murmured.

'For Simon.' It wasn't a question.

'For both of you.'

* * * *

Next morning Lawrence seemed unusually light-hearted and Katherine hoped this was partly due to what had been said on Christmas Day. For she herself was far happier than previously. In his admission that Simon resurrected unhappy memories, Lawrence had provided an acceptable explanation. Which of us didn't, at some time, try to forget unpleasantness? The man was simply behaving naturally; who was she to pry into his distress?

As for that kiss—that sweet moment when his lips claimed hers? She had scarcely allowed her thoughts to dwell on it. It may have been, as he'd inferred, inevitable. A man and a woman, both lonely, alone together; in an unguarded minute some mutual need had found expression. All she could do was bow (if reluctantly) to convention, and subdue that need.

Breakfast over, Lawrence suggested a stroll through the park, 'If you are sufficiently recovered from your accident...' She nodded, smiling, and was offered his arm.

'I suppose your incapacity entitles you to cling to me!'

Laughing aside her querying if he objected, Lawrence headed along the terrace, past the ruined East wing. Tempted to ask how the interior had been destroyed, Katherine recalled the criticism of her perpetual questioning, and remained silent.

And it was easy enough to live in the present, for he was taking pains to interest her. From the terrace they went towards the rear, which she'd not yet explored. As they walked, Lawrence related how the house had been restored by his great-grandfather. He paused occasionally, indicating carved family crests above doors, as well as details of the reconstruction, satisfying her earlier curiosity about the differences in style. Passing the kitchens they came to the stables.

'Come and see...' Lawrence invited. He paused to pat the chestnut mare she'd seen him riding, then asked if she'd ever ridden.

Katherine laughed. 'You wouldn't think so—it was atop a great shire-horse!'

Lawrence smiled. 'Perhaps that, too, is something I should teach you?'

'You ride often, don't you?'

'Used to—when I was alone here. Now—' he hesitated, still smiling—'I find it easier to be happy in company.'

Katherine didn't know how to respond, overwhelmed by these confessions to appreciating her presence.

'Well, Katherine?' Lawrence persisted. He nodded towards a stall at the far end of the stables. 'There's a mount waiting for you...'

He strode towards the filly and rubbed the animal's nose affectionately. 'Midnight doesn't get sufficient exercise—I'm too heavy for her, but you—' his eyes, with a hint of mischief, travelled over Katherine—'you and she would get along admirably together.'

Katherine crossed to him. 'Surely someone rides her?'

'One of the stable-lads, who comes in daily from the village.'

'If that's all, why did you get her?'

Lawrence chuckled. 'There you have me—simply because I imagined Reveller over yonder might feel lonely.' He noticed Katherine's astonishment and laughed. 'I know what you're thinking! Yes, Kate, I do have infinite consideration—for horses! Won't you, though, ensure none of us endure loneliness—get that back of yours well, then ride with me...'

'Thank you, Lawrence, I'd love to.'

Leaving the stables, they skirted the West side of the house, and Lawrence pointed out a row of windows on the first floor. 'The ballroom...'

'I didn't know there was one.'

He shrugged. 'It hasn't been used for years. This house is wasted on a man like myself, who lives in near-solitude. It might have been so different...'

'Then why not...' she began, then his frown stopped her.

'I've become even more of a recluse,' he said, with a sigh. But his smile returned. 'Although, for the first time in long enough,

I'm taking interest in the place. Indoors again, I'll show you the pride of it all—the library.'

This was on the first floor, along a corridor, beyond the music room.

Katherine gasped delightedly when Lawrence motioned her to precede him into the room. The lofty ceiling was of ornate plasterwork, but even more impressive were the walls, housing countless beautifully-bound volumes. Between each section of shelves were exquisitely decorated columns, rising to a height of some ten feet, surmounted by a rich frieze and a pediment.

Set in one wall, replacing books in the centre panel, was a white marble fireplace. Of elegant craftsmanship, it was enhanced by a dark marble inset, carved to depict a Roman scene. A large mirror over the fireplace reflected Gothic windows.

Lawrence smiled. 'I see you're suitably impressed—I was very fond of this, indeed proud, for it was designed by Robert Adam.' Turning, he pointed. 'And observe that writing-desk—Chippendale.'

Smiling again at her pleasure, he wandered to the window, where Katherine joined him.

As they gazed over the snow-covered scene, some movement at the lake caught Katherine's eyes. 'What's that?' she exclaimed, touching his arm, then watched Lawrence's brows draw together.

'Skaters! Villagers—they must be stopped immediately!' He swung from the window and strode to the bell-pull.

Katherine was frowning also when he rejoined her. How hard he was! They'd passed a delightful morning, with the horses, then going round his home. Now he'd spoilt it all. It seemed he could tolerate any sight but people enjoying themselves. Always, he must do something to mar their happiness. What possible harm could emerge from permitting these poor people some fun—even within the boundary of his property?

She glanced sideways at him, anticipating his mouth grim with annoyance, but he only looked...wistful. Katherine put out a hand towards his, then let it fall, instead, to her side. For some reason this man was terribly sad—and she felt totally inadequate.

She sighed, depression sweeping over her, and recalled the earlier occasion when she'd felt thus weighed down. Shivering,

150

she remembered the desolation of the ruins. How she hated them—festering like some wound in the side of the house. Lawrence's house—his home.

FIVE

Shortly after Christmas Janet was taken ill with influenza. For a day or two she struggled on, trying to fulfil her duties, but eventually had to retire to bed. By this time young Simon's streaming eyes and hoarse throat confirmed he had taken the infection from her. And he, in his sickness, became fractious and demanding.

Katherine tried to restore peace by going into his room at various times during the day—but this wasn't enough, even with the help of Isobel, the parlourmaid. And Lawrence protested (as Katherine had feared he would) that she was neglecting her own work for the boy.

Thus, Mary—a niece of Mrs Hawkins— was brought in daily to help in the nursery. Even so, the girl, who was but fifteen years old, could not manage unaided, and Katherine endeavoured to watch over the situation. She, in turn, grew over-tired, but endured this cheerfully, believing she was doing some good for Lawrence's young son.

A little before nine o'clock one evening, Mrs Hawkins came into the drawing-room, where Lawrence and Katherine were sitting before a glowing fire.

'Yes?' he demanded, coldly, and Katherine sensed he was annoyed by the intrusion.

'I'd like a word with Miss Sutcliffe, sir...'

He nodded to where Katherine was reading, across the hearth from him.

'It's Master Simon,' Mrs Hawkins began. 'Mary can't do a thing with him. For an hour or more she's tried, but he only screams...'

Katherine rose at once. 'I'll come right away...'

'Oh, you will, will you?' Lawrence enquired, curtly; then he appeared to remember the housekeeper's presence. 'You may go, Mrs Hawkins.'

He waited until the door closed behind her, and Katherine felt apprehension mounting inside her. When she met his eyes, they were blazing.

'I've had enough of this,' he declared, furiously. 'Make up your mind whether you came here to assist me—or to act wet-nurse to that spoiled child!'

'Oh, Lawrence,' she began placatingly, 'you know he's quite the opposite of spoiled. And now he's ill and needs extra loving...'

He snorted. 'Then let someone else see to it—why must it always be you?'

'With Janet ill, I'm the one he needs.'

'The fact remains that isn't why you came here.'

Katherine took a deep breath, endeavouring to still her own anger. 'So far as I'm aware, I've attended to every job you have set me today. My time is my own now!'

She watched all colour drain from Lawrence's face. He opened his mouth to speak, then shut it. He shrugged, motioned silently to the door. Reaching it, Katherine heard him draw a sharp breath.

'Just remember,' he shouted, 'you're the one who's made this choice!'

One hand on the door handle, she hesitated, thinking to calm the father before going to the son; but screams sounded upstairs, so she went on her way. Lawrence would have to wait.

Simon, lying half out of bed, covers tossed aside, was red-faced from crying and his high temperature. His nightclothes were saturated with perspiration, his dark hair clinging damply.

Mary, seated on the edge of the bed, was close to tears herself.

'I'm sorry,' she began, seeing Katherine, 'but he won't settle, won't let me near him. He won't do anything; not lie still, nor take the medicine Dr McLaren left this afternoon.'

Katherine nodded. 'All right, Mary, it's not your fault; he's so wretched he doesn't know what ails him.' She gathered Simon to her, wrapping a blanket round him.

'You go for hot water,' she suggested. 'Isobel will help you carry it. We'll bath him in front of the fire here. Then we'll put clean nightclothes on him, and fresh sheets on the bed; that should help him settle.'

The girl departed. Simon nestled against Katherine, thrusting sticky fingers into hers. 'I knew you'd come; you love me, don't you?'

'Of course I love you.'

'More than anybody?'

Disturbed, she caught herself thinking of the man downstairs. 'I told you, Simon—I love you.'

He wasn't satisfied. 'Most of all, I said...'

Katherine sighed, then smiled to herself. 'I love lots of people.'

'But you came up here specially to be with me, didn't you?' Simon sounded triumphant. It appeared he could learn nothing from his father about possessiveness. And Katherine realized that hitherto she had not recognized Lawrence's attitude as possessive. And if it was? Astonishing as the notion may be, she couldn't find it dismaying.

So, Lawrence had been hurt, unable to understand the boy had more need of her now—she'd show him that was her only reason for leaving the drawing-room. She'd rectify the matter—keep both members of the Rushton family happy.

Mary and Isobel brought steaming jugs of water—Mary would have stayed to help bath the boy, but Simon wouldn't have that; he wanted only Katherine. She was obliged to send the girl away. Katherine found that bathing the sick child took appreciably longer in consequence. Even whilst she was finding fresh linen and remaking the bed, Simon moved only reluctantly from her lap.

Once settled between the cool sheets, however, with Mary departed after her brief reappearance to tidy the room, Simon seemed more cheerful.

He was, indeed, too bright for past ten o'clock. He persisted in chattering and wouldn't quieten until Katherine promised a story.

She yawned, sitting in the bedside chair, her exhausting days taking their toll. And even when the hall clock struck ten-thirty, he showed no inclination towards sleeping. Katherine tried being firm with him then, ordering him to close his eyes now, for she was leaving. He started to cry at that, inducing such a fit of coughing that she had to fetch him a glass of water.

Simon grasped her hand. 'Stay with me, Katy,' he pleaded, dark eyes unnaturally bright in the feverish face. Thinking of his loneliness with Janet ill and nobody else in the house seeming to care, she took pity, electing to stay till sleep overtook him.

Somewhere around eleven, as Simon's eyelids were at last beginning to droop, Katherine was disturbed by a noise behind her. Glancing over her shoulder, she saw the door open, quietly. Lawrence.

Smiling, she beckoned; he hesitated, briefly, then closed the door again.

Katherine rose, worried by his expression, about to go to him. But Simon wouldn't release her fingers. 'Don't go, Katy,' he murmured huskily.

She sighed and sank on to the chair once more.

* * * *

When Simon was asleep and she felt she could leave him, Katherine dragged herself exhaustedly to her bedroom. Her injured back ached abominably from sitting so long.

Eleven-thirty—much too late to smooth over her difference with Lawrence. She'd have to accept that disturbance until morning.

She brushed her hair, then washed face and hands in the cold water, which was all she had in her room. She reached for her nightgown, kicked off her slippers and began unfastening her dress.

It was then Katherine heard the organ, sounding urgent and discordant. She wondered if it had been playing earlier and she'd been too tired to notice.

She believed she could distinguish part of a Bach Toccata and Fugue, but the rendering was too agitated for certainty.

Swiftly, she thrust feet back into her slippers and fastened the buttons of her bodice, hurrying to the music room.

It was illuminated only by moonlight, reflected from the snow outside.

Lawrence sat at the organ, his back to her, oblivious of her presence.

Biting her lip, Katherine listened and watched. She had been right—it was the Bach Toccata. His left hand fingered the keys as positively as ever, but for the rest...

Katherine gave a shuddering sigh, blinking against her tears. Lawrence was dragging what remained of his right arm mercilessly back and forth over that keyboard. Abruptly, he stopped, sank his head between hunched shoulders, to rest on the Swell manual.

Initially, she wondered if it would be kinder to leave him the dignity of remaining unaware that anyone shared his misery. Only she couldn't.

She could no more walk away from that

room than neglect to go to Simon earlier. Unsure what she would do or say, she crossed to Lawrence. And still he gave no sign that he knew she was there. And still she knew not what to do...how to cope with his distress—or her own, which his engendered.

Almost of its own volition, her right hand went to the organ. Her fingers remembered, if she did not, Lawrence's coaching through that Toccata. He raised his head, but said nothing and made no further move. He was staring straight ahead—as if seeing emptiness—or more than she could see. She knew not which. And she did not know what to say...

Instead, her left hand went to his shoulder, while the right continued playing the piece. She willed him to make a move—to say or do something that would give some clue how to proceed.

And then it happened. Perfectly in time with her, he took up the left-hand part, without turning to her or speaking. Katherine sighed with relief, and slid on to the seat beside him.

'You came,' Lawrence murmured, but that was all.

They played on, as far as he had taught her, and then she stopped. Her fingers went to still his. 'No more, Lawrence, till next time.'

Suddenly she shivered and he noticed. He rose quickly and crossed to the dying fire. Taking up the poker, he stoked the embers back to life. He turned to her then, with a hesitant smile. 'Remember that first time we kindled a fire in here?'

Katherine smiled back and went to him. 'You don't think I'd forget?'

He shrugged. 'Never sure—of anything, with you. I believe you are with me, and then...'

'Lawrence, why can't you bear to see me go to anyone else?'

He didn't reply, but his frown returned.

'I sometimes think,' she persisted, 'that you hate to see people happy together. Like the other day when those skaters upset you.'

'They were trespassing.'

'Was that the only reason?'

He sighed, and shook his head. 'You know it wasn't, don't you? Oh, Kate, if only I'd the right to claim your understanding...'

'Oh, Lawrence, don't talk of rights in

that context! I want to understand—won't that suffice?'

He went to the huge leather chair, then beckoned to her. Puzzled, Katherine went to him. He reached for her hand, squeezed it, then let it go.

'It's...difficult, owning a place like this; it cuts you off from so much...'

'It need not...'

'With my temperament?' he snorted. 'It takes a woman like you, Kate, to get near me.'

She was silent.

Lawrence continued, 'Haven't you observed that I lack something which enables people to confide in others, to win them over, to make friends...' He stopped.

'You were right,' he admitted next. 'I was miserable watching those skaters—ridiculous as that might seem. I knew that was one thing I'd never experience—sharing fun... Can you imagine it—*me*?'

'Yes, I can,' she answered quietly.

'What?' he laughed incredulously.

'I can, Lawrence,' she insisted. 'I can see you as the owner of this lovely house should be—entertaining in that ballroom, heading the table in your exquisite dining-room, taking parties of friends to picnic

161

near the lake in summer...'

He laughed again. 'Oh, Katherine, indeed...!'

'You could do it—and be happy so.'

'Alone?'

'Only if you chose that way. But you'd do it, even so. You see, I don't believe you are entirely a recluse, any more than...well, than I'm entirely a model secretary. Just as I'm also the kind of woman who must rush to Simon when...'

'Oh, yes,' Lawrence interrupted. 'Katherine, do hesitate before such action in the future...' His voice was sombre.

She tried to laugh away the warning. 'You are being silly—about a small boy who seemed to have no one.'

'I mean it, Kate. I was frightened...'

'Frightened?'

'Of my own reaction. I was determined to dismiss you—for defying me. No, rather for...for siding with the rest of them.'

'Oh. Well, if you can't bear me to...'

'My meaning has escaped you, Katherine. I am a hasty man, in a moment of fury I could well do something I would regret, I could send you away. And I never retract.'

And now Katherine was frightened—by

the prospect of dismissal. But there was more—something she must rectify without delay. 'You said a moment ago, "For siding with the rest of them." What do you mean, Lawrence? You infer everyone's against you.'

'And aren't they? Rivers, Mrs Hawkins, your friend Janet, and the rest—haven't they all labelled me the brutal master, to be despised—tolerated only because I pay their wages? They see how I treat Simon—have no friends...'

'None?' she asked, quietly.

Lawrence smiled, fleetingly. 'Or *had* none. So, my dear, my only friend—don't let me believe you prefer the company of those who smile more readily.'

When, at long last, Katherine retired, sleep proved elusive. Lawrence had revealed so much...amid the confusion in her mind, one fact alone remained clear: he needed her. His distraught playing demonstrated it, and his subsequent words verified that. But *how* did he need her? As what? To remain simply his confidante, his close companion—or did he intend more?

Did he—she hardly dared phrase it in her thoughts—did he propose making her the second Mrs Rushton? She had sensed frequently, of late, that he was holding back, restraining some feeling growing between them. Was Lawrence, too—reluctantly perhaps—conscious of this deepening of their relationship?

After the emotions of that evening, a strange peace settled over Masterton. Simon recovered and Janet returned to her post in the nursery, so Katherine was able to devote her attention to Lawrence. And he responded to this; laying aside his ill-humour, he became agreeable, charming, even witty.

Katherine was delighted; if all he needed was her absorption in his interests, that was no hardship.

And then he went off, suddenly, to London. One evening they dined as usual, then sat together in the drawing-room. Next morning he said certain business required attention, and was gone.

Katherine wrestled with unreasonable anger—he expected she play the part of a true friend, keeping nothing back, yet he could go off thus, with scarcely a word of explanation. She was hurt; although, as the day progressed, she reprimanded herself for being unduly sensitive.

But even copying his book failed to

interest her. She thumbed through the manuscript, scowling at his abominable writing—until remembering the reason for it.

Tears pricked her eyes; what must it be like—having to learn to use one's left hand? Idly, she picked up pen and a scrap of paper. Laboriously, she wrote, tongue between her teeth, *Katherine Sutcliffe*. Even she herself could hardly read it. Yet Lawrence had persevered, making one hand serve as two. How had he done it? Again, she tried, and a third time, each effort only a fraction more legible than the last. She covered the sheet of paper with this unfamiliar signature, then turned it over. Bored with her own name, she wrote *Masterton Hall*—then *Lawrence Rushton;* over and over again, until her fingers ached with discomfort.

Katherine started, guiltily, when the study door opened after a brief knock. This was no way to occupy her time in Lawrence's absence. He trusted her to work unsupervised. She pushed the piece of paper beneath others, glancing towards Mrs Hawkins, who had entered.

The housekeeper, of whom Katherine had been wary since the step-ladder incident, seemed inclined to be friendly.

'I was just wondering if you'd prefer luncheon in your room, Miss Sutcliffe, with the master away on another of his trips to London.'

'Very well, Mrs Hawkins, if that's more convenient.'

'Oh, it wasn't that, Miss. I thought maybe you'd find the dining-room a mite lonely.'

Katherine smiled. 'If that is the only reason, I will keep the arrangements as they are.'

'As you wish.' But Mrs Hawkins didn't go; she wandered round the study, as though she had something on her mind.

'Was there anything else?' Katherine demanded.

'Mr Rushton visits London frequently, doesn't he?'

'Does he?' Katherine responded coldly. 'I really couldn't say—this is only the second occasion since I came to work here.'

'Is that all? Now that surprises me— unless, well, perhaps he needn't travel to London for all his comforts...?'

'I beg your pardon!' Katherine could scarcely believe she'd heard aright.

'Now he has you to keep him company, I mean, Miss Sutcliffe—that was all.'

'I hope it was, Mrs Hawkins. And now, if you don't mind, I am very busy...'

Still the housekeeper lingered, though working her way round to the door.

'It's only to be expected, isn't it? We know what men are. And Mr Rushton must miss the joys of a happy marriage. Who can blame him for going off—they tell me there are plenty of such women in London.'

Katherine took a deep breath, trying to check the colour rushing to her cheeks. How dared Mrs Hawkins come in here to discuss Lawrence Rushton in this manner! Katherine looked to the door, pointedly, but the other woman had already anticipated that, and opened it. She knew when to make her exit; and, besides, she'd implanted the doubts she'd intended.

Although she recognized that all Mrs Hawkins had said was mere conjecture, calculated to make her uneasy, Katherine found herself unable to dismiss it. Was that—could that be Lawrence's reason for going there? She had believed this was no more than a visit to his publishers. It could, of course, be a convenient arrangement to satisfy other needs as well. She closed her eyes. She would not think of it. And it was no concern of hers. There wasn't the slenderest thread binding them. He had kissed her, that was all. A blush suffused her cheeks again, remembering. Had that too been some momentary passion?

'No, no, no!' something inside her cried, 'I mustn't believe that; it wasn't desire, but...affection?'

The next few days were, nevertheless, trying. Mrs Hawkins had succeeded in sowing doubt; scarcely an hour passed without Katherine wondering what Lawrence was about in London. Where he was—and with whom. And she missed him more than she'd imagined possible. During his previous absence she had bemoaned the quietness, the lack of interest, but much had changed since then. Now she missed his presence at mealtimes, his hand on her shoulder as she sat at the organ, the knowledge that she need only glance from her book, across the drawing-room, to see him.

★ ★ ★ ★

As day succeeded day, her thoughts

became more confused. Half-believing the housekeeper's explanation, she found it hard to imagine being quite so relaxed with Lawrence in the future.

Never in her life before had she been alone, and in close proximity, with any man unrelated to her. Only her employment with Lawrence permitted that now. And she had been aware of a certain racing of her pulses, had sensed that first day in the music room that he was teasing her by remaining near. But surely that had been *all*—seeking only to amuse himself by bringing the colour to her cheeks? It had been a joke; a little, silly, private joke.

Or was this an aspect of Lawrence Rushton that she had chosen to overlook?

Just as she was losing all confidence in him, Katherine received his letter. Brief, hardly more than a note, it allayed her fears. He had, she learned, spent a deal of time with his publishers and had had other business needing attention. Now all was nearing completion and he looked forward to returning in time for dinner the following evening.

Katherine's heart sang—this was the Lawrence she had come to know; concealing nothing. And surely, if his 'other business' involved women of ill-repute, he wouldn't even have referred to it.

Throughout the next day Katherine lived in happy anticipation of his homecoming. She dressed carefully for dinner, choosing an amber-coloured gown which he'd previously admired. Satin, it was, admittedly, dressy for a simple meal at home, but she wanted to wear something special. She brushed her chestnut hair, parting it in the centre, then spent some considerable time sweeping it up and back over her ears, allowing curling tendrils to fall loose around her face, softly framing it. The hall clock chimed, reminding her she'd be late for the meal. Hastily extinguishing the gas light, she ran lightly downstairs to the dining-room. Her welcoming smile died on her lips—the room was empty. She told herself Lawrence had probably come in only seconds ago and was changing. But she had heard no sound from that room next to hers; had he not yet returned from London?

Rivers put his head round the door; seeing her alone he went away without speaking. Katherine sighed; his attitude towards her remained unflinchingly chilly.

Half an hour later Rivers reappeared and

silently set Katherine's soup before her.

'It seems Mr Rushton is delayed,' she began.

'Apparently,' Rivers replied shortly, and left the room without another word.

There was still no sign of Lawrence when Katherine had finished eating; she remained in the dining-room, thinking to keep him company. Presently, however, Isobel came to clear away so Katherine went towards the drawing-room. She couldn't settle to the book that she'd been reading; impatiently, she crossed the hall to the study. She would find one of Lawrence's books, surely that would occupy her. Taking one of his novels from the shelf, she retraced her steps to the drawing-room.

And still he didn't come, and now she was growing anxious. Supposing something had befallen him as he travelled from Maidstone station? Only a week ago a brougham had overturned when its wheels hit a patch of ice and the horse, frightened, had bolted.

Unable to sit still, Katherine went to the music room. Here she felt close to Lawrence, even when he was away. She ran her fingers over the keys of the piano, then the organ, but didn't sit at either. If...*when* Lawrence returned she wanted to hear his familiar step in the hall.

She stoked the log fire, showering sparks on to the hearth. She smiled slightly—a fire always burned here now, this once-neglected room had become their retreat. And so it would be soon. Her days of isolation would be ended.

At eleven, though, she was alone still—sitting in the firelight, trying to suppress her childlike disappointment. Lawrence had been delayed, she tried convincing herself; tomorrow at breakfast she would see him. Tomorrow.

With that thought she sighed, then put the guard in front of the fire, about to go to her room.

Behind her the door creaked open, sending her heart pounding; half expecting to see Lawrence, she swung round.

An ancient woman shuffled in. Dishevelled grey hair surrounded pallid features, from which vivid brown eyes regarded her.

Katherine shivered.

The woman nodded, approvingly. 'So you came, at last. I knew you would.'

'Knew?'

'My boy needs you.'

172

For one awful moment Katherine thought this crone must be Simon's mother, but that meant... Oh, how could he even touch...

'My boy—Lawrence.'

Katherine started; this couldn't be his... mother?

'Surprised? Yes, I can see...' The woman settled into the leather armchair. 'He's been lonely, but I always knew...' She stared into the fire, smiling uncannily.

Katherine knew not what to say or do, if her thudding heart would have permitted any action. Again the creature spoke.

'Death there'll be, once more, at Masterton Hall—death and danger. It's a cruel place, see you take care, my dear—live—give him a son...'

She got no further for hurrying feet brought a middle-aged woman in grey to claim her charge; with no word of explanation to Katherine, her caller was taken away.

Still temporarily thrown off balance by the incident, Katherine went to her room. Bemusedly, she took the pins from her hair, began to brush it, preparing for bed, though heaven knew if she would ever sleep again! Tomorrow she must question Lawrence...

But was that fair? Having seen this creature claiming to be his mother, could she blame him for wishing to conceal her existence? Would it not be more tactful to try, without involving him, to discover how the poor soul had been reduced to this state? And surely one mystery was solved, for who but she could have been responsible for those screams? Who else be locked away?

Startled by knocking on her door, Katherine found Rivers there, carrying a candle. 'The master has sent me to fetch you.'

She frowned, puzzled; she'd not heard the front door, nor Lawrence's step in the hall. 'But surely he's still...' she started, but Rivers interrupted, meeting her eyes unflinchingly. 'How could he ask for you, if he'd not returned? This way...'

Katherine set down her hairbrush and followed. Rivers astonished her by going along the corridor and unlocking the gallery door. His candle flickered over the pictures.

'There's no one here,' she protested, but was pushed inside.

Locking the door, Rivers seized her, marching her along the echoing gallery. 'Come along, he's in here...' He was dragging her towards the room which wasn't a room!

Katherine took a deep breath, searching through confused memories of what lay beyond that door, for anything that might save her. Because Rivers intended her destruction. The man's vice-like grip told her any struggle would end with her hurtling into space.

Then she realized Rivers wasn't aware she knew about that room; she'd play on that—her only hope. He was hustling her relentlessly towards what seemed inevitable. And she couldn't give up, couldn't let certain death come. There was so much undiscovered. So much undeveloped in her relationship with Lawrence. So much unrevealed as yet. She couldn't just go, let life slip away, without learning why he was stern with Simon, why so insistent that he had no wife, why, until her coming, he'd remained aloof. She had to learn all this—and understand him better.

They reached the door. Rivers jerked back its curtain, turned the handle.

'Just step inside, Miss...' He extinguished the candle.

And he loosed his hold on her. Those were his mistakes; in darkness he, too, could see nothing. He would only sense that she hadn't gone through that door. Other than that, she could be anywhere. She lunged at him, caught him off guard, and heard him fall. But he was up again, instantly; she heard rapid breathing as he advanced on her. He snatched at her skirts, pulling her to the floor, struggling to get his fingers on her throat. Katherine scratched at him, trying to reach his eyes or nostrils, but a heavy hand came smacking into her face, stinging tears to her eyes.

He fought savagely, as with another man, hurling himself bodily upon her, attempting to overpower her; and as they struggled she realized what he was doing. Inch by inch he was edging her towards that open door. She felt for it with her feet, meaning to kick it to. Only Rivers, reacting faster, kicked it first—forcing it wide open.

Katherine felt the cold blast of night air whistling through from the ruins. Rivers gave a great heave, and turned her over. She was facing the door now, could see in the light reflecting off the snow how near it was. And Rivers's malevolent expression as he bent over her. He caught her flowing hair, rising, dragging her to her feet by her tresses. His other hand clamped iron-hard on her wrist, and she feared she was nearing the end.

He hung on to her hair, pulling her this way and that, jerking her forward and back. Down and up went her head, down and up, down and... The pain was excruciating. Her teeth found the back of his hand. Rivers gave a screaming oath as she bit. She tasted his blood—if she spat it out, she'd release him.

And then he let go her wrist, freed her hair.

He put the wounded hand to his mouth; they eyed each other, warily. Both glanced around. Simultaneously, they saw the cutlass, gleaming in the half-light, on the wall. Rivers sprang for it, and advanced, slowly, savouring the moment, towards her. Katherine knew she could no longer fight him. The other door locked, she had but one escape. She backed steadily towards the ruins.

With a satisfied smile, Rivers lowered

the cutlass but trod resolutely on at her. He was only inches away, he could have touched her—but he didn't. This would be less distasteful. He put a hand to the edge of the heavy oak door, eyeing her unflinchingly as she withdrew further from him.

Praying there was but a slight ledge—some three inches would suffice—within that shell of a room, Katherine kept on retreating.

Now the door was being closed on her—within seconds it could force her into the abyss. She leaned all her weight against it, intent on preventing it from closing. She felt resistance, as Rivers pushed from the other side. And he was on firm floorboards—her heels were in space now. Soon she'd be falling—with nothing to stop her.

Katherine grasped the door frame, to use it as leverage. Loose, the huge block of wood fell away. Involuntarily, she screamed when it crashed to the filthy stone floor—as she might have crashed. She heard laughter then from the gallery, felt an easing of the pressure on the door. At once, she understood—Rivers believed she'd fallen. She must make no sound, give no sign that it wasn't so. This demanded complete stillness, she must find something to help steady her. Quickly, she glanced to left and right in the eerie white light. If there was some foothold, somewhere to cling until Rivers had gone...

The door frame had left a cavity, maybe six inches across, and an inch deeper. Taller than Katherine herself, it presented the only possibility. Here and there enormous iron nails, originally securing the wood, protruded from the masonry. Could she hang on to them?

She inserted her right toe into the cavity, and gripped one of the nails, after testing its strength. Then, forcing herself to keep balance, she swung her weight across, bringing her left foot to join the other. Inwardly, she sighed, relieved; now she need only wait...

As if in derision, the door clicked shut; she heard the key turn in the lock.

Katherine shuddered. What use the struggle, why trouble to fight him? All was lost now. She was locked out here, to cling, like a limpet to a sea wall, until numbed fingers relaxed their grip, and dizziness stole her stability.

SIX

Katherine closed her eyes against the nausea threatening to overwhelm her, only to open them, startled, as a bat wheeled past her head. She stifled a scream. If Rivers lingered in the gallery, no clue must reveal that she lived. Only supposing he started to search for her body...then there'd be no chance...

What was that thought—chance? She could scarcely believe anything remained within her to acknowledge any such thing. Wasn't she exhausted, frightened, beaten...? But she was alive still, had not succumbed to unconsciousness. That must be to some purpose. Having lasted this far, was she to toss all away—with her own body, into the ruins? Thrown on to her own resources, would she let them betray her into dying? And now—thinking again—was it not unlikely Rivers would seek her remains? He, surely, would keep away, leaving others to discover the body—in time.

So then, time was what it gave her—and she would use it. At worst, a false step could send her plummeting; better that than giving up. Her life was worth fighting for—wasn't it?

Cautiously, she looked to the right and noticed a wooden joist, almost a foot thick, crossing towards what was left of a dividing wall. The wall, partially crumbled, had once supported a wooden staircase. Katherine noted, joyfully, the upper flight of stairs still remained. Wriggling one foot free of her skirts, Katherine bent down, gingerly, clinging to those protruding nails till she was kneeling on the joist. It took her weight.

Slowly, she began to crawl along the cobwebby beam, forcing herself to look ahead instead of down. Splinters ran into her hands and legs, but eventually she reached the other side, and knelt there, peering round her. She was panting and paused to regain her breath, then swung her left leg over the beam. Hands locked together round it, she dangled into space, feeling with her feet for the rickety steps. They were out of reach.

Clenching her teeth, she gradually eased herself down until she hung by her fingertips. First one foot touched the top step, then the other. Trembling, she clutched at the wall, waiting for the shuddering to stop. Then, glancing down, she saw the skirts of her lovely dress as the wind snatched at them: a mass of tatters. She promised herself a new gown, something superb—if she survived.

Warily she descended the steps, testing each in turn, until she grew more confident that they would support her and began to believe there would be an escape.

Suddenly the stairs swung away from the wall. Timber creaking and splintering all around her, unable to grasp anything to save herself, Katherine plunged down.

She must have fainted; it seemed some considerable time later that she opened her eyes—wondered, fleetingly, where she was. Her cheeks were wet with tears, her breath frustrated sobbing.

The biting east wind was driving snow through the gaping windows. Though she had fallen some distance from them, snow had blown across the filthy floor and her saturated dress clung miserably. Where the dress was ripped, and her petticoats beneath, she saw great gashes on her legs. Blood oozed from them. She put out her hands to the wounds and noticed that they, too, were raw and bleeding.

Finding she was unable to stand, Katherine feared she was trapped by the broken stairway. Groping around with an exploratory hand revealed, however, that this was not so. She was held by further injury to her damaged back.

So that was it—again. She must pit her decreasing strength, not against some inanimate object, nor some other person, but against pain. She must permit no defeat. She alone could ensure survival. She must summon sufficient determination to get out of here before she froze to death—or lurking rats attacked her.

Somehow, she rolled over on to her knees. Putting tender palms to the ground, she pressed, willing her back to support her. Despite the searing pain, she scrambled to her feet. She tottered a few steps, but it was too much.

Screaming with anger, she dropped to her knees again; thwarted, she beat the ground with her fists. She would get there—she would reach that wall. In here no one would discover her—outside, there was a slender hope...

Breath rasping, hands clawing at the

ground, she dragged herself inch by inch towards the wall. No matter now that her poor hands must work for the rest of her near-useless body. Awkwardly, she hauled herself on to the stone sill, and surveyed the snow-covered scene. Freedom. The grass was several feet below but, uncaring now, Katherine flung her painful self from the building.

She lay where she had fallen, oblivious of the icy moisture seeping towards her skin. Her hands throbbed, were ruined; would she ever again apply them to that magnificent machine? And did it matter—her skill with the invention had brought nothing but trouble, and terror.

In a sickening wave of pain before losing consciousness, Katherine pictured Rivers's triumph when she was discovered dead in the morning. She had no doubt that this would be her fate.

★ ★ ★ ★

Strong arms were carrying her, she was laid gently on cushions. But this unsteady, though curiously regular, jogging jarred her back terribly. She moaned, moving her

184

head from side to side, and the arm holding her against the cushions tightened. A cool hand touched her forehead. Katherine stiffened, remembering. So she had been found, before it was too late. She dared not open her eyes. Rivers?

'Kate...'

Unbelievingly, she raised her hands. 'Lawrence...'

He nodded, pressing his lips to her hand. 'Thank God we found you. We were delayed on the road; because this horse of ours lost a shoe and we had to knock up a blacksmith. It was George who saw you—heaven be praised for his keen eyes; you wouldn't have lasted the night exposed to these elements.'

His dark eyes sought hers, he pressed her face gently against his shoulder. 'Katherine, Katherine!'

Looking beyond him, when he eventually moved away a little, she discovered they were in Lawrence's carriage; he was half-kneeling on the floor, holding her on to the seat, steadying her against its rocking.

'We're taking you round to the front,' he explained. 'I'll soon get you to your room.'

When they reached the door, he swung her into his arms again, and carried her to her bedroom.

★ ★ ★ ★

Lawrence asked no questions, though remaining with her until Dr McLaren arrived to examine her and dress her wounds. And when Janet had helped wash and undress her and Katherine lay, aching and sore still, but in clean linen, he returned.

'Another accident, Katherine?' he asked, when Janet had gone.

She shook her head. 'No—and I don't believe the other was either...' He didn't appear surprised; perhaps he also had been suspicious.

He sighed, occupying the chair beside the bed. 'You must try to sleep now, Kate; you can tell me all about it in the morning.'

'But...Rivers,' she began.

'Sleep, my love,' Lawrence insisted, 'or you'll be ill.'

'But you've got to be careful as well, Lawrence—Rivers is dangerous...'

A smile played round his lips for a

second. 'I shall be here, with you, and the door's locked. I will ensure that you come to no further harm.'

Katherine wakened to find a comforting hand on her own—and remembered. Before opening her eyes, she recalled Lawrence's concern and kindness, his calling her 'his love'. Could this be real—or her own imagining? As if to answer that, she felt his breath on her face, his lips on her forehead.

She opened her eyes, and smiled at him.

Lawrence smiled, wryly. 'You shouldn't have wakened! Yes, my Kate, this is what I feel for you—although, I fear, with no right to declare it.'

Katherine frowned and he rose, stepping back from the bed to look down at her. 'That is why we will speak no more of this...affection. I only want you to know it exists.' He began gnawing at his lip, and she realized this had become a habit. Then he smiled again, 'And how are you now?'

She tried to move and winced. 'Stiff— and sore.'

'But afraid no longer—I can see by your eyes.'

Katherine smiled. 'You are here.'

He smiled back, ruefully. 'I'll call Janet to stay with you while I bath and shave, and you have breakfast. Then you must tell me all about it...'

'Now,' Katherine insisted, urgently, 'before he attacks you as well.'

'I don't believe he will do that—he'd lose too much if I were dead—at present.'

'He is...blackmailing you, isn't he?'

'Of course not; how could he?' A flush had sprung to his cheeks, but Katherine was not to be put off. 'Lawrence, don't lie to me—I heard him, or enough to form my own conclusions.'

He began to pace the room, then came to stand looking down at her again. 'And if he is—that's my affair.'

'It places you at his mercy.'

'I can handle Rivers.'

'He left me for dead, Lawrence—tried to push me from the gallery into the ruins, he...' the memory, starkly realistic, returned to her. She shivered, her eyes filling with tears.

Lawrence hesitated, seemed to reach a decision, sat on the edge of the bed and gathered her to him. 'It won't happen again, Kate; I'll send him away. Hush, now—you're safe again.'

'But you're not—he'll watch and wait till he can pounce...'

'All will be well, Kate,' Lawrence murmured against her hair. 'Nobody will harm either of us.'

'But why—why does he want me out of the way?'

She felt him sigh and he shifted uneasily. 'I can only guess that he'd seen, almost before I myself had, how fond I was growing of you.'

'But why should that matter to him, to anyone except...' No, she could not say 'your wife'—lest he no longer denied her existence.

Lawrence sighed again and moved away. 'Oh, Kate, Kate, what a mess this is! And how heartily I wish you weren't involved in it. I should have sensed what was happening—and had the foresight to understand how it placed you in danger.'

'And what would you have done?'

'Sent you away, of course—before it was too late, while I had the strength of mind to do so.'

'Then I'm very thankful,' Katherine said softly, 'that you'd no inkling of it.'

'But Rivers will be dismissed,' Lawrence

affirmed, striding to the door, 'now—before another hour passes.'

She heard him calling the man-servant as he hurried along the landing. There was no response from Rivers.

Soon she heard Mrs Hawkins's voice as well as Lawrence's.

He was frowning when he returned to the room.

'Rivers has vanished.'

'Vanished? But that's worse—he could be anywhere, in hiding, watching...'

'I think not—I've a shrewd idea where he's gone.'

'Where then? Lawrence, what is going on here?'

Momentarily, she thought he would tell her; but he shook his head.

'No, I'll fight this my way. Maybe, when it's all over—if you want to come back...'

'Come back? But you said—only just now... You can't mean it, you wouldn't send me away.' She was sobbing now, hysterically. 'And what about your work— who'd help you with it?' She had forgotten what her bandaged hands implied.

'That! Does that matter—does anything matter beside your safety? Kate, twice now, you've been injured—twice your life has been jeopardized; don't you see, I can't let you stay.'

'I see one thing—' she replied, firmly, suddenly calm—'that I cannot leave you here.'

He sighed and made for the door. 'I'll find Janet for you. We'll discuss this rationally, after breakfast.'

By the time Lawrence returned, Katherine's decision was made. 'You can say what you will, Lawrence, I am not leaving.'

'Don't be stubborn, Katherine, there's no alternative.'

'I've told you—I'm staying here.'

'To be perpetually at risk? I won't have it.'

'You'd protect me.'

Lawrence snorted. 'What would that achieve?'

'I have it resolved—we're almost always together, we'd be alert, on guard...'

'Some life, that'd be!'

'The one I choose.'

'Oh, Kate—why persist so? Can't you just go away, to your parents, anywhere, so I know no injury can befall you?'

She shook her head, biting her lip, but her eyes met his with a new brilliance.

'You'll take care of me, I know you will...'

'But what of the nights?'

'You're right next door.'

He hesitated. 'We could have this lock changed...'

'I knew it!' she cried ecstatically, 'I needn't go.'

He seemed pensive, frowned again. 'It's no use—what will happen when I must visit London?'

'I'll come with you.'

'That would set tongues wagging!'

'I see; you're more concerned about people's opinions, than...having my company.'

'That is simply not true; but there are certain proprieties; I think of your name, not my own—believe me, mine has enough to tarnish it!'

'Could we not try it, Lawrence?' She saw his eyes soften, as hers met them, beseechingly.

'If we let a month elapse,' she went on, 'even two, and then discussed it again...'

He gave a tiny grunt and sat on the edge of the bed. 'You've made it sound very reasonable—workable. But the fact remains you know nothing of the dangers.'

'Won't you tell me, even now?'

Lawrence shook his head and looked away.

Katherine touched his hand. 'Let me stay, Lawrence...'

He closed his eyes. 'I cannot...make... make you go,' he admitted, falteringly, as though despising himself.

'Good,' she declared. 'And now, if you'll leave me, I will get up...'

'But Dr McLaren will be here soon,' he protested.

'To find me greatly recovered, sitting with my...employer, talking quietly, reading perhaps. How can he possibly object?'

He cast his eyes heavenwards. 'Can't I make you do anything?'

Katherine smiled. 'I won't be long, if you'll wait in your room, Mr Rushton...'

'Mr...?' Dark eyes narrowed.

'So much wiser, don't you think? In case the servants imagine we're becoming too "fond" of each other. That was your word, wasn't it? As I said, if you wait for me, you can help me down the stairs. You can't have forgotten how competently you do so!'

Lawrence couldn't remain grave and Katherine managed a laugh. 'Besides,' she added, when he reached the door, 'my incapacity provides an excellent excuse for you to stay by my side—keeping watch over me!'

Despite her brave words, Katherine was badly scared. Who would have dreamed that, mysterious as this house was, it harboured a murderer? She was determined, nevertheless, to show no hint of her fear to Lawrence Rushton. She'd no intention of being packed off to Yorkshire, leaving him to face no one knew what catastrophe. They would stay—together. This was no time to turn from him, to run away—when he'd confessed his affection for her.

Katherine stared wonderingly at her reflection in the glass when she got out of bed. Had she really changed so much? She could detect no difference—beyond that new sparkle in her eyes. Yet this was scarcely the woman who had come to Masterton Hall a few months ago. She would never then have felt this delight on learning that some man (who might still be married) was fond of her. And she had to keep in mind that possibility; she must fight her instinct to...to...love him?

She sighed; she must not breathe the

word, must not let it into the air, for in so doing she might fan it into stronger life. He had spoken only of being fond of her; he mustn't guess she was already more than fond of him. Lawrence had problems enough. If those problems were solved, if it were proved that he were...free, then she might allow her love its freedom.

And he had said, 'I have no wife...'

Steadily, with the passing days, Katherine recovered from her terrifying ordeal; although her back was often painful, as soon as her fingers healed she returned to her desk.

★ ★ ★ ★

When Lawrence next had business in London he took Katherine with him, reserving her a room at an hotel near his club. In the morning she accompanied him to his publishers. Mr MacAndrews, head of the firm, professed delight on meeting someone skilled with one of the new typing machines.

Afterwards, learning this was Katherine's first visit to London, Lawrence took it upon himself to ensure that she missed little. Their hansom cab took them first to

Westminster, then to St Paul's and then to the Tower. And Katherine soon discovered Lawrence's knowledge of the Capital was by no means small. She'd always found him an interesting companion; now she realized she'd only half known him, had only half appreciated his talent for arousing curiosity about one's surroundings.

Indeed, when he was telling her they would attend a performance by the famed Henry Irving, she'd scarcely a chance to thank him before pointing to the enormous Gothic building they approached. 'Later, I'd love to hear about the theatre, but now I simply want to see everything! Do tell me, is that Westminster Abbey?'

It was. And as he escorted her round the abbey, Katherine found that Lawrence was fascinated by architecture. He pointed out not only its beauty but the different styles added through the ages. Outside again, they admired Barry's design of the Houses of Parliament, completed a decade ago. At St Paul's, Lawrence told her not simply of the various Christian churches preceding Christopher Wren's building, but of the legend attributing the site with a temple to the goddess Diana. Katherine marvelled; seeing, through his eyes, all the people—over many centuries—who had worshipped there.

The interest continued at the Tower, when she learned its history, reaching back past its Norman origins to suspected Roman connections. Katherine smiled and nodded towards one of the guardsmen stationed there. 'Do you suppose he appreciates just how privileged he is to live here?'

Lawrence laughed. 'I didn't think you'd be so enthusiastic about a lot of buildings!'

'Only because you make it come alive.'

He gave a mock bow. 'Anything to please you!' But a quick glance told her he was delighted to be showing her that all these places were nothing like so dull as some imagined.

By the following morning, however, his happiness seemed to have faded. He was preoccupied when he arrived to collect her after breakfast. She asked if something was worrying him, and he shrugged.

'I have an appointment with a solicitor. All will be well when that is over.'

Waiting in the gloomy outer office, in Chancery Lane, Katherine wondered what had brought Lawrence there. Was he in some trouble—something too dreadful to discuss with her? And what of that old woman, his mother? Was there truth in her tales of foreboding? In the upset of Rivers's attack, the woman had almost escaped her mind. She must question Lawrence about her. Find out the truth—if that were possible.

When Lawrence emerged, apparently more cheerful, she deferred mention of the matter, giving herself to contemplating the scene from the hired carriage, travelling towards Buckingham Palace. Once there, however, despite the reconstruction to the design of John Nash, Katherine was disappointed in its appearance, and said so.

Lawrence laughed. 'Perhaps that is why our Queen, since Prince Albert's death, prefers residing at Osborne House.'

'Maybe that's more comfortable, more of a real home—something like Masterton Hall...'

'Is that how you think of Masterton, as your home?'

'Have you forgotten you couldn't persuade me to leave—even for my own safety?' She paused. 'You seem surprised...'

'Delighted,' he asserted. 'Far from your own home...' he hesitated. 'That volume of engravings was my first attempt to make you feel...at ease, that my bit of England should become yours...'

She gazed, astonished, at him. 'So long ago...?' But his only reply was a slight smile.

That evening Lawrence took her to the theatre, and afterwards for dinner—though Katherine declared herself too thrilled by Henry Irving's acting to eat!

During the meal, Lawrence raised his glass to her. 'You've brought me so much happiness, Katherine...'

'And worries!'

He shook his head. 'They're not here—not tonight. Only you, me—away from everyone, forgetting—and remembering.' He paused momentarily, '...remembering how you came to me, how you persisted with me—against all my petty cruelties, my scorning, till you made your place—like this. But a *small* distance away.'

'Small!' she thought. 'But still a chasm, separating me from you—from loving...'

She forced a smile. 'And you, Lawrence, have become...my dearest friend.' She didn't say more—how could she?

Appearing pensive, Lawrence was staring into the street. He sprang up suddenly and stood between her and the window, shielding her. 'Oh, God!'

'Lawrence—what is it?'

His face was ashen. 'Rivers! Here, of all places. He's passed now. But we must hurry. Pack, leave London...get away, go home. He must not see you.' Leaving the restaurant, his arm went round her shoulders. 'He shall not harm you, Kate.'

It was, indeed, too late to leave London that night, but Lawrence was uneasy until George met them in Maidstone with the carriage. As they settled against the cushions he drew her close, her head against his shoulder.

He gave a long sigh, then smiled. 'Safe now, my Kate, soon we'll be at Masterton. We'll shut out the rest of the world again.'

'But I've loved our trip to the "rest of the world",' she protested. 'You've shown me so much.'

Lawrence laughed indulgently. 'What a child you are, my sweet, with a child's capacity for enjoyment. Let nothing spoil that—no worries, nor fears. I'll do the worrying for us both.'

'No, that's not fair. That isn't how I want it.' And nor was it; she dreamed of a shared life—burdens and all.

As the mansion, dominating its hill, came into sight, Lawrence raised her fingers to his lips. His eyes, when she turned to him, were melancholy.

'Remember,' he murmured. 'Remember —when I'm prevented from doing this.'

★ ★ ★ ★

For almost a month Katherine was supremely happy. Their visit to London appeared to have deepened their understanding. And the fact that Lawrence had taken her had vanquished all Mrs Hawkins's insinuations about his reasons for going to the Capital. Lawrence was also, for a while, attentive, whenever they were alone together—and at all times concerned for her welfare. She told herself this was all she needed—the knowledge that he cared for, and would protect, her. As time went on, however, her alert mind started questioning his behaviour.

Whilst studying to perfect her secretarial skills she had observed other people's ways—and what prompted them. Katherine was no country miss, educated simply to domestic life, with no curiosity beyond the next meal, or if the weather would be fine that day. She had worked with intelligent men and women; had discovered that a woman's part is not necessarily that of an unquestioning domestic. And she had gloried in that discovery.

She had been taught to use her intellect; to acquire the talents she would need—and to go further in learning about people. It had been her custom to interest herself in the persons of her immediate circle. Silently watching, noting, and caring about them, she'd seen how their problems, their joys, successes and failures, contributed character—and explained their behaviour.

And now, watching, noting and caring about Lawrence, she was disturbed to uncover much that was inexplicable. Never before had she met anyone, man or woman, who feeling affection did not show it. Who, seeking happiness, did not go after it. Who, knowing fear, did not seek aid in fighting it. And he did not. Repeatedly, she saw him start at some sudden noise or glance uneasily over his shoulder. Yet he denied this, even to her, was adamantly opposed to her suggestion to alert the police to watch for Rivers. He seemed determined to ignore normal methods of warding off criminal attacks. And what more incriminating than attempted murder?

Lawrence refused to do more than give himself to enduring her safety. Her safety, too, appeared now to be his only concern. He gave no sign of need to express his feelings. The passing weeks since their return decreased the times he raised her hand to his lips. And rarely did his eyes hold hers lingeringly, speaking that which he declared must not be voiced. It was as if those tender moments had never been.

Katherine wondered sometimes if she'd imagined them—or, worse, if Lawrence regretted his affection. Had it been an expression of pity even, on finding her thus bruised and bleeding? Had he demanded their emotions be concealed because her initial fears were justified—that he was still legally bound to another?

Confused, oppressed by doubts, and irked by his insistence that she should not venture outside alone, Katherine took things into her own hands. She would walk across to the lodge. Over the months she had come to count Sarah and John among her friends at Masterton. What more natural than seeking their company? And if she chanced, whilst there, to throw more light on the mystery surrounding Lawrence, all the better.

Before reaching the lodge, however, Katherine changed her mind. The sun, this crisp February day, glinted on the gilded weather-vane crowning the church steeple. It seemed to beckon. She recalled the stillness within; could she still her disturbed mind there?

The heavy door creaked as she opened it and crept into the dim building. The sun, sinking now, for it was late afternoon, shone on the carved crucifix alone. Katherine experienced an eerie sensation that it was bidding her think of Lawrence, the man who'd designed it. The man whose exterior frequently belied his ability to create beauty. The man who appeared aloof from love, yet confessed affection for her. The man who fathered a child, only to deny him a father's tenderness. The man who...

She sighed at her continuing perplexity about him, and went to kneel in the front pew, drawn towards that carving.

She must calm her bewildered thoughts, let light into her brain darkened by doubts, quell the anxiety, dismiss her misgivings about Lawrence.

Only she couldn't. There seemed no way to check her mind's disturbance. Back and forth it went, over the events since her arrival. And all that stood out clearly at the end was Lawrence—unhappy, in danger, in need of her.

'And I of him,' she murmured, tears springing to her eyes. But, like this, with so many difficulties, his enigmatic ways, how could they help each other?

She must understand him better—for her sake as well as his. But he would not let her. He'd once cared enough for family, for this church, to provide this monument—yet now he shied away. Was his conscience intolerably burdened? Did this necessitate concealment of their relationship? It didn't make sense—Lawrence didn't...

And all she did was question his motives, try to analyse his behaviour, yet all the while she would have given anything to trust him.

Burying her face in her hands, Katherine wept.

When, at long last, she again raised her eyes to the crucifix, the sun had set. In shadow the face spoke of suffering, of the suffering love endures—unquestioningly.

So that was her answer. She dried her

eyes, got slowly to her feet. It wouldn't be easy to follow that example, but she had to.

Nearing the back of the church, she gasped. In the semi-darkness a man knelt, his eyes never leaving her. Lawrence.

He rose, taking her arm as she reached him, but said nothing till they were outside.

'Why do you weep, Katherine?'

She bit her lip, turned away her head, but slender fingers went to her chin, forcing her to meet demanding eyes. 'Why?' he repeated.

She sighed and shook her head. His chestnut mare was tethered at the lych-gate; without a word, he helped Katherine into the saddle, then mounted behind her. 'We'll talk,' he said, into her hair, 'at home.'

Lawrence held her to him, riding through the park. She felt him warm against her back, a comforting contrast with the keen headwind.

At the stables, Lawrence dismounted, silently, and assisted her from the saddle. He hesitated, his face close to her own, then turned, attending to the horse. Katherine made as though to return to the house.

'No—wait,' he bade her.

Satisfied the mare would take no chill after her canter, Lawrence patted the beast's side, as she'd seen him do before, then crossed the stall. He reached down a lantern from a shelf, but changed his mind about lighting it. He leaned his tall frame against a bale of straw, taking up a stalk, fingering it, regarding Katherine anxiously.

'You're not happy, then?'

'I...?'

He made an impatient sound. 'Don't pretend, Kate.'

'I am content.'

He snorted. 'If that's the truth, it's more than I am!'

'Have I asked more of you, have I said I'm not happy? Have...?'

Shouting, Lawrence interrupted, 'Because you wouldn't, you'd endure it all, you wouldn't flinch from staying with me! Why, Kate, why? I offer you nothing...' He flung down the straw, irritably, turned his back on her, his dark head bowed miserably.

She went to put a hand on his arm; still he refused to face her. 'I want to understand you, Lawrence.'

207

'When I don't understand myself?'

'We could try—together.'

He shook his head and Katherine sighed, then leaned against him impulsively, her cheek against his back. 'You could confide in me, stop shutting me out...'

He swung round.

'And have you judge me, like the rest of them... Lose what little there is between us...?'

Katherine closed her eyes, breathing deeply, before responding: 'No matter what you have done, or said, or caused to be done, I want only to be with you. But I'm not, am I? We stand as close as this and we're not close...because I do not know you. And I want to know...I yearn with all my heart to know everything about you.'

'So you can learn to hate me.'

'*Love.* Lawrence. Hate—never!' It was out now, she had said it; there could be no retracting, no going back. Only forward, together—or right away from him. A long way away.

He was a long time silent, examining her expression in the gathering dusk, as though seeking confirmation of her sincerity. He must have found it; he sighed, 'Ask me, then...'

'I'm worried about you,' she began, and he snorted.

'You need not worry yourself.' His voice was an icy blast in her face, but then it dropped to a murmur, 'And worry is not what I'd bring you. But continue—I'll answer, if I can.'

'You speak of my unhappiness, Lawrence, but what of your own? That goes deeper. It seems like a great unease...'

He nodded.

'What are you avoiding? You shy away from all gentleness as if it would harm you. You...' she hesitated, then went on. 'Well, today was the first I've seen you in the church, yet I'm sure you once felt a great deal for it...'

'That's my Kate—how can I conceal anything from you! Maybe, though, that's something I can talk of...' He paused, sorting out the words carefully. 'Can you understand being unable to face the spot where all one's hopes began so joyfully, and ended in misery? Can you, Kate, picture a man, no longer young, wishing now to avoid cruel reminders? Can you imagine a man of faith, losing it—when too many things went wrong, too quickly, driving him near to madness, to the brink of self-destruction...'

'And now unable to find peace any-where...' she murmured.

'Yes, Kate.'

'Let me be your peace, Lawrence.'

He sought her eyes in the last glimmer of daylight. 'You could be—and only you.'

'Then...'

'When I'm rid of the threats, clear of the danger, for that I will not expose you to...'

He embraced her fiercely. 'I have to shield and protect you, my love, my happiness.'

'And not permit me to share...?'

'Only the joy, my sweet, when the troubles are over. When I'm free...'

The word stabbed her. 'So, you are not yet...free?' she began, her voice tremulous.

Lawrence sighed. It was quite dark now, but she knew he would be frowning. His voice was low, dreadfully sad. 'Then you have not believed me...'

Katherine did not answer.

'I have no wife—I told you.'

Still she said nothing.

'Let's go in to dinner...' He spat the words out impatiently, turning on his heel and making for the door.

Katherine followed him, distressed, and feeling inadequate.'

Lawrence faced her suddenly and pulled her roughly to him, his arms closing round her. 'This is how I need you, Katherine—how I need and love you.'

His lips sought hers, their gentleness surprising her until, as she returned his kisses with warmth and fervour, his grew more searching and demanding, as though to draw life itself from her.

Abruptly, he raised his head. 'I swore I wouldn't...' He sounded very upset.

'I had to know, Lawrence.'

His fingers went to her hair, running caressingly over it, then pressing her head against his chest. Holding her, as if for ever. 'Trust me, my Kate—only trust me.'

SEVEN

That evening they sat in the music room, not at first turning to either piano or organ, but talking quietly, impersonally. Katherine noticed Lawrence appeared more than usually preoccupied. Eventually, he urged her towards the console of the organ. 'Time you did some practising...'

He stood behind her while she played the first few bars of a Handel Oratorio, then returned to his chair beside the fire, telling her to go on playing.

For over an hour she continued, then grew restless, sensing Lawrence wasn't really listening. Quietly she rose, crossing to the door. 'Good night, Lawrence,' she murmured, feeling suddenly weary and dispirited.

He hurried to detain her. 'One moment...'

From his pocket he drew a tiny box, and held it out without opening it. He smiled a little then—the only smile she'd won from him since they had left the stables—and raised a quizzical eyebrow.

'Has curiosity deserted you then, Katherine—or do my revelations so displease you that you risk questions no longer?'

She shook her head, smiling back at him. 'Remember I said I would know everything about you—only when you are ready.'

He inclined his head, smiling again, seeming relieved. 'Still you don't ask what this is—who it's for?'

'I might not like the answer!' Katherine retorted, lightly, her laughing eyes showing she was confident he wouldn't disappoint her.

Lawrence's brown eyes mocked her. 'This might, indeed, annoy you! For it is yours, Kate—a token. Here, take it...'

She did so, then pressed the catch—revealing a ring, a cluster of diamonds and sapphires.

'...My grandmother's—now yours...' He hesitated, his smile fading now. 'I will not place it on your finger...until you know all about me, and only then if you ask it.' He took her left hand and raised the third finger to his lips. 'This is where I hope it'll sit one day. With a gold ring to anchor it.'

'Oh, Lawrence...' Breathless, Katherine was lost for words.

About to embrace her, he glanced over his shoulder, irresolute, then went to lock the door.

'Furtive, underhand,' he muttered, brows drawn together, 'What a way to love you!' He made no move to touch her, his brooding eyes on hers, as though seeking something.

Katherine went to slip her arms round him, holding up her face for his kisses. 'Thank you, my love, for your gift, for your promise, and your love...'

His mouth, crushing hers, sealed that.

Next day Lawrence gave her a fine gold chain to suspend his ring about her neck; frequently she smiled to herself, feeling its light touch between her breasts. It was not easy, though, as both had anticipated, to have this love which must not be declared. Hurt came in concealment of what she would have everyone know—in not sharing her delight with Janet, or old John and Sarah. It came also in working with Lawrence, sitting endless hours with him, and showing him little affection. For that, she—he—they both, as if by some unspoken agreement, deemed wisest.

And if, in the silent hours of darkness, she lay longing for his kisses, for reassuring arms about her, wondering if he, too, lay sleepless, but a wall's thickness away, Katherine believed this test would strengthen their love.

Her emotions were strangely mixed; alternating between delight that Lawrence returned her love, and despair because he could not, or would not, reveal why their love might not reach its logical conclusion.

★ ★ ★ ★

February blew itself out in a flurry of snow showers and icy winds, leaving the ground so hard that their horses' hooves—for Lawrence was schooling her in riding the black mare—thudded through the park.

They learned a new kind of love in sharing such pleasures; in walking together as well as riding. And always, as ever, working in his study, then spending quiet evenings together, reading, talking, or in the music room.

Looking up from her treasured book of engravings one day, Katherine found Lawrence watching her quizzically.

'You love that book, don't you?' he remarked.

She nodded. 'There are so many beautiful places, I wish...' she stopped speaking.

'Yes?' Lawrence prompted.

'You're too busy.'

He smiled. 'You wish to visit some of them, is that it?'

'Well...'

'And so you shall—on the first warm day, we will lay work aside, take the brougham...'

And so it was that Katherine found herself drawing in a breath of pure delight at seeing Leeds Castle, mirrored by its surrounding lake. She felt Lawrence's eyes on her and met them, surprised by the tenderness in his expression.

He appeared a little confused, almost as if he'd have preferred her to remain in ignorance of his emotions, so she made no comment.

It wasn't until their next outing, to Allington Castle, that he made any allusion to that moment. After an exhilarating hour or two wandering about the castle grounds, then walking along the towpath, they sank back into the carriage, and again his eyes were on her.

Presently he nodded, smiling a little to himself. 'It is all quite sincere, isn't it—your interest in going about in this way, seeing different...'

'Of course,' she interrupted enthusiastically. 'Sometimes I wish we neither of us had to work, so we might spend every day just...exploring.'

Lawrence laughed, shaking his head in surprise. 'So—I haven't bored you?'

'Not for one tiny second. How could anyone...?' She broke off, aware suddenly that he was telling her something. That his wife maybe had not shared this interest?

As if conscious of her thoughts, he nodded. 'You're the first, Kate, to want to come out with me—except for social occasions.'

'But why...?' she started, then realized this was scarcely a tactful question, and avoided his gaze.

She sensed that he shrugged, then he laughed again. 'I suppose, my dear, that everyone else must have taken me for a dull old writer—which perhaps I am!'

'Never dull,' she asserted, smiling across at him. 'And you may take me anywhere—I'll be only too happy to learn about any place with you.'

His eyes held hers, teasingly. 'You may regret that—when I've wearied you with tramping over every historic site within a hundred miles radius!'

Later, handing her down from the carriage, he smiled once more. 'It is good to see your pleasure, to know that...well, that I am capable of bringing happiness.'

But, suddenly, his mouth was a firm line once again, his eyes had clouded. He sighed.

'We'd best go in—prepare ourselves for dinner.'

All evening Lawrence was withdrawn and Katherine sought to say something which might restore the smile to his lips. It wasn't until he escorted her to the drawing-room door, when she'd bade him good night, that he gave a clue to the trouble.

He caught her hand. 'Promise me one thing, Kate—don't ever be dishonest with me. If you grow tired of...the way things are here, say so. Deception, whatever the motive, is the ultimate cruelty.'

She met his look frankly. 'I don't lie,' she assured him, 'nor pretend to be other than I am. And I am happy, Lawrence—happier than ever.'

He raised her hand to his lips, then drew her to him. 'I cannot believe there are so many ways in which we are attuned. Pray God we may live to see the day when...'

His voice had trailed off, he cleared his throat.

'Sleep well, my Kate. Good night.'

And he almost pushed her from the room.

March came in mildly, belying its reputation. Going through her wardrobe,

Katherine decided she needed more suitable dresses. Now that she and Lawrence were going out so often, she loved dressing for the occasion. He complimented her only rarely, for he was not a man to lavish praise on anybody, but she knew well enough by the look in his eyes when her appearance pleased him.

Several weeks having passed since Rivers's attempt on her life, without any sign of his return, Lawrence relaxed his diligence for her safety. He took little persuading that George take her into Maidstone in the brougham, so she might purchase dress materials. He appeared, indeed, more than content to let her go alone, saying he had matters requiring his immediate attention.

Katherine was puzzled at first, wondering what these matters were, for of late Lawrence had taken her into his confidence.

She dismissed her momentary disquiet, however, as soon as she began exploring the shops. Happily, she compared one fabric with another, then made a final selection of materials and sought trimmings for them.

As she planned what she would make, she pictured the evenings when she would sit at her sewing whilst talking with Lawrence.

The domesticity of the scene attracted.

Glancing at her watch, her purchases completed, Katherine found she had some fifteen minutes before she was to meet George at the coaching inn. She wandered from one shop window to the next, looking at their wares, interested, but her attention not completely held.

Then her attention was caught, forcibly, bringing a pounding to her pulses, by a familiar figure. Despite the intervening crowds of the street market, she knew at once the set of the head, the swing of the stride. It could be no other.

What had prevented his mentioning that his business also was here? Surely he would have preferred that they journey together? And how had he got here—by hired carriage?

She would cross to Lawrence now—and watch the smile come into those dark eyes at the prospect of her company.

Momentarily, people moving between the market-stalls in the twilight concealed him, then she glimpsed him again. Horrified, Katherine saw his companion. A woman, about her own age, fair curls springing from beneath a feathered hat. She gasped; his arm went to the woman's waist as they mounted the steps of a fashionable hotel.

Katherine pressed her knuckles to her mouth. She would not weep, here in the street, for all to see. That Lawrence should thus flout discretion made her the more determined to show no emotion.

Nothing, though, could quiet her rapid heart, nor the startled sobs that were her breathing. She leaned against a shop doorway. Her distress must have been apparent, a kindly elderly soul paused to enquire if she were unwell.

Katherine shook her head. 'A little breathless, that is all—it will pass.' She thanked the woman and watched her go on her way—wishing that she too were old and finished with love's vulnerability.

And now what should she do? Enter that hotel and confront Lawrence and his companion? She could not trust herself to do so calmly. Instead, she'd return to the house, demand an explanation on *his* return.

Between her breasts, she felt his ring on its slender chain. Only so recently had he given it to her, protesting at her assumption that he was still married—and asking her to trust him!

Katherine gazed unseeingly ahead. He'd even begged her to be truthful. How could she believe one word he uttered in the future? And this meant they had no future—together; just as surely as—so her heart dictated—she'd no future without him.

George discovered her thus, agitated and heedless of the time, when he started searching, because of her absence from their pre-arranged meeting place. He stared, anxiously, at her worried expression, assisting her into the carriage. She was thankful to escape his curious eyes, by withdrawing into the obscurity of the brougham.

All Katherine could see was Lawrence's arm about that woman—and her fair curls, so like the ones in that portrait.

She was unable to weep, even now she had privacy; the hurt was deeper than tears. She felt numb, and sick with revulsion.

There had been, too, the look George gave her. It had seemed...pitying. As if he knew how torn she was. And pity she would not endure. No one must learn of this—except Lawrence himself at the appropriate moment. She would not reveal to Janet, or anyone else, how bitterly she'd been humiliated.

When George helped her alight at the front steps, she thanked him composedly, then asked him to convey her excuses for absence from the dinner table. Pleading a headache, she would remain in her room. Nothing would induce her to eat with Lawrence Rushton tonight.

Crossing the hall to the staircase, head bowed pensively, Katherine encountered Lawrence, leaving the study.

Startled, she wondered how on earth he'd arrived home ahead of her. Then she recollected how, after seeing him, she could easily have allowed time to slip away unnoticed. Distress was oblivious of minutes.

'Katherine...!' he was saying, with a smile. 'You were miles away—I asked if you'd had a satisfactory afternoon...'

She glared at him. 'Does it matter?' she demanded furiously, 'I'm sure you have!'

'What?' He appeared surprised, 'seeking the solution to something insoluble? Alone.'

She sighed. He was a hypocrite, too—

trying to convince her he hadn't stirred from the house!

'Katherine, what is it?' He was approaching her, but she refused to look at him.

'Let me pass, please; I must go to my room.'

His fingers brushed her sleeve as she pushed past him, she felt his eyes on her face, knew they would be grave, anxious; but she kept her head down. Staring hard at each tread of the staircase, she left him.

In the sanctuary of her own room, she found the tears which had refused to come earlier. They poured down her cheeks as, without removing cloak or hat, she sat at the dressing-table, her face buried in her hands. It had been difficult before, living with this new-found love which could not be declared, now to live without it would be impossible.

★ ★ ★ ★

By morning, the sleepless hours presenting more than sufficient time for re-examining the situation, Katherine had decided against speaking to Lawrence of the matter. He knew where he'd been—and with whom. If conscience didn't tell him anything to explain her changed attitude, nothing would.

Before dressing she removed the chain which, for so short a while, had held his ring next to her skin. Despite herself, she held the ring to the light, watching myriads of beams emanate from its precious stones. She swallowed hard, realizing how precious, indeed, the jewel had become. She couldn't give it back—not yet. Something deeper than love of the ring prevented her.

Over breakfast, Lawrence was solicitous about her headache.

'But I see from your face that you are far from well. You must know, Kate, that I don't expect you to work if you are not recovered.'

She shook her head impatiently. 'There is no need for concern. I'm perfectly able to carry out my duty.'

She saw him wince at the word—and was glad of it.

Until the end of the week, Katherine maintained her cool indifference whenever she was with him, but in her room gave way to the overwhelming misery. That this should happen now—just as she was so enjoying accompanying him about the countryside, sharing his life...

There was no alternative—she must leave Masterton Hall, cut herself off from Lawrence, be rid of the torture of his daily presence and its reminder of his deceit.

First though, she would solve that mystery surrounding him—if necessary see he was brought to justice. No man could prove so evasive in living out his life unless concealing something heinous.

Rising early on Saturday, she breakfasted before Lawrence and made for the lodge. Alone, John was re-potting plants in the rear porchway. They exchanged a greeting and she stood, watching his gnarled, though nimble, fingers. Something about his task reassured her; perhaps its symbolism of continuity. All else might change, but she liked to believe John and Sarah would always pursue their roles here.

'I know you're reluctant to discuss Mr Rushton's affairs, John, but I need your help. Do you believe me when I tell you it's more than curiosity that prompts the questions you're unwilling to answer?'

John nodded.

'You are loyal to your master. And like and respect him.'

As I once did, she thought, and more...

'He's been fair to Sarah and me, Miss Sutcliffe—mostly. He let us stay on, when he dismissed the others.'

'So he did dismiss them?'

'...Er, yes, that is...' He coughed, bent again to his plant pots.

'All except Rivers?'

'Mr Rivers, yes. He stayed on.' John was frowning.

'And when was this departure of all the staff?'

'After the fire, of course...' John clapped a hand to his mouth. 'Now look what you've made me say! Pretend you've never heard that, will you, Miss?' He caught her sleeve. 'Please, I beg you, don't let on to the master.'

'I won't say a word. But why, John, why doesn't he want this...fire mentioned? That was, I suppose, what destroyed the East side of the Hall?'

John nodded. 'Only remember what I said—don't talk of it...'

'I've promised. But, you know, John, I

don't believe you need go in fear of Mr Rushton...'

Even now, she defended what she'd once believed to be a true assessment of him.

John smiled slightly. 'Perhaps you're right—with Mr Rivers gone. It was him put the fear of God into me—though he swore what he did was in the master's name.'

'And what did he do?'

'It was threats mainly, I suppose, looking back on it. Only at the time it kept us fair nervy. Never took to Mr Rivers from the day he came here.'

'And how long ago was that?'

'Something like four year now, I reckon; he came along of Mr...' He stopped.

'Yes...?'

But John shook his head.

'No. I've said too much already. If Sarah knew she'd be wild. We made this pact, see—nobody'd learn anything from us—on account of Mr Lawrence's kindness letting...'

Katherine feared he'd launch into another discourse over their tenancy of the lodge—and that must wait. She had discovered merely that there'd been some fire—and she'd already guessed that. So why the secrecy? It seemed obvious there was more to be unearthed. And, today, John Saunders appeared a more ready informant than his wife. While she had him in talking mood, she meant to extract every possible relevant detail.

'And this fire, John, was it the accident where Mr Rushton lost his hand?'

'Dreadful, it was—his wrist trapped by blazing timber. And all through trying to save that good-for-nothing...'

John turned away, setting pots on a shelf, fiddling with the plants in them. 'I've said more than enough. You must excuse me, I've work to do. I bid you good day...' He kept his back turned.

'Very well, John.' Katherine sighed, disappointed by their conversation's abrupt ending. 'Thank you,' she added, leaving. 'Be assured no one will learn of this.'

Slowly she walked across the park, through the copse, to the house. All the time thinking of Lawrence, of the horror of being pinned, helplessly, by the burning wood, forced to watch while the relentless fire robbed him of his right hand.

Had the shock of that incident done irreparable damage to him, making him unreliable? Already, she was finding excuses for his behaviour, her doubts about his integrity fading.

Letting herself into the mansion, Katherine realized anew that she could not fail, whenever thinking of Lawrence, to see how desperately he needed understanding—and compassion.

And what had John inferred—that it all occurred while Lawrence was rescuing someone? His wife? Rescuing, that is, or trying to rescue. There'd been no clue to its success or otherwise.

She could only presume success, since Lawrence's companion in Maidstone had resembled his wife's portrait.

But why was she absent from Masterton? Only in bed that night did Katherine think of a possible explanation. Supposing that rescue had been *partially* successful? Supposing Lawrence wasn't alone in being injured. Katherine hadn't seen the woman's features. Might she have been disfigured, then chosen to live away from the hall—in seclusion? In that Maidstone hotel? This seemed to fit in neatly, as though Katherine pieced together the truth. And—giving some reason for the reluctance Lawrence showed to acknowledge a wife—John *had* mentioned, hadn't he, '...that good-for-nothing...'

And was it not, in her earlier estimation of him, a typical reaction of Lawrence Rushton—remaining faithful to that woman? She could imagine him gritting his teeth, and vowing he would not abandon her.

It made sense that way. Lawrence was caught, as surely as his arm had been caught in that scorching trap—who was she to judge him for electing to alleviate the dismal life of a wife who—though proved disloyal—was now suffering. Enigmatic Lawrence might remain, but today a little light had been admitted—it showed her he deserved some regard, respect, even perhaps affection.

For the first in a succession of nights, Katherine slept.

★ ★ ★ ★

With morning came her decision to offer him the opportunity to explain the situation. She could see no reason that he withhold the truth. And if the difficulty be brought into the open, they might then more readily help each other to accept and endure it.

Only that evening it chanced that Lawrence gave her the cue she needed. All through dinner Katherine was aware of his eyes on her, his silent pondering. Later, after sitting almost an hour in the drawing-room, still scarcely speaking, he broke the silence, abruptly.

'I've observed of late, Katherine, a certain...cooling of your attitude to me. I've tried to discover the reason for this—indeed, have examined my conscience for some way I might have offended you; but have found...nothing. I'd be obliged if you'd tell me what is amiss.'

'Can't you guess, Lawrence, when I too was in Maidstone that day?'

'What day? What are you speaking of?'

Katherine sighed. So he was evasive already; well, she wouldn't permit that. This time she would have the truth.

'I saw you going into that hotel—with your wife.'

His dark eyes became veiled. 'I see. Still, you do not believe me, still you doubt my every word!'

'And with just cause, it seems—even now you're pretending!' What was the use, trying to keep calm with a man who was determined always to make *her* the one doing *him* an injury!

'Shall I never convince you?' Lawrence persisted.

'But I saw you...'

'Saw me? But I wasn't...' And then he stopped. He nodded, gnawing his lips, his brow furrowed. 'Kate,' he said at last, 'you've got to believe me, there is an explanation.'

'Then give it,' she begged, her eyes filling. 'Only tell me...I want to believe you.'

Lawrence gazed at her and sighed. 'Yes, Katherine, I think you do; so there is hope. But you must bear with me—give me time. From what you've just said, I think the day approaches when you'll know the whole truth. First, though, I must attend to certain matters...'

Rising, Lawrence started pacing the room, perturbed. 'You must take particular care, there will be no more wandering off alone—not even through the park. If I cannot accompany you, you must ask Janet or one of the maids.' He stopped pacing, and faced her. 'You see, my Kate, I do care...'

She nodded. 'Very well, Lawrence.'

He sat on the arm of her chair, his hand going to her shoulder. 'I'm serious about the danger; a...crisis looms ahead. Be especially wary of Rivers returning to Masterton.'

* * * *

Katherine was bewildered after the conversation—pleased by his continuing concern, but equally distressed by his refusal to confide further. What was he concealing? And why had he shown the astonishment of someone learning something new when she mentioned that unfortunate encounter in Maidstone?

For days Lawrence scarcely left her side. His book was progressing well, so they spent longer than normal hours in his study. And daily they took some exercise together, usually riding, for Lawrence's love of horses had aroused in Katherine a similar enthusiasm.

During Saturday breakfast, however, Lawrence revealed that urgent business would occupy him all day. He wouldn't even take luncheon with her.

Disappointment washed over her. Although no longer so completely relaxed together, Lawrence was an interesting friend still. And the man she loved—albeit unwisely.

Feeling lost, after her solitary luncheon, she sought out Janet, who—since Simon was asleep—agreed to take a stroll.

Walking in the spring sunlight towards the lake, they were deep in conversation. Janet, betrothed now, was full of plans for her marriage to George.

Glancing away from Janet's radiant face, Katherine glimpsed some movement among the lakeside trees. Too big for one of the deer, the shape puzzled her, till it drew nearer. It was horse and rider; the man erect in the saddle, unmistakable.

As she watched, he reined in the horse, waiting. A woman, fair hair streaming in the wind, cantered towards him. Katherine saw her face. It was unblemished. So, that theory might be discounted!

Instinctively, she clutched Janet's hand, unintentionally revealing what she'd observed. The girl followed her gaze, frowning.

'Is that the elusive Mrs Rushton?'

'I think it must be.' The calm of her own voice surprised Katherine. She forced her now-trembling legs to carry her on, trying all the while to control the fierce throbbing attacking her head.

'You see now, don't you,' Janet went on, 'why I dreaded your becoming devoted to the master...'

'And now you know that all I ever felt was an employee's loyalty,' Katherine lied, wishing it were true.

She endeavoured to make sense of Janet's conversation, to recover from the interruption, and to ignore the two riders galloping towards the mansion.

That evening Katherine again ate alone, thankful to be spared meeting that woman, though wondering where Lawrence was entertaining her. About to rise from the table, she heard the carriage passing the window. It appeared he was taking her out.

Katherine was too disturbed to remain alone in any of the rooms she used to share with Lawrence—for now, surely, the end of their relationship had come. And so again she joined Janet, who, with George away from the house, appreciated company. George had, it seemed, been informed at short notice of Mr Rushton's requirements.

Katherine was puzzled. With few friends apparent in the locality, was it not unlikely that Lawrence would take his wife out thus, after carefully concealing her existence?

Or had the time come for her to take her rightful place, beside him...?

The prospect depressed her. Discounting Lawrence's professed love for her, what would her position be if there was a mistress at Masterton? Too late now to remind herself she'd believed that to be so on accepting the post. Now, she would miss those cherished quiet evenings, the hours spent in the music room...

And the memories that room held—of the first touch of Lawrence's lips. How could she have let this man, his married status in doubt, kiss her? Was it because she'd believed him free—or because she wanted to believe that?

Tortured again by the misgivings pursuing her for weeks, it was impossible to concentrate on Janet's conversation. Pleading tiredness, she retired to her room.

Lawrence, it seemed, had returned, and repaired to his room. Though not alone. Or was he? It was most extraordinary; Katherine could not avoid hearing his voice, raised angrily. But each response was in a similar tone, she knew it too well to be mistaken. Was he now talking to himself? Furiously?

At length, determined to dismiss the man from her thoughts, Katherine prepared for bed, pulling the patchwork quilt over her ears, excluding every sound from that next room.

The following morning she spent in church, without first seeing Lawrence at breakfast. She had, indeed, scarcely been sorry.

His attitude was so perplexing, his behaviour so secretive, that she was glad to escape him. And to consider what she must do.

In happiness, she could try overlooking the forbidding atmosphere of Lawrence's home, could pretend those screams in the night, those attempts on her life, never happened; but in misery...? All that remained was fear.

And just how afraid she was could be ignored no further. No longer would she endure the situation here.

She emerged from the church into the brightness of mid-day April, the weather more settled than expected that month.

The house, surmounting its hill, against a cerulean sky, looked beautiful—deceptively tranquil.

She forced her eyes away. She'd made her decision; nothing—this time—would deflect her from it.

She passed through the lych-gate to find Lawrence waiting on Reveller's back; Midnight, her mount, beside them. He tossed her the reins he'd been holding, then offered a hand as she swung into the saddle.

As their fingers touched she bit her lip; he shouldn't have done this, he was only making it harder.

Lawrence smiled. 'I couldn't wait to see you, it seems an age since Friday.'

'I'd have thought you too occupied yesterday to miss me!' She was amazed by the man's imperturbability.

She watched his expression take the familiar frown, steeling herself to remain unaffected. She had been right in her resolve. She could stand no more of his mercurial behaviour. She'd continue as his secretary only until obtaining another post, then put the creature from her mind!

'I've a surprise for you, my Kate,' Lawrence began, as they dismounted at the stables. 'I'm giving a party—in your honour, next month.'

Katherine stared at him, her mouth gaping open.

He laughed. 'You might appear pleased —instead of thunderstruck! Is it so inconceivable I should wish to demonstrate my regard? And show everyone how you've brought fresh life to me?'

Somehow, Katherine found sufficient voice to murmur thanks.

Going to her room to prepare for luncheon, her mind was in turmoil. How could she leave now? It was almost as if some secret force were keeping watch over her thoughts and warning Lawrence when something was needed to retain her here.

Could that be? She shuddered. Was there some 'presence' at Masterton, some ancestral spirit aiding him as he pursued his mysterious purpose?

Was that old woman less substantial than she'd believed—was she the *spirit* only of his mother, giving him supernatural means of achieving his ends?

Katherine gave herself a mental shake, she was becoming altogether too fanciful— she who'd poured scorn on the notion of a

Masterton haunting!

And, as she might have anticipated, Lawrence, by airing plans for the forthcoming function, soon had her wondering that she'd ever entertained misgivings about him.

But was this ability of his to reverse her opinion of him precisely where the danger lay?

★ ★ ★ ★

One dark, damp Thursday when Lawrence was absent for the day in London, Katherine was startled by a figure disappearing into the gloom at the rear of the hall.

Her heart pounding, she hurried after. Even in this poor light that arrogant bearing was easily recognized. He must be challenged.

'Good day, Mr Rivers...'

She saw him start. He froze, then turned, a cool smile on his lips. 'Good morning, Miss Sutcliffe.'

He was a calm one.

And she, too, must be. 'Mr Rushton is not at home,' she continued, her expression inscrutable. 'But perhaps you are aware of that? No matter, I'll tell him of your visit.'

He inclined his head, without speaking, then left her.

EIGHT

Fearing now something more tangible than any spirit, Katherine avoided the deserted dining-room, making for the nursery. She could not eat alone, waiting and listening for Rivers to seek her out.

Throughout the day, trying vainly to concentrate on her typing, she expected him. But he did not come.

By early evening there was no further sign of him. If they had not exchanged those few words, Katherine would be doubting that she had seen him. As it was she longed to share the news, and dared confide in one person only.

Later, the drawing-room door ajar, Katherine listened for Lawrence's anticipated return. She heard the outer door open, then close, and recognized his step in the hall. She ran to the doorway and beckoned him.

He came immediately, tossing his cloak on to the chair just inside the room, without taking his eyes from her. Katherine closed the door behind them, leaning against it.

'It's Rivers, Lawrence—he's been here. May be here still.'

'Did he see you?' he demanded anxiously.

'I ensured that—and told him I'd inform you.'

Lawrence frowned. 'That was unwise; now he knows for sure you are still alive.'

She snorted. 'Do you suppose he didn't already, that he isn't fully informed of everything that takes place here...'

'I can't think that anyone...' Lawrence began, but she interrupted.

'Not Mrs Hawkins? That incident with the step-ladder was no misadventure!'

'Then she must go...' Lawrence reached for the door handle. 'I should have dismissed her as soon as there was any suspicion.'

Katherine covered his hand as it lay on the handle.

'No, Lawrence—not yet. Don't you see while she remains we have the advantage over them?'

'But it's endangering you,' he protested, his dark eyes grave.

Katherine smiled. 'I have survived for long enough—in danger; I shall continue to be more than cautious.'

He searched her face. 'You must take every precaution—and come safely through this—for me.'

Suddenly, he leaned towards her, his lips finding hers, his lean body imprisoning her against the door.

'Oh, my Kate,' he sighed, into her hair, 'if only I could protect you like this, with myself, from all harm—make you mine, have you with me every moment, in safety.'

Again his lips claimed hers, bruising them in the intensity of his emotion.

He gave a long-drawn-out sigh and moved away. 'Go to your room,' he ordered, over his shoulder. 'Leave me, Katherine, for a while.'

'But you've only now returned,' she protested, and was surprised when his expression, on turning to her, showed amusement.

He nodded. 'Returned to the sweetness of the woman I love, from whom I have been too long absent...and who must forgive me if I employ stern measures to curb the eagerness of my feelings. Go, Kate, please. I will wash, change. And do not frown so, join me here in an hour—to find me my cool, circumspect, self again!'

Katherine returned his smile, humour tugging at her mouth also. She went happily to her room. So he did still care, he needed her as much as ever. More, it seemed, in some ways. Enough, too, to wait undemandingly for her.

But to wait how long? Some black devil inside her persisted. Until he was free of his wife?

* * * *

She observed, during the ensuing days, that Lawrence was becoming progressively more worried. Even while they were working his eyes darted nervously about the room, as though constantly on the alert. His temper was short, too—though he was careful not to vent that on Katherine.

Worst of all, though, his creative powers were deserting him.

One morning, after working three hours,

they'd achieved but a page and a half of typescript.

'It's no use, is it, Kate?' Lawrence sighed. 'Yet I must work, cannot give up...'

'Is something wrong, Lawrence? More than before, I mean...'

Again, he sighed. 'I expect an answer within days to a...proposition I've put forward. Don't ask me more, my dear, when all is settled, I'll tell you. Only bear with me—make allowance for my ill-humour.'

Katherine nodded; in that moment loving him, if it were possible, more than ever. She longed to hold his troubled head against her, to comfort and reassure.

'Meanwhile,' he went on, 'you must force me to work. It's time this book was bringing in money.'

For a while the words appeared to flow more readily, till they were interrupted by childish laughter from outside the window. Katherine smiled to herself; Simon and Janet must be returning from their daily walk.

'Will you kindly order that child to be silent!' Lawrence roared, his lips then tightening into a line.

Katherine crossed to open the window. 'Would you mind quietening Master Simon, Janet?' she called, then felt Lawrence at her elbow.

'Out of the way,' he said, curtly, and then shouted, 'In here, boy!' to the astonished Simon.

The child remained anchored, trembling, to the spot.

'This instant!'

Janet brought a terrified Simon to the study door, which Lawrence had flung open in readiness. 'No, you wait in the hall,' he commanded Janet. 'He must learn to stand on his own feet.'

He took the child by an arm, dragging him inside the door before slamming it.

'Well?' he demanded. 'Why must we suffer this infernal noise?'

'He was only laughing,' Katherine protested.

White-faced, Lawrence swung round to face her: 'Be silent!'

He returned to the tiny figure before him. 'Answer me, child—I will not tolerate your silent insolence.'

Still Simon didn't respond; he appeared to be too frightened.

Hand on one hip, Lawrence rocked

on his toes, looking down at the boy: 'If I have one more instance of your unruly behaviour,' he threatened, dark brows menacing, 'you'll be banished. Understand?'

Simon nodded, tears running unchecked down his rosy cheeks. 'I'm sorry, sir,' he muttered, looking hopefully to the door.

'And so you should be. Oh, stop snivelling, boy—and get out of my sight— you sicken me!'

With that, Lawrence barked to Janet to fetch the child, and returned to his desk. 'How am I expected to create anything in a house that becomes daily more like a bear garden!'

All Katherine's sympathy for Lawrence vanished, and with it, her ability to work. She felt his eyes on her, knew he would order her to continue, but she couldn't help that.

'You're a hard man, Lawrence,' she remarked, quietly.

'And who asked your opinion, Miss?' he retorted.

'Simon looks to you for love and affection, and all you give is...'

'Discipline! And, Lord, how he needs it!'

'That is not so.' Katherine insisted, still speaking quietly. 'You keep him shut away in abnormal solitude, then protest when he shows any boyish high spirits. You're the most unnatural father I've ever met.'

'Indeed, Kate,' he replied, icily, 'I'm even less of a father than you imagine. Oh, go to your luncheon—tell them I'll eat in here. You make it plain I'm not fit company for anyone!'

Sadly, Katherine left the study, but when she later, somewhat reluctantly, returned, Lawrence was all contrition. He caught her hand as she passed his desk.

'Forgive me, Katherine,' he begged, brushing her fingers with his lips. 'I know I'm harsh with the boy, but there are reasons...'

'That's what you always say, isn't it, Lawrence? Reasons why you're unkind to him, why you shrink from any tenderness, why you...'

She stopped; she'd been on the point of saying, 'Why you cannot marry me.' And her lips on that, must remain clamped.

'...do not ask for your hand?' Lawrence enquired, reading her thoughts yet again. He sighed; his voice, when he spoke, was hushed. 'And that there are reasons for that

I would most of all, and most earnestly, have you believe. Katherine, things are not always as they seem.'

'Then tell me...' she pleaded.

'I cannot.' Lawrence rose, wearily. 'Come—let us exercise the horses. I must have some air.'

She shook her head. 'You go,' she suggested, wanting time to think.

'Please, Katherine,' he persisted, 'I need you.'

★ ★ ★ ★

From that day Lawrence made some effort to be more amiable, and even—to please her, he said—began spending time in the nursery before work each morning. Indeed, by the night of her party, Katherine had almost forgotten what it was like having life disrupted by Lawrence's anger.

She dressed carefully that evening, in a dark green silken gown—not previously worn, because of the lack of entertaining at Masterton. The colour enhanced her eyes, and showed off her hair to good effect. She turned this way and that to catch every aspect of her reflection in the glass, noting with satisfaction how the material was moulded to her neat hips, in the latest fashion. The fullness at the back of the skirt served to emphasize her tiny waist, and she smiled, thankful for the excuse to wear such finery.

Today was *her* day, different from any other since her arrival. She had, hitherto, devoted her time and attention to Lawrence and his needs. Now it was her turn, her night of enjoyment—all the happier because Lawrence was giving it. She felt, and looked, radiant.

Katherine left the mirror, about to go downstairs. At her door, she stopped, turned back, and opened her jewel casket. It seemed appropriate to wear his ring again, for so long she'd felt compelled to lock it away.

She had the chain in her hand when the knock sounded on her door.

Lawrence stood there. For a moment he gazed at her, as though surprised, then she noticed his eyes, running over every inch of her gown. She felt her colour rising as they travelled to her neck, her hair.

He seemed to collect himself. 'May I come in—just for a moment?'

'I'm almost ready, I was coming down...'

'I know,' he hesitated, then observed

the ring, dangling from its chain; 'I came about that...' He nodded towards it.

Katherine stood aside to admit him, wondering fleetingly, with sinking heart, if he would say it had been a mistake—that she'd never be entitled to wear it. But Lawrence was smiling; he took her hand and stepped back, admiring her.

'First though, I must comment on your...beauty; and words fail me.' He swallowed, 'You're a lovely woman, Katherine; tonight...exquisite. How proud I'll be to have you on my arm.'

Lawrence drew her to him then, sending her pulses racing, as his lips covered hers.

'I scarcely dare touch you,' he whispered, 'lest I spoil you.' Katherine could feel his heart pounding against her, then he let her go, taking the gold chain from her.

'Slip the ring from it—now, give it to me...'

She hesitated, wondering why, and he laughed.

'What? You don't entrust it to me? It's yours, Kate, I'll never take it from you.' His eyes smiled, with gentle amusement. 'Give me your hand—the left one.'

He slipped the ring on to her finger. 'I told you I would, didn't I? That it was only a matter of waiting.'

Katherine turned shining eyes to him. 'Lawrence! Does this mean you're free, that we...?'

'The questions must wait,' he responded lightly, laying a finger on her lips. 'Our guests will be arriving...'

With that, he offered his arm, and they descended to the hall.

From that moment, Lawrence proved kind, attentive, amusing, all the things she'd known he could be. He helped her greet their visitors; then, taking her arm, led the way upstairs. Katherine was surprised. She saw him smile.

They went through the music room, everyone talking and laughing as they followed, then next through the library. Lawrence released her arm to open double doors, after crossing an ante-room. Katherine gasped. This was the ballroom, which she'd only seen from outside when Lawrence indicated its windows.

Magnificently proportioned, it was clearly designed by none other than Robert Adam. Who but he could have conjured up such beautiful plasterwork—and so splendid a fireplace? The room was a haze of white and gold, its enormous chandelier sparking rainbow lights to reflect from gilt-framed mirrors. The red of velvet curtains, sweeping to the floor, was the only other colour.

Katherine became aware of Lawrence scrutinizing her expression. 'It was well worth it!' he declared. 'I was too ashamed of the place before to bring you in here. It's been locked up for some long while and sadly neglected. I...never intended setting foot in it again, but this night will lay all ghosts.'

Across the far end of the room stood a long table, with two smaller ones at right-angles at either end. All of mahogany, their finish was similar to the one Katherine had long admired downstairs.

The tables were set with exquisite silver and glassware, their brilliance proclaiming that a deal of care had gone into preparing the occasion. She turned to Lawrence.

'This is wonderful—how can I ever thank you!'

His lips twitched with unaccustomed merriment, his eyes lighting. 'You asked that before, I remember; let us hope we're nearer the day when I may claim all I wish, by way of your thanks!' Still amused, he turned, inviting their guests to be seated.

Katherine found herself at one end of the long table, with Lawrence far away at the other. On her right was his publisher, Mr MacAndrews, whose wife sat to his right; and on Katherine's left, the Rector, Adam Chandos, with his wife Susan beside him. Looking round, Katherine realized that only these few of the people present had she met previously. Indeed, she had difficulty recalling any other names, despite the short time elapsing since Lawrence made the introductions.

At first, nervous among so many people after the quiet life since coming here, she spoke little. Gradually, though, aided by the wine, her tongue loosened until she was talking freely, not only with near neighbours but those farther away. By the end of the meal she'd made several friends among these friends of Lawrence's.

And that he, who rarely went out and never entertained, had so many friends surprised her.

The meal ended, Lawrence rose, bidding them drink to her health, and the good fortune bringing her to Masterton. 'For look around you,' he continued, 'and you will see a room that has been restored—as I myself have been—because of her interest.'

Her eyes swimming in tears, Katherine wished Lawrence was beside her, so she might whisper her thanks instead of being content with nodding to him and smiling.

A four-piece orchestra had slipped into the ballroom, and could be heard tuning up against the background of conversation. Katherine felt a hand on her arm and turned to find Lawrence behind her.

She smiled. 'Oh, my dear,' she murmured, 'you're so good to me!'

His smile widened. 'Save that for later—in private.' He nodded towards the highly polished floor, indicating the orchestra which was now playing. 'I think we should dance, don't you? Then others will follow suit.'

With a sudden trepidation, Katherine took a deep breath before going into his arms. Apparently sensing this, Lawrence smiled reassuringly. 'Relax, Kate—soon they'll join us, then we'll be forgotten.'

He was right, of course; other couples began dancing, until only the elderly remained as onlookers.

Katherine discovered Lawrence was an accomplished dancer, and imagined his love of music ensured this. She sighed contentedly, then felt his silent laugh.

'I was just wondering what you would have said if you could have foreseen this on the day you arrived!'

She glanced up, amused. 'I'd have said "never"—for I thought you quite the most arrogant, insufferable boor of a man!'

'An opinion which has never varied!' He laughed, and caught her closer to him.

After that first dance, Katherine partnered several guests; and although they lacked Lawrence's special appeal, she enjoyed becoming better acquainted with them, and moving to the music. She learned many were from the literary world; one had even been a friend of Charles Dickens.

Sitting out a waltz, Katherine heard something stir behind her.

'Katherine!' came a loud whisper from a nearby doorway. The door, ajar, showed no light beyond. A figure beckoned. The old woman.

Her dark eyes were smiling and she nodded approvingly as Katherine went to her.

'A fine bride you'll make—keep yourself safe till then...'

Before Katherine could protest, the woman continued, 'I see it all, my dear—death… Now you wear that ring, take particular care.'

She must be closely related to Lawrence; there were no secrets from her. Unless…but no, she refused to believe the woman had some supernatural knowledge. How, though, could she possibly foretell danger…?

Allowing no opportunity for questions, and with a speed astonishing for her age, the old lady vanished. Only a dreadful uneasiness remained. Katherine forced herself to dismiss those ominous words, lest they spoil the whole evening. For weeks she had forgotten the old woman, she must forget her now.

When a polka was played, towards midnight, Lawrence again claimed her. Taking her hand, he smiled—indeed, he appeared to have smiled perpetually for hours. 'I want to show you,' he confided, 'that I'm not nearly so staid as you always think!'

Katherine was laughing and breathless when the music stopped, and had laid aside all gloomy apprehension. Instead of releasing her, Lawrence drew her to his side. 'Now everyone has seen how happy you make me.'

If she'd once entertained numerous

doubts about this man, they were banished now. Again, she'd defer questioning him about that woman purporting to be his mother. Tonight he looked so carefree, so much younger.

All too soon they were escorting their guests to the door. Descending the staircase, a hand on Lawrence's arm, Katherine turned to him, her eyes shining. 'Thank you for a lovely evening; I've never been happier.' She looked at the ring on her finger, recalling how its presence had delighted her—as well as the knowledge that others were eyeing it.

At the door, Susan Chandos was missing a glove, so—leaving the Rector and his wife talking with Lawrence, Katherine returned to the ballroom seeking it. Nearing the ante-room, she noticed somebody speaking and couldn't avoid overhearing.

'...she's passably attractive, and has secured a position above the menial ones normally open to her sort...' Katherine hesitated, but before she could warn them of her presence the conversation continued.

'Did you observe the Rushton ring on her finger?' another female voice demanded.

'Yes—*and* you looking askance at it!'

'You are aware, I suppose, its rightful place is on the hand of Lawrence Rushton's wife...'

His wife. Katherine didn't wait to hear more; she ran, through the library and along the corridor. His wife. It was all ruined; he wasn't free, he'd placed that ring on her finger, but still it belonged to another. His wife.

She longed to scream, but couldn't. She wanted to sob, but dare not—till she reached her own room. Remembering Mrs Chandos's glove, she rang for Isobel and sent her to find it. Her duty attended to, she retreated to her room.

Katherine took one last look at the ring, then tossed it on to the dressing-table. How could Lawrence have given it to her, when it belonged to another? How could he avow his love for her, have asserted, time and again, that he had no wife?

She heard his voice, and couldn't endure it. She covered her ears—but, of course, that didn't exclude it. The voice was inside her head—mocking her, it seemed... 'Kate, my love...' He had called her that. 'You're so good for me...' '...and a gold ring to anchor it...'

Promises, Lawrence's promises. Oh, he was good at making them, he turned a fine phrase, wooing her! But making words serve him was his profession. He ought to be able to express anything—and that, convincingly! Well, she'd have no more of it. She wouldn't heed him, from this night forward.

Eventually, he knocked at her door. 'Katherine—are you indisposed? I haven't seen you since you went seeking that glove. I haven't said good night, and there's something else I must say...'

'In the morning,' she replied, firmly, vowing that when morning came, and subsequent mornings, he'd find her deaf to his smooth words.

★ ★ ★ ★

Avoiding further discussion of the situation proved easier than she'd have believed. At breakfast Lawrence was amiability itself, intent on re-living the highlights of the previous evening, but at her calculated indifference he withdrew into silence.

During luncheon, he tried again, but again she froze him. At length, returning to the study, he sighed. 'I'm sorry,

Katherine...I don't know how, but I appear to have disappointed you...'

She felt his anxious eyes on her, but didn't meet them. What was the use in covering yet again the same ground...to be told the same lies, coaxed back into the same fool's paradise? Disappointed...? Exactly.

'That's it, Lawrence,' she replied coldly. 'You have.'

That ended his geniality—and his attempts to learn what distressed her. For days he went tight-lipped about the house, treated her as merely his employee—until Katherine was thankful she wasn't tied to so morose a man.

Meanwhile, she was planning to leave Masterton, sighing wistfully for the occasions when she'd made similar plans only to have them dismissed by Lawrence's. That last time she'd almost left, to be dissuaded by Lawrence arranging the party. Why not abide by her decision, and avoid being hurt?

But that evening had been good; she could not wish it had never been. Good—to see the trouble he had taken, having the ballroom renovated, inviting interesting people; good, too, to see him really happy, for the first time—carefree.

And how could he—with a wife some-where? How could he ignore his legal partner and set that ring on her finger? The ring. She'd have to do something about it.

The morning following the party she'd locked it away again, shedding more tears for its brief spell on her finger. She'd pretended it didn't exist, subconsciously denying the distress it had caused. But days had passed, she'd observed Lawrence looking at her bare finger, had seen him hesitate, then decide against the obvious question. The time for pretence was over.

Katherine went down early that morning, placed the ring, in its box, beside his plate.

'Oh, yes...' Lawrence remarked, when he noticed it. 'We've brought the matter into the open, have we? I wondered when that might happen. Why insult me thus? Isn't my ring good enough for you?'

He paused, dark eyes flashing angrily, nostrils flaring—and Katherine reflected how easily she could hate him, as she had on arriving.

'This ring, let me inform you,' he continued, haughtily, 'has been in my

263

family for generations. I told you—my grandmother's; well, it was hers before that, hers before...'

She snorted. 'And still it belongs to another...!'

'Indeed?' He seemed taken aback. 'To whom?'

'Your wife! And this time you owe me that long-overdue explanation, Lawrence Rushton! Without it, I shall remove myself from your wretched house, its mysteries, its unanswerable questions...and from you, its glib-tongued master!'

'Katherine, calm yourself—what is it? What has turned you against me?' He was feigning surprise, distress even, but she wouldn't soften.

'The other night I heard your fine friends discussing me—*us*, as though I were trying to usurp somebody's position here. I will tell you as I could not tell them that I have no intention of doing any such thing. I came here content to be your employee, you were the one who wanted to make more of it. But you should, I'd have thought, have waited until the place at your side was vacant before offering it. You see, I'm susceptible to having a ring placed on that particular finger, because I can't help loving you.'

Without a word, Lawrence rose. White-faced, he took her arm and marched her to the hall. He snatched her cloak from its hook and tossed it to her. 'Put that on...'

'But I...' Katherine began.

'Do as I say!'

He grabbed her arm again, forcing her to the front door. He drew back the heavy bolts and flung it open, leaving it gaping behind them. Down the steps he ran, dragging Katherine hurtling after him—but for his hold on her, she would have fallen headlong.

His fingers biting into her arm, he strode across the lawns, through the copse and the meadow, towards the church. All the while compelling her to run in order to keep up. She was sobbing with fear, and the pain his fingers were causing.

Lawrence released her only to open the church door, then turned aside to a smaller one leading off from the porch. Taking a key from his pocket, he unlocked it, and reached a candle and matches from a ledge inside.

'Light that,' he ordered.

Stone steps descended sharply, chill

damp air wafting up, as Katherine followed him into the vault.

At the foot of the steps she stood still, gazing around at the monuments, the carved tombs, graves set in the floor.

Lawrence crossed to a huge marble sarcophagus, and set the candle beside it.

'Here...' he beckoned, and she crept towards him trying to suppress her echoing footsteps in the eerie stillness.

'Read that...' he commanded.

Katherine read.

Here lie the mortal remains of Samantha Victoria Rushton wife of Lawrence Rushton of Masterton Hall died 30th March, 1873

Katherine bit her lip to control the weeping, now threatening to shake her body to fragments. She closed her eyes, thankful to know the truth at last, though hating Lawrence for the way he'd revealed it. Now perhaps, he'd take pity on her, she would feel comforting arms round her. He had made her suffer, because she'd hurt him—now, surely, compassion would return...

'Now, will you believe me?' Roughly, Lawrence grabbed her hand, pulling her with him to the steps. He did not speak further, and Katherine could not.

Lawrence slammed and locked the door inside the church, then opened the outer one. Still he said nothing more. Taking her by the arm again, he forced her at a brisk walk back the way they had come. The front door of the house stood open still, but he ignored it. Round the side to the East wing he went, appearing oblivious to her, though relentlessly holding on to her.

Unlocking a creaking door into the ruins, he nodded to her to go inside. He removed his coat, placed it on one of the fallen slabs of masonry.

'Sit!'

Katherine obeyed, thankfully.

'She died here,' Lawrence began, eventually, his voice devoid of sting, sounding dreadfully tired. 'A fitting place for recounting it...'

'There's no need...' Katherine protested.

'You say that—now. I think differently! I know not, Kate, to what you're accustomed. But *I* cannot live like this—having my every word questioned. I have shared with you, Katherine, more of what goes on in the heart of me, than with any other—alive or dead. Yet it takes this to make you believe me.'

He sighed and walked away, looking down, stirring the dust with the toe of his boot. After what seemed an age, he continued, over his shoulder, avoiding her eyes.

'I became aware of somebody beside my bed—in the dressing-room. It was Samantha, attired for going out. I asked what was amiss, but she only shook her head and made for the door. I pursued her to the gallery, calling her to stop, but she ignored me, she...'

'Had there been some...trouble?'

'Trouble!' Lawrence snorted, facing her. 'There was never anything else—but that's another story... She carried a candle, didn't light the gas mantles. She went through the gallery to my study—that room just beyond.' He glanced up to the door Katherine recalled vividly from her struggle with Rivers. 'I reached the doorway as she was rifling my desk. I realized she had taken my keys, was seeking my recently completed manuscript. I understood. She was leaving me and taking it with them—*her*,' he corrected, paused, then continued: 'Well, she found it, and I crossed to try snatching it from her. We...fought, I suppose; the candle was overturned, setting light to the pages. I made another grab for them, but she was the nearer. She smiled, triumphantly.'

'Triumphantly?' Katherine interrupted, and Lawrence seemed startled to find her there still.

'Don't you understand? She'd found the way to destroy me—by destroying my work. Better even than stealing it, as first intended. I salvaged some of the leaves, stamping out the flames, hypnotized by their charred remains. Now she had this...weapon, she laughed wildly, holding the pages she'd retained, one by one, to the candle, then tossing them on to the burning heap. Bigger and bigger the bonfire grew, and each time I went towards it she fended me off with blazing paper. I tried to drag her to safety; time and again I'd seen her skirts swing near that fire, but she was insensible to danger, obsessed by this great urge to hurt me.'

Lawrence stopped, closed his eyes momentarily, then continued: 'I seized her arm, intending to force her back to the gallery, but she fought like a vixen. I hung on—then, just when I believed I'd overpower her, she reached for my silver inkstand. I felt the blow on the back of my head—knew nothing further. Some while later, I opened my eyes. Flames surrounded me. I looked around, couldn't see Samantha, and concluded she'd escaped. The heat was intense, smoke filling the room making my eyes stream. I tried crawling along the floor, but now the carpet was smouldering. Coughing, scarcely able to see, my head reeling still, I got to my feet.'

Lawrence paused, turning his horrified gaze to Katherine. 'From the far corner, a sheet of flame detached itself, began moving towards me. It was Samantha, her gown ablaze—only her eyes recognizable as human; terror-stricken eyes, beseeching me to help...

'Somehow, I reached her, dragged heavy curtains from the windows, wrapping them round her, then rolling her on the floor to extinguish the flames. All the while she was screaming, till her screams turned to moaning. And the flames wouldn't go out; each time I smothered them they broke out afresh, nothing would beat them.

'At last, they were quelled—then I

270

discovered the room was an inferno. Glass cracked in the windows, the air fanning the blaze the more with each pane that broke. The curtains still hanging had caught fire, from them the panelling, pictures on the walls...'

'But what of the rest of the household—did no one hear or see the fire—come to your rescue?'

Lawrence studied her for a minute, and sighed. 'Rivers came—eventually, after the panelling had come tumbling, blazing from the walls and the ceiling started to cave in. When the beams were burning...'

'Surely you could have run to safety?'

'And left Samantha...?'

Katherine nodded. 'Of course, she was your wife...'

'No!' Lawrence contradicted, vehemently. 'Not for a long time—not really. But she was another human being, unconscious. I was her only hope—' his voice dropped, miserably—'I failed her.'

'But you tried, Lawrence, nobody could have done more.' It sounded so trite, how could it comfort?

'I've told myself that ever since; only at times I...wonder. Did hatred hold me back, prevent me trying hard enough?'

Katherine went to slip her arms round him; shaking her head. 'It wouldn't—you're not like that.'

She felt him shrug, but his arms enveloped her, as though given something to cling to.

'I made another attempt to drag her out, but the carpet was setting light to the curtains I'd wrapped her in. I swung her into my arms and, staggering against scorching furniture, stumbled towards the door.

'The beam fell as I reached for the handle. We were trapped; I was pinned by the shoulders and—' she sensed him look down to it—'this arm, as flames inched along that beam towards me...'

Katherine hugged him. 'It's over now, Lawrence, you survived—and I'm very thankful.'

He laughed—without humour. 'When I bring you nothing but unhappiness and difficulties? Oh, my Katherine, you were made for a young man, carefree, with a light heart...'

'Don't you want me?'

'Want?' Lawrence hesitated, decided to say it. 'I'll never stop wanting you.'

She raised her lips to be kissed, but

instead he kissed her forehead. He looked miserable.

'And now it's almost three years ago—behind you. Why let it haunt you?'

'Haunt?'

'Don't pretend with me. Why haven't you had this part of the house restored?'

'It will remain as it is—as a reminder.'

'A...memorial? Isn't that macabre?'

'I said a reminder,' he replied, harshly, 'of her treachery.'

Katherine swallowed back further questions. Nothing mattered now but Lawrence's future happiness—and her own, dependent upon it.

'So, now you've told me,' she began, slowly. 'There's nothing to hold you back...' She moved away, to stand by a gaping window, looking out over the park. When he made no response, she took a breath, she needed his reassurance... 'How soon will we be married?'

She heard him sigh, he hesitated, then came to her. He tilted her chin with a gentle finger, till she was looking into his eyes.

'When all this is really over—the fire—and its repercussions. Then, my Kate, and only then, we will marry.'

NINE

Subdued, Katherine joined Lawrence for luncheon, noticing the lines etched even more deeply, or so it seemed, around his mouth. She felt obliged to apologize for forcing him to re-live that dreadful experience, only she couldn't.

She had longed, almost from the start, to share everything of his—pain too. Now she'd done so, she couldn't regret any part of it. She felt older, though scarcely wiser, and exhausted; but she was, nevertheless, glad he'd confided in her.

She smiled wanly when Lawrence looked up as she came in. 'It seems an eternity since breakfast...'

He nodded grimly. 'Although I cannot pretend it has sharpened my appetite!'

'It can't hurt *us*, Lawrence,' Katherine began, hoping to cheer him.

'I wish I believed that.'

'How can I convince you?'

He sighed. 'That, I'm afraid, is not in your hands.'

Katherine frowned. 'My dear, there's more, isn't there? You haven't told me everything.'

'I've told you as much as is good for you—and as much as I intend, for the present. Don't aggravate me by pursuing your interrogation.'

She went to stand behind his chair, her hands on his shoulders. 'How can I help, Lawrence?'

Eventually, he reached for the tiny box, still beside his place. 'By wearing this—if, after consideration of all it signifies, you choose. But you have to be sure, Katherine; I can't build on false hopes again. Think about it—tell me your decision. The ring's waiting, if...'

'There's no "if", Lawrence. I love you—give it to me now...'

She faced him, extending her left hand, eagerly. Slowly, he sprang the catch of the box, looked from her to the ring and back again to her. She took it out and handed it to him. Lawrence's fingers were icy. When he'd slipped the ring in place, she took his hand in both her own.

He smiled faintly. 'Yes, Kate, as I've already said, you're the warmth in my life. And that ring on your finger my only chance of happiness. Stand by me, Katherine—stand by me, through the rest...'

'I'm here, Lawrence,' she responded, gently, 'and will be as long as you need me.'

With that reassurance Lawrence seemed content. Their routine returned to normal. And it was then Katherine found difficulty in stifling the questions. Lawrence may have told her a great deal of what had occurred but it did not complete the picture. Still Katherine wondered if that weird old lady was his mother; still she queried the identity of his female companion that day in Maidstone.

Would mystery always surround him? Would the love he professed be perpetually clouded by doubts. Would she accept his reluctance to reveal everything?

One thing was certain—nothing would induce her again to ask Lawrence how soon they'd marry. She might have risen from a humble background, but she'd pride enough to restrain further eagerness!

She found it hard, though, to withhold her instinctive affection, and became more reserved with Lawrence than was her nature. And so, although they still spent most of their recreation together, pursuing their mutual pastimes, an uneasy atmosphere developed.

Spring gave way to summer; Lawrence's absences from home continued, but always he returned by nightfall. Katherine told herself this was in consideration of her, hoping it was so. They both, indeed, remained alert for the accident which might not be an accident. And for the return of Rivers.

★ ★ ★ ★

At her typewriter, weeks later, Katherine was puzzled when Lawrence abruptly ceased dictating.

'I've got that; go on...' She glanced across: he was scowling. He flung down his manuscript and stood up.

'Oh, I'm weary of this!'

Katherine smiled. 'We'll pause for a while—take the horses and...'

'No!' Lawrence roared, startling her. 'You misunderstand—and purposely, I shouldn't wonder. I don't mean I'm weary of this book, though heaven knows it crawls along. It's this situation between us that disturbs me.'

Her heart began racing; had he, at last, found marriage alone would satisfy him? Had he overcome the difficulties—the *secret* difficulties, preventing that?

Lawrence strode to the window, stared out, then swung round, facing her. He spoke very quietly, but his eyes were cold, wary.

'Believe me, Katherine, I understand— can see how, given time to reconsider, you've reached a certain conclusion.'

'Lawrence, what do you mean?'

'That you've made your decision.'

'Decision? But all decisions are yours, I've accepted that.'

He sighed. 'I hate hypocrisy, Kate, even if you seek by it to spare my feelings. It's plain enough; for weeks you haven't even mentioned our future.'

'Only because...' she began, but he interrupted, heatedly.

'And I, too, have been thinking— imagining what goes on in that head of yours.' He paused, turned to gaze over the park again, his voice coming quietly, with considerable effort. 'It's...all right, Katherine—I release you from any commitment to me.'

'Lawrence!' She couldn't believe it.

Hesitantly, he faced her once more. 'It is what you want, isn't it? To continue solely as my secretary...'

'Of course it isn't!' She must use her reeling brain, rationally, to discover the reason for his strange assumption.

'I read it in your whole attitude—with some hold on me you're content. You prefer your position in charge of that piece of machinery. It gives you...authority. But I warn you, your value will drop when the typewriter becomes commonplace. Soon, there'll be hundreds of women like you—full of their own importance!'

'You're so wrong—this machine's useful to you—that's all I care.'

'I think not, Kate.' Eyes flashing, Lawrence advanced on her. 'You worship that thing because it strengthens your security here.'

Beside her desk now, his breathing was agitated. 'Well, I have no such awe, this is my opinion!' A sweep of his hand sent the typewriter crashing to the ground. His eyes, meeting hers, were challenging.

Katherine sprang back, surveying the wreckage. 'Look what you've done!'

'I'm fully aware. What does it tell

you—this contempt of mine for your precious toy?'

She hesitated, reluctant to express the awful thought. 'That...that you've no further use for me...?'

Lawrence's anger appeared to drain away; he turned from her.

'As you will,' he murmured.

'And what of your book?'

'To the devil with it! There you go again—don't you see?' He swung round, brown eyes searching her face. 'Don't you? You won't let go of me...' He stopped, swallowed, then continued, his voice strangled, 'And yet you don't want me.'

'Don't want? Lawrence, what is this?' How could he have reached this conclusion?

'Katherine, Katherine, be honest—I can face it. Tell me the truth now—all of it.'

She breathed deeply, trying to marshal her disquieted thoughts, to find words for all he was to her. Only she was not quick enough.

'Then I will tell you.' His hand on her shoulder forced her to sit at her desk. 'Maybe it was...pity, at first, made you imagine yourself...fond of me; fond enough to...despite my low spirits, my impatience, my...past. You're kind, Katherine, you give affection eagerly. But it isn't enough, is it, not enough to—' he sighed—'take me on, the way I am.'

Katherine was puzzled, what could he mean? 'Because you must keep me waiting...?' she asked.

'Because of this!' He thrust his right arm under her nose. 'Maimed as I am, how could anyone love me!'

She tried to speak and choked. He saw her weeping and misinterpreted it.

'That's it.' He strode to the door, as if unable to bear any more.

'Lawrence!'

'Well?' He paused, hand on the door handle. 'Must you prolong it?'

'I will have my say—you've ensured yours!' Something inside Katherine overruled her shaken emotions, her respect for him, quelling all but her love. 'And I suggest you sit down.' The calm of her voice, despite her aching heart, almost made her smile. 'This may take some time.'

She waited until Lawrence returned to his desk, thankful his hesitation allowed more time for thinking. Now she'd reveal everything she felt.

'I asked you, weeks ago, when we would marry. Your reply, I thought, forbade further reference to the matter. I told myself I would wait patiently—that having you as my husband was...the only thing I wanted...'

'But now you've changed...'

'Be still!' Her temerity amazed her. 'I've said it before but it mustn't have reached you...' She sighed, then went to him.

'I love you, Lawrence, I have almost from the start.'

Relieved to be speaking so freely, she knelt beside his chair, taking his right arm.

'This,' she whispered, 'means only that you've been hurt—giving me excuse for extra loving. And don't belittle my love, calling it pity! You're a hard man, Lawrence, you almost made me hate you, but I've always had this admiration...'

She felt his hand caressing her hair, the fingers slid to the nape of her neck. He kissed her.

'So you haven't changed.' He sounded scarcely able to believe it. Smiling at last, he nodded. 'Very well, Katherine—so be it. We will be wed—now I'm sure you, also, desire it.'

'When?' she ventured.

He sighed. 'Before long. Be patient, my Kate, through what must precede that.'

He drew her to her feet, embracing her with the passion she'd once feared had vanished.

Lawrence smiled ruefully, regarding the heap of tangled metal.

Katherine laughed. 'Maybe the type-writer is commonplace already...'

'Then order a new one, tomorrow—a small price to pay!'

★ ★ ★ ★

Happier than she remembered, Katherine found the days racing by. And, although she noticed Lawrence had difficulty concentrating still, he appeared more cheerful.

He spent some time outlining his plans for restoring Masterton.

'A fitting residence for you; as I told our guests, you've given me incentive to use the place again.'

About to go to her room one evening, Lawrence called her back.

'Would two months hence suit you?'

Katherine smiled. 'For our wedding?'

'The very same. I should by then have attended to the...matters outstanding.'

'It would suit me admirably,' she responded, her eyes shining.

She had to tell someone. She would have burst otherwise. Choosing not to write of it to her parents before every detail was settled, she confided instead in Janet.

The girl was delighted. 'At last! I'm so happy for you. And thankful he's not letting you face it alone.'

'Face what?' Katherine demanded, frowning.

Janet dropped her eyes. 'Oh, dear, I've let it slip again. Katherine, please don't be cross. I can see now that none of it's true.'

Katherine sighed. 'So they're spreading rumours again, are they?'

Janet coughed awkwardly.

'You can tell me,' Katherine persisted. 'I know it wouldn't be your doing.'

'One of the maids was informing Mrs Hawkins of something she suspected...'

'Do they listen at doors now?'

'Well,' Janet spoke reluctantly, 'Mrs Hawkins rewards them for anything they learn.'

'Rewards! I can believe she would!' And,

doubtless, relay information to Rivers and his fellow-conspirator. But why? Even if she were carrying a child, what possible interest could that be to them?

Eventually, Katherine smiled, wryly. 'Whatever started that story, the passing of time will prove its falsity. But I hope, for Mrs Hawkins's sake, Lawrence does not hear of it.'

Returning, grave-faced, however, from a day's absence, he called Katherine into the drawing-room.

'Have you heard...an unpleasant rumour, Kate?' he began, quietly, searching her expression for distress.

'What rumour?' she enquired, although guessing.

'A vile, hideous tale that I am giving some poor changeling a name. Oh, Katherine...!'

He appeared astonished when she laughed.

'So, you have heard, and, I suppose—yet again—you decided to bear the unpleasant-ness alone?'

'We know it's unfounded gossip.'

Lawrence shook his head at her. 'My plucky Kate—but this you shall not endure...' He strode to the door.

'Lawrence—wait.'

He turned, an eyebrow raised.

'Why say anything? They will not believe you. And what possible harm can it do?'

'Harm? To your good name.'

'I shan't be tied to the stake as a wanton, on mere rumour! Give them their fun, then we will laugh, nine months from now—when I am childless!'

'Fun? Your sense of humour and mine must be vastly different!'

'Can't you imagine them, eyeing me, willing my figure to round out a little...?'

'I can! And find the idea extremely distasteful!'

'We've done nothing to offend the most strait-laced dowager. I almost wish we had—how I long to startle this stuffy society!'

'Katherine!'

'Don't you think some of these restrictions unnecessary?'

Lawrence smiled, but said nothing.

'Let the rumour die, Lawrence—when they mark no developments.'

★ ★ ★ ★

Katherine continued amused by speculation on her condition, especially when

Mrs Hawkins professed a sudden interest in her health, enquiring after it at every encounter.

Lawrence, meanwhile, grew more perturbed, as though summoning all his resources to face some ordeal. An ordeal he would not disclose.

One Saturday, tending the horses, she felt him watching her.

'What troubles you, Lawrence?'

Sighing, he leaned against the side of the stall. 'Only that...Katherine, my dearest Kate—trust me, believe in me...'

She smiled into his worried eyes. 'Now don't be foolish—I have told you repeatedly, I shall not change.'

'Not even...' he shook his head, hesitated, then continued. 'You mustn't doubt me...even if it seems the evidence is heaped against me.' Gazing beyond her, he murmured, half to himself, 'I might, I just might, have neglected some way, not obvious to me, of...averting it, but more than that...never!' He looked her straight in the eyes. 'My conscience is clear, I swear to you. You do believe me...?'

'Of course,' Katherine asserted, though uncomprehendingly. 'Lawrence, what is this? I don't understand.'

'And no more you should. Don't trouble your pretty head with it, Kate.' And more than that he refused to say, anger threatening when she pursued it.

But Katherine was disturbed. Why did this man she loved forbid her to share his problems? And what, precisely, were they? For some hours that night she lay awake, trying to guess what might be causing his anxiety.

★ ★ ★ ★

Leaving the church next morning, she was feeling happier. The sermon from the Reverend Chandos had been no more uplifting than ever, but some serenity within the building, and time for reflection, had compensated. It was plain what she must do. Lawrence had begged her to believe in him—the fact that she didn't know what prompted that was immaterial. She must do everything possible to demonstrate her complete faith in him. And in a matter of weeks she'd be his wife, then, as never before, entrusting herself to him.

Bewildered, Katherine looked all around for Lawrence, after her brief word with the

Rector in the porch. It was Lawrence's custom to meet her there and escort her safely to the Hall. When he didn't arrive after she'd stood at the lych-gate some five minutes, she began strolling home, thinking to meet him on the way.

Skirting the trees surrounding the lake, she thought she saw someone move, and paused to watch. A man was leading a horse, his tall figure, glimpsed through the trees, easily recognizable.

'Lawrence...' she called; then observed the woman at the other side of the animal. A woman with fair curls—the person she had seen in Maidstone.

'Oh, no!' She put a hand to her mouth, uncertain whether she'd spoken the words aloud. The man started, then leaned towards his companion, saying something.

Katherine had no wish to witness more. She turned away and hurried towards the house.

Half-way across the meadow, she sensed somebody following her, and suddenly she didn't want to see. If it was Lawrence she wanted only to get away from him. Snatching up her skirts, she ran for the cover of the copse.

A hand came down hard on her shoulders, biting into her flesh, imprisoning her.

'Lawrence!' she screamed. 'Stop, you're hurting me!'

He grappled with her, his strength frightening her; she'd never been aware of such power in his arms. If this was some game, she saw no reason for it. Then she remembered that woman. This was no game—Lawrence intended to be rid of her.

She tried to wriggle away.

'No, you don't!'

'Let me go,' she pleaded. 'I'll free you—you can go to her.'

He laughed—an odd sound, unlike him; had something unhinged him? And still he wouldn't release her. She bent almost double trying to escape.

He slid his fingers along her shoulder towards her throat. His grip tightened; it seemed to be squeezing the life out of her.

She heard hooves, pounding through the trees, then...nothing.

★ ★ ★ ★

Later, much later, Katherine opened her eyes to find she was in her room; with a start, she saw Lawrence standing by the window. Her throat ached abominably; she put a hand to it, trying to swallow.

As though alert for the slightest movement, he turned and came towards her.

'Katherine, thank God...' He made as if to sit on the edge of the bed.

She was petrified. 'No, Lawrence, keep away!'

'But, Kate,' he protested, 'I've waited here for hours—or so it seemed. I've sent for Dr McLaren, I've...'

'But why? When a short while ago you wanted only to be rid of me?'

His eyes were solemn. 'Listen, Kate, that wasn't...'

'Not you? Come now, I'm not stupid.' She paused a second. 'I know now what you meant—about doubting you. This time, I'm afraid it is too much.'

'I can explain it all,' he interrupted, but Katherine, shaking her head, refused to look at him.

'Not any longer. You see, Lawrence, I've listened to your last explanation. There can be no possible justification for your attack on me. I told you—you only had to say,

I'd have let...let you...go to her.' A lump came into her throat, precluding further speech. She closed her eyes, then forced out the words. 'Please leave me...'

Katherine heard her door click open and close. Lawrence's footsteps receded along the corridor and she began to breathe more easily.

She opened her eyes to survey the room. Her tiny gilt clock read one-thirty. She would wait—until she believed Lawrence was eating luncheon—the servants resting after Sunday's heavier meal; with luck, she'd leave unobserved.

She dragged herself towards the washstand, putting a hand to her head as she almost fainted again. She splashed cold water on to her face, then gasped in horror, seeing the great fingermarks at her throat. Why had Lawrence seized her thus violently—why stopped short of killing her?

She sighed, shaking her head. All was utterly baffling, and she in no state to unravel it. She could only flee from here—and quickly. Before nightfall she must be miles away. But how might she effect her escape? She couldn't walk any distance—she could scarcely cross the room.

Then Katherine remembered the horse—she would take Midnight, leave a note stating her intention; no one must believe her capable of stealing the mare. She would ride to...

To where—that was the problem. She could turn to nobody in the vicinity. Anyone connected with Masterton Hall would feel obliged to inform its master. She must simply disappear—with no risk of being followed. She would ride into Maidstone, leave Midnight at the coaching inn, then take the London train. From there, she'd sometime, somehow, make the necessary changes of train for Yorkshire.

And what would she tell her family? That, too, would be difficult; during the journey she must find some explanation.

Katherine took a small bag from the wardrobe, cramming into it her clock, hairbrush and nightgown. More than that she could not carry—and, indeed, could spare no time for. What money she possessed she thrust into a pocket in the bag, then tied a kerchief round her neck, concealing those marks. She slipped from the room with no backward glance—leaving the place was distressing enough, without adding further pain.

It was a simple task to hurry downstairs and out through the side door. Murmuring voices confirmed the servants were in their quarters, and going this way she'd avoid the dining-room windows.

Reaching the stables without detection, she saddled Midnight, swiftly, talking soothingly to the animal. Then they were away—galloping towards the North Lodge, this being unoccupied. It was useless thinking to pass Sarah and John's home.

Out on the road, Katherine sensed a certain reluctance in Midnight who was accustomed to the softer parkland. It was of her mount that Katherine thought during much of her furious ride towards the town. She had loved those early lessons, riding bare-headed, the wind in her hair. What freedom—exhilaration. And now she'd grown to love this beautiful black creature; to be delighted when Midnight recognized her, to laugh as soft lips nuzzled her palm for sugar. Now this was ending, just as the rest was over already—how she would accept a different existence she couldn't contemplate. But it must be so.

Following her hasty departure, Katherine found herself, nearing Maidstone, willing things to slow down. Despite all that had happened, scared though she was, she dreaded severing this final link with Lawrence.

The inn came in sight. Soon she would dismount, call one of the lads, hand over the reins to him.

Exactly as Katherine imagined, a scruffy boy of about twelve received her instructions to care for the horse, pending collection by Lawrence. And that was it. The end.

Only this time she couldn't just walk away.

Midnight was a living creature—her friend almost. She laid her head against the horse's neck, then patted her—and was reminded of a similar gesture, frequently repeated, from Lawrence to his mount, Reveller.

Katherine turned, hastily, running from the inn's courtyard. She reached the street, thronging with families taking a Sunday stroll.

The animal neighed. Katherine stopped, almost turned back; but, blinking rapidly, hurried towards the station. She must get right away from anything and everything that could remind her...

Past the jewellers' where she'd bought Lawrence that silver tiepin, the place where she'd purchased Simon's farmyard.

Simon. If only she could have seen him just once more...

Thankfully, Katherine at last stepped aboard the London train; now there would be no changing her mind, no going back. She'd won this last battle with Lawrence Rushton, and with her love for him.

TEN

Katherine was scarcely aware of the fast-changing scenery as the train carried her northwards—home. She could now only vaguely recall the ride into Maidstone, and the night spent in a London hotel was but a blur. She sat motionless, feeling ill and too exhausted to care where she was or to observe the stares she invited by thus travelling alone. Suddenly 'Keighley', on a station platform, roused her to the realization that she neared her journey's end.

Rapidly, she reached for her bag, then the carriage door—but the train was about to move off. Seeing her plight, an elderly man, who had alighted, took her bag so she might gather her skirts and step hastily down. She thanked him, and he opened his mouth to comment on her abrupt decision to leave the train, but his wife spoke, beside him. 'Are you feeling quite the thing, my dear? I noticed in the train that you appeared somewhat...dazed.'

Katherine tried to smile. 'Thank you, but I am only...tired.'

'And have you far to go now?' The man eyed her anxiously.

Katherine gazed in astonishment at him. This must be the measure of her distress—right up to that moment she'd not given thought to the rest of the journey. And it was all of ten miles.

She closed her eyes, longing to be transported there. How in the world would she reach her parents' cottage?

The woman put a hand on her arm. 'Is no one meeting you?'

Katherine hesitated, reluctant to admit it, but what else could she say?

'Our carriage should be waiting in the station forecourt; we will take you to your destination.'

'Oh, but I couldn't let you...' she began.

'It might be out of our way, dear,' the man started to protest.

'Charles, how could you!' his wife reproved, taking charge. 'The girl needs help—now, you take her bag again...'

So it was that Katherine's mother glanced out of the window to discover who had drawn up outside their cottage in so fine a carriage.

'Henry!' she called to her husband, sitting beside the kitchen range. 'It's our Katherine—and by the look of her she's poorly!'

Katherine's elderly rescuers refused the invitation to come indoors; assured she'd be cared for they'd be on their way. She thanked them sincerely, wondering what she'd have done without their aid, then obeyed her mother's instructions to come inside this minute.

She gave her parents a wan smile, after greeting them. 'I'm all right—really I am. You must not fuss so.'

'Then what are you doing here, my girl?' her father asked, in his bluff North Country way: 'You haven't left that fine job of yours, have you? Your letters always spoke well enough of that Mr Rushton...' Hazel eyes anxiously searched her tired face.

Katherine sighed; even here, it seemed, she wasn't allowed to forget the man.

Her mother stopped, half-way to the hob with a kettle, awaiting her answer. Katherine looked from one to the other; wishing they'd delay their interrogation. 'You mustn't worry, either of you. I...I'm here for a holiday, that is all.' There; that would give her time to think.

During her absence, Katherine had forgotten how her parents' concern expressed itself in a need to know the ins and outs of everything. She wasn't prepared for that—she couldn't yet accept the situation herself, much less explain it.

To ward off their probing while drinking tea, Katherine turned the questions on them, enquiring how her sister, Clare, was faring—teaching at the local school. They eagerly related how well-liked their younger daughter was by headmaster and pupils. And so, albeit temporarily, Katherine was spared further quizzing.

After the tea, she made the exhausting journey her excuse for going to bed.

This set her mother flurrying to heat a warming-pan.

'That bed must not be slept in without a thorough airing!'

Before Clare joined her in their room beneath the eaves, Katherine was asleep. So she awakened next morning to the girl's curious questions. Katherine told her the story she'd given her parents and she also appeared to accept it. Katherine wondered how she would explain when time elapsed and she did not return to Masterton Hall, but that could wait.

Immediately her sister went downstairs, Katherine crossed to pour water into the wash-stand bowl. The looking-glass revealed that the red marks were turning colour, becoming bruises; and how un-sightly they were! She must continue using that kerchief to hide them, until finding an old, high-necked dress. She re-examined the marks. There were so many—all round her throat.

This way and that she turned, scru-tinizing the purple fingerprints, counting... One, two, three, four, five, six, seven, eight, nine... She stopped.

There couldn't be—it was utterly im-possible!

How could a man with but one hand leave more than five such prints? Her heart jumped—it hadn't been Lawrence!

Only she knew it had—she'd recognized

him, had looked into his eyes at that last awful moment, had heard his voice, his laughter. Only *that,* she remembered, had sounded strange...

'Katherine!' Her mother's voice, calling from the foot of the stair, recalled her to the reality of breakfast.

'Coming...' Hurriedly, she washed face and hands, slipped on her dress, knotting the kerchief over it. During breakfast she forced her attention to the conversation, away from the events bringing her here.

Presently, Clare departed for the school and their father, after his break for food, returned to the fields, leaving Katherine with her mother. She felt the older woman's eyes—green like her own, though fading with age—on her. And wasn't surprised when her mother cleared her throat, awkwardly.

'Katherine...is there anything you want to tell me? Something you couldn't say in front of your father?'

Katherine shook her head. 'I am perfectly well, thank you—there's no reason for concern.'

'But you're so pale—has he been working you too hard?'

'Perhaps,' she replied, evasively, 'I told

301

you—I've come for a rest...' She took a deep breath, the inquisition was never-ending. Yet she understood it. She had travelled farther than any member of her family and, although writing frequently, had not previously returned on a visit. And now, here she was, turning up without prior arrangement.

Oh, she could see how peculiar it must seem.

Katherine smiled. 'When I've helped with the dishes, I'll prove I'm fit by taking a walk.'

'You'd best fetch that young pup out of the barn then—don't let him worry the sheep, mind.'

'A puppy—you mean old Martha's had another litter? You didn't write of it.'

'Like as not, I did and you've forgotten. Three months old, he is, and we're stuck with him. The rest of the bunch went easy enough, but he's...a funny little thing. One leg shorter than the rest—though he moves fast enough...'

'What's his name?'

Her mother laughed. 'Haven't found him one yet—happen you will.'

Opening the barn door, Katherine whistled. A small black object hurled itself at her. She went down on one knee to scratch the top of his head, while he twisted this way and that, trying to lick her hands and face, tail wagging furiously.

She stroked the glossy coat, its puppy curl straightening into adult doghood. Why must he be black? Tears stung her eyes, remembering her—*Lawrence's*—fine mare, Midnight. She looked down, ruefully, at the frisking animal. Maybe he'd be good for her—something to love, something new to think about. She frowned, noticing the peculiar limping run as he made for the gate, though it didn't inhibit him. He seemed to skip along.

'Skip!' she called, and he turned, panting, head on one side. Katherine smiled—he had a name now.

She took her favourite path for the tarn which, mid-week, should be unfrequented. She'd a deal of thinking to do; away from worried eyes and perpetual questioning.

The wind was keen at the top of the rise, but the sun tempered it. Katherine gazed beyond the tarn to the valley, with moors to one side, limestone peaks to the other. She used to spend hours absorbing the serenity of this view; why, now, did she only feel very alone? Would serenity elude her for ever?

She walked to the edge of the tarn to sit on a boulder, listlessly tossing stones into the water. Spreading concentric circles went reaching out from them, out of sight; if only she might reach out... No; she mustn't even think of him.

Skip snuffled in the grass, hither and thither, following different trails. Was this how she'd been, searching and never finding, only to return to the beginning? Was there to be no fulfilment of hopes, only...emptiness? Skip settled at her feet, yawned, then laid his head on his paws. Katherine fondled the short hair behind his ears, thinking—but not of Skip.

How was Lawrence reacting to her disappearance—was he distressed? Or would his impassive expression reveal nothing, as at their first meeting? Would he always, now, conceal every emotion?

But he'd expect me to run away, she reminded herself; he knows why I've left. Only it didn't coincide with her imagining; she saw Lawrence plainly—hurt, puzzled, unhappy. And why had she this dreadful sensation of failing him?

For the first time in weeks, she recalled

the old woman; why had she been adamant Katherine belonged at Masterton? Was she truly Lawrence's mother?—it seemed scarcely credible, yet she'd a mother's concern. She'd foretold danger at the Hall. In that she'd proved correct. Was she some...witch or something? If so, what did that make Lawrence?

She'd been concerned for Katherine also—begging her to keep safe. To bear Lawrence a child! There was no possibility of that now—maybe there never had been. Except...well, Lawrence had given her that ring—the ring destined for his wife.

Why hadn't she realized the night of the party that that was what he intended her becoming? Was she the one so confused that she always fell to doubting him? She had been wrong, after all, as he'd shown conclusively, in believing his first wife still alive. About what else had she been mistaken? Not this attack on her—that was certain.

Instinctively, Katherine touched her throat, recalling the interruption whilst trying to determine how two sets of fingermarks got there. It *had* been Lawrence, walking the horse; she'd known his stride, the set of his head, and heard his voice. She'd even looked him in the face, before she'd heard...what? Still she could not remember, though believed it connected with Lawrence. Yet there he'd been, starting to squeeze life itself from her...

Katherine sighed; these wild fancies were but a trick of the brain, because she longed to trust him. She must dismiss them. Reason told her, firmly, that the evidence of her own ears and eyes and...

What had he said? '...even if it seems the evidence is heaped against me.' Surely he didn't mean that attempt to kill her? Premeditated, it was worse than ever. And why resort to violence? He wasn't a violent man.

No? What of his anger with Simon? What of dashing her typewriter to the ground? Thumping mercilessly at the organ?

Skip was wandering restlessly—she must return to the cottage.

'Oh, Lawrence,' she thought, 'why try to kill me? You need only have said you loved someone else; I'd have left...'

During luncheon, feeling out of place at her parents' table, Katherine repeatedly had to retrieve her straying thoughts from a certain dining-room—and the man eating in solitude. For that was how she saw him, despite commanding herself to remember the fair-haired woman. Oh, what a nonsense it was! And, away from the terror of those hands at her throat, how she wished she hadn't fled so precipitately.

Lawrence had begged her to hear his explanation—for perhaps the first time since her arrival at Masterton, he'd wanted to reveal something. And she'd refused to listen.

Annoyed by this wavering, Katherine wrote to Janet that afternoon, asking that she pack her possessions into her trunk and send it after her. That way no belongings of hers would remain at Masterton. She would discipline herself, eventually, to withdraw her thoughts as well from Lawrence Rushton.

And she needed the clothes left behind there—before anyone remarked on how few dresses hung in the bedroom.

Day succeeded day, each bringing Katherine more strength, recovering from the ordeal—and each increasing her misery. She missed Lawrence, wakening in the night from the sound of his voice, the touch of his lips. By day, walking alone, she fancied he walked beside her. And this was so wrong, she should be setting her mind to securing employment. Her family could not support her. Already, Clare had asked when she'd return to Kent, soon they'd all be asking. Oh, if only...

Lawrence could be so gentle...

After Rivers's attempt on her life he'd stayed with her, after Mrs Hawkins scared her. And it was Lawrence himself, shortly after her arrival at Masterton, who'd prevented her plunging to her death in the ruins. He would never have harmed her.

Would he?

Her trunk arrived, heralded by Janet's letter, of which snatches haunted Katherine for days...

Why did you leave so suddenly? Master Simon keeps asking why you don't come to play—he thinks you're cross with him... After you were found missing the master had us into his study, one by one. Mrs Hawkins, George, me, Isobel and the others—to ask if we knew where you were... He's more bad-tempered than ever... It's so eerie here—an old woman terrified me, clutching my arm in the shadowy corridor. 'Get her back,' she urged, 'the green-eyed girl, my boy's fretting for her.' Then a woman in grey took her off, hurriedly. Who is she, Katy, do you know her? The master strides from room to room, hardly sits at his desk at all... Sometimes I hear sounds from the music room, not music, though—a dreadful thumping on the organ...

Katherine sighed; and she had not been there, no one would have gone to him, no one calmed him.

But he knows why, she persisted, to the empty room. She wrote back immediately, nevertheless, not so much to thank Janet for sending the trunk, as to express concern about Mr Rushton. Maybe, somehow, he would learn of it.

Returning from the tarn, Skip at her heels, one morning, Katherine realized with a start that it was a month since her arrival in Yorkshire. Every mark had vanished from about her throat. She was glad; the mirror no longer reminded her there was reason for doubting Lawrence had been her attacker. Nothing would make her recall her rashness—how she alone might have tossed aside happiness.

She had re-read Janet's letter repeatedly, confirming the girl made no mention of any woman at Lawrence's side. Every word, indeed, stressed his isolation.

Despite the passing weeks, nothing made

sense for Katherine. Without Lawrence there seemed no reason for anything—certainly none for living. Her family may have accepted her presence, but she was far from accepting this way of life...this unhappiness. Yet she'd made no effort to find another post—perhaps because something within her refused to release her hold on the last.

A letter awaited her at luncheon. Recognizing Janet's hand, she tore open the envelope.

My dear Katy,
(it began)
I must let you know that all is not well here. You do not say why you left, but that I am sure you still care about Mr Rushton, and I'm afraid something is very wrong. The whole house was roused by a dreadful row one night. The master was in the hall, shouting at—who do you think? Mr Rivers! Yes, he'd come back. None of us knows why, but there he was, large as life. The master took a pistol to frighten him off, then Mr Rivers ran from the house—and Mrs Hawkins with him! What do you think to that?

But the worst of it is Mr Rushton looks so ill, as though Mr Rivers brought him bad news. I've been helping with the cooking and he doesn't eat enough to keep a sparrow alive. And, Katy, oh Katy—he does look so miserable. My heart aches for him, it does really; and you know there's no love lost between us on account of Master Simon. (Oh, yes, he still asks after you.)

But, Katy, I am worried—Mr Rushton is so unlike himself. At first he was always angry with somebody, but now he seems to have lost all spirit. He wanders about the place as if searching for something—or somebody—he'll never find. I saw him out in the grounds this morning, just standing there, looking...at the windows of your old room.

Couldn't you forgive whatever wrong he has done? You loved him once, can that love have died so easily?

Unable to read further before the curious eyes of her family, Katherine excused herself from the table and went to her room. She read the letter again, tears streaming down her face.

She longed to go to Lawrence, to reassure him—as he'd needed her reassurance previously... But how could she?

That night she scarcely slept; tossing this way and that, trying not to visualize

Lawrence's eyes—infinitely sad, as she knew they could seem. Unwanted—as she knew he could feel. While she was here, and despite everything, wanting him.

As day began to break, Katherine wakened from a light doze. She dressed quietly, not to disturb Clare, and, as soon as her father had gone to the fields she crossed the yard. Opening the barn door, she called Skip, then watched him run ahead in the direction of the tarn.

She walked all the way round it, taking some time because she moved slowly, deep in thought.

Might she not write to Lawrence, enquiring after his health? Give him a chance to explain. Again, she recalled regretfully her refusal to listen before leaving...

Though what possible explanation could there be for trying to strangle her?

Suddenly she didn't care. So much had gone unexplained, yet through it all had come this love they shared, a love she could neither stifle nor ignore, even miles away from him. It refused to lie down under anything that occurred. No disaster could extinguish it. She heard his voice, sounding so close he might have been beside her, 'Only trust me...' And now she did trust him. Knowing that, her heart was exultant.

Katherine sat beside the tarn, the comforting warmth of Skip across her feet. She must plan, think this out carefully. It might be dangerous. Yes—if Lawrence had sprung on her, would she feel safe with him—ever? And did that matter? For without him she would linger in this pointless existence till she was old and uncaring, all love for anybody withered.

What a waste!

She shivered. It was early yet, the sun had no heat in it. The wind swept across the top of the hill, as always here. Katherine rose, began throwing sticks for Skip to retrieve, laughing at his lop-sided run as he brought them to her. Now she had this half-formed scheme to contact the man she loved, she felt light-hearted. Later, she would re-examine the details, but for the moment this was sufficient.

Besides, she dared not inspect the idea too closely, lest caution creep in and make nonsense of it. And that she couldn't bear—she had to believe she'd see him again. And if her letter brought no response? She would know she had tried, would have nothing with which to reproach herself eternally.

She laughed again at the dog and went down on one knee to fondle him.

'You go for the cripples still, I see!' The voice, from behind her, carried some distance by the wind, was unmistakable.

She put both hands to suddenly feverish cheeks and turned, slowly, afraid to have the emptiness of space mock her. But he was there.

Stumbling over tussocks, Skip frisking excitedly round her, she ran to him.

'Lawrence!'

He stood looking at her, uncertainly, scowling, worried, but she came straight on at him, running still—and he opened his arms to her. He caught her to him, to hold her hard against him, without speaking.

His dark eyes were moist when she leaned back to look up into them. 'You ran to me,' he said. 'You ran to me!' And hugged her to him.

Katherine raised her face again, and when he didn't kiss her was puzzled. Then she put a hand to either side of his face and drew it towards her own. Their lips met, but only with the warmth of her kisses did he start to show any feeling.

'Lawrence, why...?' she began, and heard him sigh.

'It has to be what you wish, Kate—and only that.'

She smiled a little and went into his arms again. 'I wish this,' she murmured, and his mouth claimed hers once more.

'Your coat's wet,' she remarked, at last, when he released her.

'Only with dew. It's of no consequence.' He was smiling now, his eyes almost laughing.

'But how...what on earth...?'

He laughed then. 'Oh, my Kate, I was so afraid...'

'How did you get here?' she asked, not taking in all he was saying.

'Train to Keighley—I threatened Janet with dismissal if she didn't tell me where to find you. I'd seen your trunk go off, you see. Not very loyal to you, is she? Will you reprimand her?'

Katherine shook her head, gazing at him, unable to believe he wasn't some figment of her imagination.

'Why did you decide to come, Lawrence?'

'Isn't that obvious? But the thing that gave me heart to...'

A tiny smile played round his thin lips for a second—he brought a scrap of paper from an inside pocket. Dog-eared, as though from much handling, he straightened it before giving it to her.

Katherine frowned, then recognized it. She had sat one day, hadn't she, trying to sense what it was like—having only the one hand for writing? Interrupted by Mrs Hawkins's maligning gossip, Katherine had slipped the paper away, had never again found it. But Lawrence had.

She met his eyes.

Lawrence nodded, his voice became hushed: 'It was like a message from you—although I told myself it wasn't any such thing. I couldn't dismiss it, though. For a whole evening I sat in our music room, gazing at this. It seemed to say there was still just a little...hope. That someone with enough compassion to try and learn...how...' He stopped, gestured awkwardly with his left hand, shrugged. 'Well, you might be sufficiently understanding to...hear me out...'

Unable to speak, Katherine nodded, blinking hard. She cleared her throat, managed a smile.

'And when do you say you arrived?'

'Last evening; by hired carriage from the station to your home. Then courage deserted me. I walked for a time, round the tarn here—telling myself the worst that could happen would be that I'd be shown the door. Only that wasn't the worst—and I knew it. I dreaded having you turn from me again. But you didn't, did you?' His arm about her shoulders tightened, as they descended the hill.

'What did you do—since you daren't knock on the door?'

'Walked some more—thought, a great deal—slept, just a little.'

'But where?'

Lawrence chuckled. 'There's a sort of sheep-fold, I suppose, way over there—beyond the scree...'

'Oh, Lawrence, you didn't!'

'And if you mention one word of that I *will* strangle you!' Eyes grave again, he turned her to face him. 'You do know it wasn't me?'

Katherine nodded. His arm about her again, they walked on.

'I'll tell you who it was and then...'

'No, not yet,' she interrupted.

'But, my dear, you have to know. I have

to make it right—if I can. I can't go on living like this...'

'You won't have to, Lawrence. Later, I'll listen—but not yet.'

He sat on a boulder, pulling her down beside him. 'I won't chance anything going amiss, Katherine—not now I've found you.'

'One moment, Lawrence,' she insisted, 'leave it this way—there is a reason. I want you to tell me—as I've told you before I want to know everything about you. But not yet. I want to prove something to you...'

'You did, my sweet—back there. And I couldn't believe it, till I held you.'

'Oh, do listen, please. I'd made up my mind—it was uncanny—only a minute or so before you spoke. I was going to write to you, ask how you were, give you an opening to salvage whatever there was—if you thought it worth salvaging...'

Lawrence's fingers tightened on hers, and she needed no words from him. 'Only it has to be this way, Lawrence. I questioned too much before, kept doubting you; well, I've been taught a lesson. I trust you without knowing anything further. You say there are explanations—that is sufficient.'

He shook his head, then rose, drawing her with him. Skip, bounding up at the first sign of life, was running in circles round them. Lawrence laughed. 'He's mad—I swear it!'

'Or like me—deliriously happy.'

He frowned. 'Katherine, don't be too incautious; don't make decisions you'll regret later. I can't lose you twice, it'd finish me.'

'You won't lose me.'

As they wandered hand in hand down the hillside, she asked how long he could stay.

'I wish I could say, "until I've persuaded you to return to Masterton Hall," but I can't—there has to be a time limit. I must go back tomorrow—to be in court the day following.'

'In court?' She took a swift breath, trying to steady her uneven pulse.

'You see—there are things you must know. Too many things out of my past. They must be cleared, as I told you before. So that when...if—' he paused and then sighed—'if you marry me, it'll be with everything wiped clean, starting afresh; I won't have it any other way.'

'But you can stay overnight—so my

family may get to know you?'

'I can't imagine they'll extend a very warm welcome!'

'You don't know them. They'll love you—because I do!'

'When they know how I've driven you away—made you miserable?'

'They were told nothing.'

'You must have said something...'

'That I'd come home to rest.'

Lawrence halted and caught her to him, kissing her again. 'Your loyalty is encouraging. It gives me new heart—hope for the future.'

'For *our* future, Lawrence.'

'There you ago again! Katherine, what has got into you? You must treat this seriously. I'm sorry, my love, but it is very serious—when I've faced that court, you may not wish even to know me.'

'Nonsense!'

They had reached the cottage gate, and he hesitated. 'Do I take you strolling past here, so I've time to tell you what it's all about?'

'No, you do not—not yet awhile,' she replied, firmly, leading the way to the door.

It was breakfast-time in the tiny kitchen,

which surprised Katherine; she seemed to have been away for hours.

Somehow, during that rather strange meal, Katherine's parents learned Lawrence Rushton was not only her employer but the man she loved. As conversation progressed, introductions led to a cross-questioning, which Lawrence accepted good-naturedly. When Mr Sutcliffe left for the farmyard, however, and Clare departed schoolwards, Katherine noticed Lawrence appeared thankful. He nodded towards her mother's back at the sink.

'Where can we talk, Kate?' he whispered.

'A walk on the moors will invigorate you, after your restless night!' she suggested, laughingly.

Skip fairly sprang along through the heather as they walked, suddenly scarcely speaking. They gained the crown of the moor, pausing to admire the view over ranges of hills to distant, even wilder heights.

The sun was warm now. Katherine touched Lawrence's arm. 'There's a hollow, see—sheltered from the wind. Let's sit.'

For a long time she felt his eyes on her, but didn't meet them, simply waiting until he was ready.

'I love you like this, Kate,' he eventually confessed. 'Out in the open—away from the cares of my home.'

'Cares...?' she began.

He sighed. 'That wretched place...'

'Do you really hate it as much as that?'

'Sometimes. But there have been occasions—at the organ, in the drawing-room, only having to raise my head to see you—when it might have been...home. And having you beside me at that party was wonderful, till it turned sour on us.'

'It'll be like that again, Lawrence, with nothing to sour it.'

'If you can accept the truth.'

'Don't spoil it; this is my beautiful day—my love is here—he is come to take me home.'

Lawrence touched her fingers with his lips. 'If you wish to come—when you've heard everything.'

'You're not very romantic.'

'Life isn't, Kate—certainly mine isn't. And you must listen—at least, to this...' He paused, as though now he'd come to the telling of it, he dreaded the consequence. 'There is to be an exhumation. At my request. There have been certain...rumours since Samantha died...'

'So, Rivers *was* blackmailing you.'

'He—and another, yes. It didn't alarm me greatly. I could pay, while I continued working, and I love my work. There was money enough to go on paying for the rest of my life, if the need arose. I'd no guilt weighing me down, and didn't care—then—what people whispered. Then you entered my life: I learned what treasure there is in the love and comfort of a good woman. I...wanted you. So, everything changed. I had to stop these accusations before they drove you, my love, away.'

Lawrence hesitated, gnawing at his lip, then continued. 'I tried to buy them off, once and for all; I'd have given them anything, excepting the house... Well, they took what money I had and returned for more. It couldn't go on. I tried—you might remember—to write more speedily, to accede to their demands. But that's no way...'

Again he stopped, staring beyond her to the hills, then appeared to collect himself.

'What I ought to do was so obvious I wondered I hadn't thought of it before. I searched until I found a solicitor willing to defend me if...if I'm charged with murder.'

'You wouldn't be.'

'Ha!'

'So that was the reason for those business visits to London?'

Lawrence nodded. 'Partly. He took some finding—the evidence is weighted heavily against me.'

'But, my dearest, why?'

'I alone know what occurred in that room the night of the fire. It's my word against theirs—and numerous witnesses could testify I'd every reason for being murderously angry with Samantha.'

'But I don't understand...'

'I know—that's why I've got to tell you. Be patient with me: I came because of this. Listen, Katherine, I love you—want more than anything to marry you. But this is why I wouldn't do so earlier, why I'm not asking you to come back with me today. Stay here, with the people who love you. When—*if* I come through, I'll return, take you home—we'll have such a wedding!'

'Now, Lawrence—please...' Katherine, in tears, pressed her face against him. 'I must be with you.'

He shook his head. 'I'm sorry—no. I will not give you my name till I know it will sit honourably on your shoulders. I cannot leave you, Kate, to face my disgrace.'

'What disgrace?' she demanded indignantly. 'You've said you've nothing on your conscience.'

'I know that and, thank God, you seem to believe it; but others won't. No, Katherine, it's my way—or not at all.'

'But I will return with you, to be in court.'

'Alone? Oh, Kate!'

'There'll be others—on your side...witnesses to the fire.'

'Two—Rivers and Barnabas.'

Barnabas? Where had she heard that name before?

'You mean there's nobody to speak up for you?'

Lawrence looked down at her hand, clasped in his. 'Only those two know about the exhumation—or what might follow.'

'You shall not endure this alone. I will come—you shall not stop me.'

Lawrence looked hard into her eyes. 'You're set on this, I see. Very well, Kate, I'll be glad you're there. I came hoping for...some indication of your continued faith in me—to uphold me. This...this devotion is beyond my dreams. Your strength makes me seem weak, I...' His voice faltered, but he took charge again, continued, 'But I order you—order, mark you—to give your name to no one in that courtroom. No newspaper reporters, absolutely no one. I will not expose you to scandal. Do you understand?'

Katherine nodded, raising shining eyes to his. Although perturbed by the ordeal Lawrence must face, she was above everything thankful to be with him.

Beside the tarn again, he put a gentle hand to her head, holding her close. 'How fortunate I am—to be warmed by your love, cheered by your smile—and heartened by your trust.'

Before they reached the gate, Katherine's hold on his arm tightened. 'Lawrence, it'd be better for you, wouldn't it, if we departed for Kent today?'

'What?' He sounded astonished. 'How will you pack your trunk so speedily?'

She smiled serenely. 'I shall not. I will take only sufficient clothing for the next few days. Mother will send on the rest. We must go home to Masterton.'

ELEVEN

George smiled on seeing Katherine, when meeting them at the railway station. 'I'm pleased you've come—and Janet will be delighted.'

'We're all delighted, George,' Lawrence remarked, his hand at Katherine's elbow, assisting her into the brougham.

On Lawrence's insistence, they had brought Skip, who settled between their feet. Katherine noticed Lawrence's smile as he contemplated the animal.

'What are you thinking?'

'So—now you've a black dog—matching that mare of yours.'

'How is Midnight?'

He shrugged. 'She'll be somewhat livelier on renewing acquaintance with you.'

'How I hated leaving her,' Katherine sighed. 'I nearly turned back.'

'Whilst I refused to fetch her myself, sending one of the lads instead. Then every time I went into the stables I tried to ignore her. You understand, Kate, how bitter life was without you. I've maybe kept some things from you, but not—for a long time—my feelings. About my emotions I've tried to be honest.'

'Take heart, Lawrence, we need only emerge from that courtroom ordeal now, to be free of every problem.'

'Yes.' He appeared thoughtful. 'And now I can endure it.'

'Now?'

'Knowing you'll be waiting for me afterwards.'

'You'd have faced that still, even if I'd refused to see you.'

But Lawrence was shaking his head.

'Lawrence,' Katherine's eyes narrowed. 'What do you mean?'

'It is simple enough. Cast back your mind, Kate—was I a happy man when first you saw me?'

She did not answer.

'Well?' he persisted.

Katherine shook her head. 'But...?'

'Without you, there was a far easier escape. I had contemplated the alternative already, only...that would've been only if...' he sighed and continued quietly, 'if there'd have been no hope of happiness with you.'

'Lawrence! You wouldn't have...?'

'Even left-handed, I could scarcely miss at point-blank range!'

Her hand flew to his arm. 'Oh, my dear...'

He smiled at her. 'Don't trouble yourself. That is all dismissed. I have much to live for...'

It was a clear, moonlit night and, nearing Masterton Hall, Katherine sat forward, eager for her first glimpse of the house.

Observing this, Lawrence shook his head, amusedly. 'How can I hate the place when you're so fond of it! And I admit to fighting certain parties who wanted me hanged to lay their hands on it.' He paused. 'However, I've made...arrangements, preventing it going to them. I'll tell you about that once we arrive.'

While George was opening the huge gates, Sarah appeared at her door. Katherine waved and the woman came running to them.

'Why, Miss Sutcliffe, I'm ever so glad you've come back!'

'You see,' Lawrence asserted, as they continued up the drive, 'how everyone is happy to have you here.'

He ordered George past the front door

and round to the stables. 'You can turn in now,' he said, smiling at the coachman's surprise; 'I'll attend to things here.'

Lawrence opened the stable door. 'Midnight,' he called, 'look who I've brought for you...'

Katherine rushed to fling her arms round the black mare's neck.

Presently, aware of Lawrence's scrutiny, she glanced towards him. He laughed.

'I'm glad there's one creature here that you've missed whilst away in Yorkshire!'

'Oh, Lawrence!' she exclaimed, going to him. His lips found hers, lingering on them. He gazed into her eyes.

'I shall try—pray God I'm not prevented —to thank you for returning. No words adequately express my gratitude. You make what has to be endured...bearable. And it's of that visit to court that I must speak. I'm grateful you're determined to be with me. But, my sweet, it deepens my concern for you. If, following the exhumation, I were charged with murder, you'd be returning here alone.' He hesitated. 'You do love this house, don't you?'

'It was like coming home just now.'

'And so it is—and would be, whatever the eventuality. You'd be mistress here.

You see, Kate, I've willed it to you.'

Katherine was astounded. 'Lawrence, you shouldn't have.'

A tiny smile tugged at the corner of his mouth: 'Are you telling me what to do with my own property? Listen, Kate—we hope to live out our lives here, together. If we're denied that, there's nobody else to whom I'd leave it.'

'Have you forgotten, Simon?'

He shook his head. 'I'm never allowed to. Don't worry, he's provided for.'

He drew her to him again. 'So, you're back with me—and with my problems. Bless you, my Kate. Try not to wrestle with them all night! You need rest, we both do, to face what's ahead.'

★ ★ ★ ★

Tired by travelling and excitement, Katherine did indeed sleep, awakening at dawn to glance contentedly round the familiar room.

She'd never cease marvelling that Lawrence cared sufficiently to fetch her home; that he'd declared life without her wasn't worth contemplating; that her love encouraged him through this ordeal.

And what an ordeal! How he must have suffered already—at the hands of his blackmailers, and thinking ahead to the possible outcome of the exhumation—but if he faced a murder charge...! Katherine bit her lip. She must be strong now...must dismiss the vision of a lone figure, cross-questioned, with nobody to give evidence on his behalf.

Her worries were interrupted by a rap on the door. Opening it, she found Isobel holding a jug of hot water, and a note.

Dear Miss Sutcliffe,
(the note ran)

Me and my John have been so anxious about the goings on here. We saw them take a body from the church vault, and can guess whose it was.

People in the village are saying Mr Rushton must face charges about his wife's death. We pray that isn't true, but if it is, he should do more to clear himself. He is making no effort to find witnesses to what happened the night of the fire. We were up at the house, and John saw more than most people reckon. We'd do anything to help the master, but don't know how.

Could you maybe talk to him, tell him we are with him, and will help all we can.
Sarah Saunders.

Katherine gave a sigh of relief. Here it was—the first sign of someone coming out on Lawrence's side. She was tempted to knock on his door and show him the note, but decided against that. Disappointment would be bitter if it came to nought. Instead, she'd discover what John and Sarah knew, then impart the news to him.

Quickly she dressed, crept past Lawrence's room, down the staircase, and out of the house. Already her heart was beating faster; supposing they had substantial evidence—their word might prevent charges being made. She offered up a hasty prayer that it would be so, as she hurried through the estate.

Katherine shuddered passing the copse where she'd struggled with her attacker, and recalled Lawrence hadn't yet revealed her assailant's identity. Today she would ask him, but not until she'd done everything possible to establish his innocence.

Finding the grass wet with dew still, she

was surprised John was already wielding the pitchfork in the meadow. They exchanged a wave but she didn't stop. The note was from Sarah, she'd go to her.

Nerves taut as a spring, Katherine approached the lodge. 'I'll soon know now,' she thought. Some movement in nearby bushes attracted her attention, but before she could investigate the lodge door opened.

Sarah smiled. 'I'm that glad to see you, Miss—come right in, sit down...I'd a feeling you'd be here at once, the kettle's on. Have you spoken to the master yet?'

'Not yet, Sarah, I...well, wanted to discover what you knew first. So he wouldn't be disappointed.'

Sarah's old eyes met hers sympathetically. 'That's just like you, Miss Sutcliffe. Well, I think what John saw would help a lot. You see, Rivers got to that room...' she paused, kettle poised over the teapot: 'You heard about the fire, did you?'

'Lawrence—Mr Rushton told me.'

'Rivers ran through the gallery; but he wasn't the only one who'd noticed crackling and the blaze. We were living up at the Hall then, over the stables. Normally we'd have been in bed long since, wouldn't have known a thing, only that night there'd been a big dinner on. They'd used the ballroom, nigh on a hundred guests they'd had, but that wasn't unusual in them days.

'We stayed very late, tidying up. We was all a bit upset, like—grumbling about her, because there'd been some bother on. The meal wasn't served quick enough for her ladyship's liking. Well, because we was annoyed, talking it over among ourselves, clearing up took longer.'

Katherine stilled her urge to tell the woman to come to the point. She thought she'd die of anxiety before then.

'I was going to go to my bed when John remembers he'd not checked the doors. That was his responsibility then. One was round the East side, in the part as is ruined now. So, *he* discovered the fire, as well as Mr Rivers. It was well alight—smoke billowing through broken windows, sparks flying up off the roof. The rooms there were extra high, with no attics over them. Anyway, John rushed inside and up a flight of steps...'

'I know the one.'

Sarah gave her a surprised look, before continuing.

'Opening the door he saw Mr Lawrence wrapping his wife in the curtains, trying to put out the flames. John called to him, but he didn't hear, with the noise of the fire, him being so upset, and all.'

Sarah passed Katherine a cup of tea, then went on. 'She was still alive then, John heard her moaning. He tried to get into the room and aid the master, but the heat was too fierce. John did try, Miss...'

'All right, Sarah. Go on now...'

'He shouted to Mr Lawrence that he'd fetch help. John glanced back—the master had her in his arms then, coughing as he was with the smoke, staggering towards the gallery.'

It was true—exactly as Lawrence had related. Katherine smiled.

'He wouldn't have done that, would he now—' Sarah asked—'if he'd meant her any harm?'

'Of course he wouldn't.'

'And do you think it might be some use?'

'Might? There's no doubt. You see, all along, it seems to have been Rivers's words against Mr Rushton's.'

'And Mr Barnabas—but for him, that there Rivers...'

That name again.

'Sarah—who is this Mr Barnabas?'

'You mean you don't know?' Sarah looked disbelievingly at her, then shook her head. 'You'd better ask Mr Lawrence; it's not for me to tell. But, like I said, he was the only other witness. What a night that was, Miss. They managed to put the fire out, after sending for Dr McLaren. Only there was nothing they could do for the mistress. Never regained consciousness. Perhaps it's as well—badly burned she was. They took the master off, said they might manage to save his poor hand; but you know what happened. A crying shame, the way he tried to save that...woman! Fair plucky he was, too, all the time he was waiting for the doctor. I know. Sitting in my kitchen, he was. Couldn't stop shivering, see, what with the pain and shock—and it was warm enough there, from the range, still. He knew what was going on, talked lucidly all the time. And never a murmur of complaint.'

Sarah smiled suddenly. 'There's lots as say as he's a hard man, but that's as maybe. I know he's a brave one.'

Katherine drained her cup. 'I'll hear the rest some time, Sarah, I'd like to... And

I'm glad you were there to help look after Mr Rushton. Now, though, I must tell him of this—quickly. I'll speak to John on my way, perhaps he'll walk back with me.'

'It's only since the fire Mr Rushton's changed, you know,' Sarah persisted, accompanying her to the door. 'Seemed as if he trusted nobody. That hurt, but we—John and me—put it down to the shock. It wasn't till this trouble started we wondered if somebody'd been...well, threatening him all along. I said to John then, "Maybe that's why he's turned in on himself. It's up to us to show there's someone'll speak up for him." '

'I'm very relieved, Sarah—and he will be. If this clears his name, we'll never be able to thank you.'

Leaving the lodge, Katherine experienced a great lightening of her heart. Seeing John still at work, she hailed him. He acknowledged with a wave, and she waited by the hedge while he crossed the meadow.

An arm came round her throat from behind, so quickly she'd scarcely a chance to cry out before her breath was taken. A hand seized one of her flailing wrists, but she struggled frantically to free herself.

This time she was not going to panic, rendering her attacker's task easier.

She turned slightly, attempting to get an elbow into his ribs, and managed to wrench herself away from the arm that was threatening to choke her. She swung round, using all her weight, ducking. With only the wrist ensnared, she thought she might break free, but he caught her hair, holding her by it.

Angry, as much as terrified, Katherine looked into his face. Brown, almost black, his eyes met hers, unflinchingly—in complete antagonism.

'Lawrence...I don't believe it!'

He laughed in her face.

'No, no!' she screamed, every part of her protesting against what sight revealed. He mustn't be responsible for these attacks.

He studied her expression, gloating over her misery; jerked her closer by the hair, till she felt his rapid breath on her forehead. Abruptly, he released her. She watched him reach down to his side, his eyes never leaving her.

Katherine waited, as one hypnotized, immobile, expecting some word, turning this nightmare into a macabre joke. But he only laughed. She noticed the riding-whip tucked in his boot. Its lash cracked through the air, as he swung it near her face.

'Now for some sport,' he snarled, 'before we stop your over-generous love, for ever!'

He swept the lash sharply across her cheek, but Katherine felt no pain; only horror and disbelief.

'Lawrence,' she began, urgently. 'You're not yourself, you're ill, deranged...'

'Deranged, eh?' His eyes flashed loathing, but fear as well now. He caught her by the throat again; she felt the blackness taking her...

With a tremendous snapping of branches, John plunged through the hedge and hurled himself at the man. Cowering in the ditch, she raised her head to see John lunge, with the pitchfork, at her assailant's throat.

'John, don't!' Katherine screamed, then knew no more.

★ ★ ★ ★

She opened her eyes slowly, hardly daring to look about her. Sarah moved from the rocking-chair to the sofa where Katherine lay.

She tried to smile, felt the weal left by that whip—and remembered.

'Lawrence?' she asked, hoarsely, as Sarah reached her, 'is he...did John kill him?'

'Of course not, Miss Sutcliffe, what are you thinking of?'

'But I saw him—John came to my aid when he attacked me. I saw it, I tell you.' She sobbed hysterically. 'Why, Sarah, why does Lawrence want me dead? He says these things about loving me and then this happens—as it did before. Oh, it's terrible, terrible. It's still the same. Why, Sarah, why?'

Tears precluding further words, she clung to the older woman. At last Sarah said, soothingly, 'You've had a nasty fright, Miss, that's all. It'll be all right—you'll see.'

'It won't—ever, because Lawrence hates me. I don't know what I've done, but he wants to get rid of me!'

'Now, you listen to me,' Sarah began, firmly, sitting on the sofa and putting an arm round her. 'I told you from the start—you've got to trust him. I know a fine man when I sees one, and I've been with the master long enough. He loves you, Miss—more, perhaps, than he's ever loved anybody. And he's straight as they come. He'd no more harm you than...'

'But he *did*, I tell you, it was him. I prayed it wasn't, but I saw him—heard his voice.'

Sarah sighed. 'Didn't you notice anything else? That whip—which hand was it in?'

Interrupted by loud knocking, she went to answer the door. Katherine lay back against the cushions, trying to concentrate on Sarah's words. She couldn't quite recall, but was almost sure the whip had been in his right hand. It had caught her left cheek. She fingered it.

Voices murmured on at the door. She could hear Sarah's; the other was a man's but was hushed and, from this distance, unrecognizable.

In a few quick strides, Lawrence reached the sofa, took her hand, went down on one knee.

'Katherine—thank God!' he exclaimed, fervently.

She stared in amazement at him. He was his normal self, eyes full of concern, and love. She gazed uncomprehendingly.

'Kate, my love—listen, while I tell you about Barnabas...'

At last. She'd learn who he was, where he came into the matter. But why now...?

'He's my brother—my twin.'

So that was it. 'You mean...?' Already she was aware of her smile.

'We are very alike.'

'Oh, thank heaven, thank heaven!' Katherine flung her arms round his neck, burying her head in his shoulder, to find gentle fingers stroking her hair.

'But why, Lawrence,' she asked, drying her eyes, 'why did you not speak of him sooner?'

He shook his head, looking away. 'For years we were forbidden to mention his name, and since then...' He closed his eyes, briefly, then turned to her again: 'I will tell you all, dearest, only believe I could not bear to utter the word "Barnabas".'

'Later, later will do...' Katherine took a deep breath. 'But it was him...and the other time...'

Lawrence nodded. 'Because of me—all my fault.'

'That isn't important,' she interrupted, 'don't you see? I knew it couldn't be you—yet there you were—or so I thought. I fought against reason, for it declared you wanted me out of the way.'

'And now you know I don't—that I only want you here, as close as this.'

'Lawrence, is Barnabas...?'

He nodded. 'Dying, I'm afraid. John came swiftly to your aid—thank the Lord!' Again he avoided her eyes. 'I don't know what I ought to feel. My brother...but I can't. Maybe because for years he's been lost to me. I was...startled, that's all, seeing him injured. It was always like looking in a mirror... But there's no feeling—nothing.'

'Why *me* though? What possible threat could I have been?'

'I imagined, at first, they intended intimidating me through you, the only way they could touch me.'

'And wasn't that it?'

He shook his head. 'The servants had the rumour—it soon spreads. They believed there'd be another child at Masterton, didn't they? Legitimate, or otherwise.'

'But Simon's the heir, surely?'

'Yes, but...' Lawrence shrugged. 'I'll explain later, at the house, where you'll be safe. Though Rivers is the only one to fear now, and I doubt if he'll appear. You'll be all right with Sarah—I'll fetch the brougham.'

'Don't leave me—I can walk.'

'After all you've endured? I think that unwise.'

'Let me, please. I'd prefer it. If I find it too much, then you can get the carriage.'

Lawrence smiled. 'You've a will of your own; what am I to do with you?'

He drew her to her feet. 'Come then...thank Sarah, and I will, then we'll be on our way.'

'Lawrence—about John,' Katherine enquired, remembering. 'What will happen?'

'About his wounding Barnabas? It was plain enough. Barnabas attacked you, John came to your rescue. John's with the police now; I told them what had happened, after sending George for them.' He frowned. 'It does mean you must endure interrogation, I'm afraid. But they said that could wait till you're recovered from the shock.'

'I am well now, if they want, if it'll help John...'

'We'll see. They'll come to the house when they're ready.'

They took leave of Sarah, Lawrence assuring her that the questioning of her husband would be a mere formality. Then they began walking back through the park.

Katherine started, seeing the recumbent figure Dr McLaren was tending.

Lawrence's arm tightened about her. 'The doctor said he'd have him moved...'

Laughter rang through the trees to their right and, turning, Katherine saw Simon, with Janet hard on his heels, racing towards them.

'Oh, no!' Lawrence exclaimed. 'He mustn't see...' He broke off and called, 'Simon—come here, son...'

Eagerly, the boy ran to him and Lawrence gathered him into his arms, hiding the boy's face against his chest.

'Take him another way round, Janet, will you?' He jerked his head towards the injured man.

Lawrence looked down at the boy, ruffled his hair, rather awkwardly. 'Run along with Janet—I'll see you soon...'

His face was pale when he stood erect, and Katherine observed a softening of the lines round his mouth. 'Poor little fellow—he'll be an orphan soon...'

'An orphan?' Katherine was puzzled.

'You haven't guessed then?'

'You mean he isn't yours? But he's so like you...'

'...*and* Barnabas.'

'Oh.' What else could she say? But she was glad—glad Lawrence hadn't treated his own son so harshly, only...

'Let's return to the house.' Lawrence put

an arm round her shoulders again. '*I* need to sit down, so you must—to say nothing of not yet having breakfasted.'

★ ★ ★ ★

Lawrence glanced up from his plate and smiled. 'You see, you were able to eat. Are you ready now, to listen...?'

Katherine nodded. 'I'm almost restored. This bacon is good—who cooked it?'

'Janet, I should think—she's a Jack-of-all-trades since Mrs Hawkins left.' He clapped a hand to his forehead. 'That was why I went to the lodge. I didn't care what meals were like while you were missing. But in bed this morning I concluded something must be done about the domestic arrangements. I decided to ask Sarah to take over the house again. Oh, well—I'll speak to her afterwards.'

'Did Sarah tell you—why I was there?'

'There wasn't time.'

'John saw what happened, the night of the fire.'

'He what...?' A wavering smile touched his lips; he leaned forward.

'He came through that east door,

climbed the stairs, opened your study door. He called to you, but you couldn't have heard...'

'I certainly did not. Go on...'

'He couldn't reach you. But he saw you trying to extinguish the flames, carrying her to safety. Oh, Lawrence, he'll stand up in court, he'll... Oh, I'm so delighted.'

'That may not be necessary—now. When Barnabas has...gone, I don't think Rivers will carry out the threat to make me face a murder charge.'

'Is that how Rivers comes into it—with Barnabas?'

Lawrence nodded. 'It began years ago...' He hesitated, took a deep breath: 'We were...six years old. There was a swing, out on the terrace. One dreadful day, we were called in for tea—but Barnabas refused to leave the swing. Nanny said we would ignore him. She was buttering bread when we heard the screams. I ran downstairs after her. Barnabas was on the ground unconscious. For weeks he knew no one—then, gradually, he returned to normal. Or so we thought.'

'But...?'

'First it was a pheasant, found with its neck wrung, then...a young deer, its head caught in a noose, then...Lord, it was awful!'

Katherine saw how the memory pained him still.

'Nanny had a love-child, Matthew, who'd been accepted by everyone from the day she brought him here, when he was a few weeks old. Matthew was almost two when—you know what children are—he borrowed a toy fort belonging to Barnabas and somehow smashed the thing. Barnabas flew into such a rage it took Father as well as Nanny to quieten him.

'Next morning,' Lawrence swallowed hard, 'Matthew was found, his skull fractured, beneath the nursery window.'

'Oh, God!'

'Nanny was distraught, we all were, but believed it was an accident until... Barnabas boasted to me that he'd pushed the boy.'

'No!'

'I had to tell somebody. That night Barnabas was taken away—to a special place, they said. And Father forbade mention of his name. He was an influential man—when he ordered the local people to forget Barnabas existed, it was so.'

'Then how...' Katherine started asking,

and Lawrence snorted.

'I was too soft. After Father died, I let Barnabas return, though keeping his presence here a secret from the villagers. He was supposedly cured. Father's will, after provision for Mother made the two of us joint heirs. I believed that, allowed to pursue my writing, nothing else would disturb me.'

'And Barnabas has been here, concealed, all these years?'

'Indeed not—he soon grew restive and demanded his share at once. The family solicitor drew up a document in which he waived his claim on the house, the whole estate, for an equivalent amount of money. He went off—to the Continent, initially, then heaven knows where—but always gambling, keeping his women happy...' Lawrence laughed, mirthlessly. 'Always women in his life—and always the same kind, like the one you mistook for Samantha: blue eyes, fair hair...' His eyes blazed angrily, he lowered their lids for a second and then continued, quietly. 'He returned from time to time—when his money ran out.'

'Ran out? But...' Katherine's Yorkshire thrift was outraged by such irresponsibility.

'Yes, it was a considerable sum. But when my brother was destitute I finally gave him a home.'

'And Rivers?'

'*And* Rivers—because Barnabas claimed he kept him out of trouble. So we made Rivers our man-servant and tried to live as an ordinary family—within the confines of the estate—outside it, still, he no longer existed. And I was too preoccupied to worry overmuch about him, having only recently married Samantha.'

Lawrence rose to stand at the window, his back to her. 'I didn't know my brother! He wanted—my bride. I wouldn't see it at first, told myself he was making her feel one of the family. One of the...!' He almost choked over the words. Katherine went to slide her hand through his arm.

'I'm sorry...'

'I'm not,' he replied, at length. 'I'm thankful now it resolved itself this way. Without his return, the subsequent revelations of what...she was, the dreadful consequences...there'd have been none of this.' He turned to her. 'I'd never have known there were other women who, unlike her, give instead of grasp. Women who love...not wisely, but well; eh, my dear?'

351

'Love...happens, whether we will it or no.'

He raised an eyebrow. 'So it was against your will?'

Katherine laughed. 'At first. I didn't even like you, but as that icy wall around you began to thaw, I became quite fond of my unpredictable, but always interesting, employer.'

'But the love, Kate, when did that start?'

'Now that is a question!'

'I'd like to know.'

She felt her colour rising: 'When you began being honest with me...' Her hand went to his right arm.

His mouth, crushing hers, stopped her. 'And I was convinced it would keep you off.' He continued holding her, whispering against her hair. 'I didn't know there was such tenderness, she...' He sighed, then went on: 'I was younger than my years—naïve. The people in my books had been more real to me than girls. Samantha, when we met, seemed like something from a fairy-tale. Dainty, pretty, delightful—when she wanted something. First it was me—or the house, we went together, you see...' His voice was hard, bitter.

'Once we returned from our honeymoon tour, I discovered her true self. Impatient with the servants, excepting Rivers—when he came I believe she imagined he added a certain...tone. I used to watch her, watching him, when we were entertaining, sensing her satisfaction as he impressed. Oh, many's the time he's won me compliments for his exquisite bearing. He'd have been excellent—in a palace. Only this wasn't...and neither was it a home. Indeed, as time wore on, I felt I was the one out of place. She and Barnabas were always laughing together, whispering in corners, eyeing each other across the room... She even insisted he had portraits painted, installed alongside mine...'

'Poor Lawrence.'

'I wasn't giving her what she wanted. She had my money...' He glanced around. 'All this...but she'd found I wasn't her kind. Barnabas was. I soon learned that what I'd once thought of as her special way with me was her way with all men—and particularly my brother. Those blue, coquettish eyes sought his now, not mine; although I did not recognize the full significance of what was happening then. I told myself she was a flirt. I didn't like the idea, but I could live with it. Later, I learned something I couldn't live with.'

'Simon?'

Lawrence nodded, biting his lip. He released her and walked away, towards the sideboard. He poured himself a drink, an unusual requirement so early in the day, and a clear indication of distress.

He returned to sit at the head of the table, toying with his glass before drinking from it.

'Vivid as my imagination was, I'd never seen myself as a father. But when I first glimpsed that infant something happened inside me.' He was deeply moved; Katherine went to sit near him. 'I could have wept—he was red, wrinkled, and screaming like the very devil, but he won my heart from that moment. I was a fool over the boy—fooled!'

Lawrence reflected, then went on. 'The party the night of the fire celebrated his Christening next day. All through dinner, Samantha looked radiant, excited, more beautiful than I'd ever seen her. But nothing pleased her; she complained about the food, the way it was served—then went on to tell everyone how I neglected her. You know what I'm like when I'm working—but I'd warned her, from the start, what she was marrying.'

'And...' Katherine prompted, for he was silent again.

The glass went to his lips once more, then he continued. 'She began hinting—about her and Barnabas. The first time he'd been present before guests, I'd introduced him as recently returned from abroad. Then it happened. Barnabas was to be one of the godfathers. Somebody was ribbing him about taking on a serious responsibility. That's when she announced, her eyes challenging me: "Barnabas is responsible for Simon." I couldn't believe my ears! Looking round the table, I saw embarrassment on every face, and the gasp that sounded confirmed it to be more than my imagination. I told myself Samantha had had too much wine—that it was a particularly tasteless joke. Until we were alone—and I taxed her with it.'

'Oh, Lawrence...' Katherine sighed, feeling what he must have felt.

'She laughed in my face. "Calculate it yourself—he was conceived during one of your precious visits to your publishers." I tried to believe that could not be. But I knew it was possible—that she had it in her to do that to me. Each time I look at the boy, I see her mouth reminding me, and *his* eyes, his hair—so nearly mine, but not!'

He looked up and Katherine drew in her breath at the sadness in his eyes. 'I did try with Simon, after you came—because you despised my treatment of him.'

'Lawrence, I shouldn't have—I was entirely wrong.'

'And wasn't I? Punishing an innocent child because I saw Barnabas in every tiny wilful action. Anyway, Samantha and Barnabas were leaving after the Christening. But Simon would remain, to inherit. Maybe they intended my demise, planned to return... At least, I anticipated her taking the manuscript: she'd been unduly interested in its completion. I realized she and Barnabas would have to raise money somehow.'

'But Mr MacAndrews wouldn't have...'

'...paid him, masquerading as me? Come, Kate—*you* know how easily he was mistaken for me.'

'Oh, yes.'

'Well, that didn't arise. Maybe that would have been less painful. It's not...

356

pleasant, being blackmailed, by your own flesh...'

'So that's gone on since the fire...?'

Lawrence nodded. 'Barnabas made off immediately afterwards, but returned the day of the funeral—demanding money; he and Rivers had this tale that the fire and Samantha's death were not accidental, but my revenge for being made a laughing-stock. And its plausibility could be upheld by everyone at that dinner.'

'And now we've the answer.' Deciding Lawrence must brood no longer, Katherine rose.

'At last, yes—I think that's possible. You wouldn't believe, Kate, how long it's seemed. Even since you came—and life has been so much better than before.'

Katherine covered his hand; Lawrence smiled, ruefully. 'I never dreamed it'd be so serious. I fondly imagined I need only wait—rid myself of all reminders. The staff here was changed—excepting Rivers, nothing would move him. Oh, Kate, Kate, I forbade mention of their names—his and Samantha's—but overlooked the constant reminder, growing daily more like the pair of them...'

'Don't, my love...'

Lawrence ignored her protest: 'Forgetting Barnabas wasn't achieved by removing portraits...'

Katherine recalled the spaces on the gallery walls.

'...even when he wasn't demanding money, he took to coming here, reserved a hotel room...'

She drew in her breath; Lawrence nodded.

'Why didn't you tell me?'

'Almost, I did—but couldn't trust myself to control my emotions. You see, he'd been here earlier that day, flaunting his latest woman, because she's so like Samantha.'

'Later then—when you'd regained your composure?'

'And have the whole story emerge—before I could prove my version?'

'How long...has Barnabas got?'

'Dr McLaren says he may linger for hours. I'll do my duty—be with him at the last.'

'Then first let's learn how John's interview with the police ended. And ask Sarah about keeping house for us. Then, more important, discuss their testifying for you.'

Lawrence shook his head. 'Something

must take precedence over that. I don't think my future is nearly so precarious now—but someone else's is.' He stood up, frowning. 'It has been for far too long. I'll rectify that. Today. It's time he knew some security, in this confusing world he's come into through no fault of his own.' He extended a hand to her. 'Come with me, Katherine.'

She was not surprised when Lawrence led the way to the nursery. Outside the door, she hesitated.

'Please...' Lawrence insisted, 'I shall need all the support I can muster.'

Simon glanced from the window-seat, where Janet, sitting beside him, was indicating pictures in a book.

Lawrence looked at them and cleared his throat. 'Er...'

Katherine exchanged a glance with Janet, moving her head almost imperceptibly towards the door. Janet handed the book to Lawrence.

'I won't be long, Simon,' she said, on her way out. 'Your father will read to you.' Katherine blessed her for her intuition.

Lawrence looked down at the book, at Simon, then to Katherine. She nodded and he crossed to sit by the boy.

'You'll have to turn the pages, I'm somewhat clumsy.'

Swallowing hard, Katherine turned away to sit at the table.

Simon gazed at Lawrence, nervously, and made as if to edge away a little. Don't move, child, Katherine prayed, holding her breath.

'This is an interesting book,' Lawrence began. 'How grown-up you're becoming.'

Simon smiled. Instead of moving away, he rested an elbow on Lawrence's leg, leaning across him to point with a chubby finger.

'This is the best story.'

'Indeed? And is this your favourite book?'

Simon nodded. 'Only I haven't got many. Only...four, I think.'

'You shall share mine—I have lots of books, some kept since I was your age. You must get Janet to...' he stopped. 'I'll take you to see them... Would you like that?'

'Yes,' Simon replied, and then added, 'please.' He pondered. 'Can Katy come too?'

Before Lawrence could answer, she went to them. 'I'm sure that's something you men can do on your own.'

She felt Lawrence's eyes entreating her, but refused to meet them.

'There's another thing,' Lawrence continued, after clearing his throat. 'You're rather old for nursery meals—you must join me in the dining-room. For...luncheon, first of all.'

Simon didn't respond. Katherine held her breath again.

She saw Lawrence ease a finger round the inside of his collar. She longed to rescue him, but knew she must not. She stared hard at the carpet.

'Father...' Simon began, tentatively, 'will...?'

'Katy will be there too,' Lawrence said quickly. 'Won't she?'

'Oh, yes.' Glistening green eyes sought Lawrence's; she smiled. 'Always.'

TWELVE

As soon as she got into bed that night, Katherine knew she wouldn't sleep. Too much had happened that day, too much hung in the balance until tomorrow.

Earlier, with Lawrence, she'd shared his optimism that nobody would make charges against him after the exhumation. She'd readily believed that, with Barnabas dying, Rivers would keep away from that court-room. But was it so simple? Supposing there was some doubt about Samantha's death—reason for the authorities to suspect it hadn't been accidental, grounds for opening an enquiry?

Katherine sighed and turned over, trying to make herself comfortable. But she felt the room was closing in, walling her in with apprehension. How would she face life if Lawrence were convicted of murder? People had been wrongly charged in the past, hanged for crimes they had not committed. Who could say this wouldn't happen to him? And if it did? How could she bear this house, with its memories, every room alive with his presence? Yet how could she not accept it—his gift, willed to her...yes, even while she was far away in Yorkshire, doubting him.

This was proof of his love, this great mansion, but would she be able to love it—sharing this home of theirs—or would it be to her, as it had been to Lawrence, a torment?

She got up and went to the window, drawing back the curtains. The moon shone, as it had last night on their return, and she gazed over the grounds. She could just make out the lake, in its encircling trees, and the Lodge, Sarah's and John's home. Bless them—for their loyalty to Lawrence, their willingness to speak on his behalf, for their aid to Katherine herself only that morning. Whatever transpired, she knew she could rely on those two. They, and others like them, would become an integral part of her life—here. Only she didn't want that, *without* Lawrence. Only at his side here would she be happy.

She sighed; dear Lawrence—employer turned lover—or almost. 'Let us not be denied fruition of that love,' she prayed. And longed to hold him.

She should be with him now, sharing this wearisome night, during which she was convinced he would sleep little. If only he had agreed to their immediate marriage. But then, even that couldn't have been arranged this quickly. She returned to bed, to toss and turn once more.

Only of late had the idea of marriage attracted her. Earlier, before knowing

Lawrence, she had scorned women who—
to her mind—had no thought beyond
getting that ring on their finger. She had
trained for a career, believing that would
be all she needed; bringing, as it would,
emancipation...

An emancipation that would be surren-
dered gladly, the moment he made her
his wife, an emancipation already almost
forgotten.

To hold him, to reassure, to comfort...
Not at some future time when he had
less need of her; but now, when he—they
both—should have mutual support. This
night she would give everything, her
whole being, if he needed that. And
if it flouted convention? She'd have no
regrets; she longed to change these prudish
restrictions, threatening to smother warmth
and understanding.

With a sound barely perceptible, even
to her over-alert ears, the door of the
next room opened—and closed again. Soft
footsteps went along to the music room.
She heard the click of a latch again—then
silence.

Katherine was out of bed in a second,
pushing feet into slippers, thrusting arms
into her robe.

Lawrence, in the huge armchair, started nervously as the door opened. A single candle lit the room. His face, in shadow, was tense, drawn—as she had known it would be.

'Kate...' he murmured, without smiling, 'I'm sorry...'

'Sorry?'

'You, also, disturbed, restless—after all you've already endured on my account.'

She shook her head, standing looking down at him. 'That's of no consequence—only this, being with you.'

He gave a laugh, devoid of humour: 'I'm foul company!'

Again she shook her head, uncertain what to do.

Lawrence, staring into the empty grate, spoke as though thinking aloud, 'I always feel nearer to you in here...'

'And I to you, when you're away.'

'It's all I ask—you and me together. One room would suffice—I need none of this. Empty of you, this mansion means nothing. I've never lived simply, that wasn't the way here, but I do love simplicity.'

'But you do live that way,' she argued, 'quietly, with your books, music, conversation...'

He smiled, fleetingly. 'Is that how you've seen it? Is it, Kate?'

She nodded, and he reached for her hand. 'Only through you. That wasn't the way with...anyone else. But you're different, you'd...'

'...marry you for one room—as you said.'

He made as if to draw her into the great chair with him, but a sharp rap sounded at the door.

Lawrence started to his feet.

'Stay where you are,' he whispered, 'anyone finding you here with me, like this, would give it the worst interpretation.'

She heard Isobel's voice at the door when Lawrence opened it.

★ ★ ★ ★

Katherine rose to meet him when Lawrence returned an hour later.

'Barnabas?'

Lawrence nodded: 'Peacefully, at the end. He...regained consciousness.'

She noticed he was bemused, seemed to smile.

'Here...' He handed her a note. 'He couldn't speak,' Lawrence was saying, 'but he was conscious,' he reasserted, 'and knew what he wanted to tell me. Read it, Kate...'

The handwriting, shaky, was scarcely discernible.

Forgive us both. Samantha devised the plot. She had to have Simon, you see, as well as me...knew you'd never relinquish your own son. We were to disappear, together—returning for Simon when you'd rejected him. Lawrence, the boy is yours—we were lovers, Samantha and I, but I could not sire a child—result of an old illness. Ask Dr McLaren. Love the boy, Lawrence. Forgive...

The words trailed off to nothing.

Katherine raised questioning eyes to Lawrence's. He nodded, 'Dr McLaren confirms it.' His voice was husky: 'So, I've further reasons to survive...God, I wish it were morning!'

'It will come—we'll wait like this for it.'

'My dear, I cannot let you. I must send you to your bed.'

'To what purpose? I wasn't sleeping.'

'Well, here, you certainly won't.'

'No matter. This is so little—when you've been so good to me.'

'I?' He sounded bewildered.

'Teaching me the organ—and to ride. Taking me all over...'

'Utter selfishness! A mass of excuses to have you with me more often. And the satisfaction of seeing you interested and—or so I hoped—happy.'

'Happy indeed—more than ever before.'

'You're a strange one!'

They talked until the candle spluttered and died, then sat on in the darkness, still talking—of Simon, of everything except the ordeal before them. Gradually, a faint glow crept across the sky beyond the uncurtained window. Katherine left Lawrence and went to gaze across the park, to the hills—crowned now with slashes of early morning light. She felt Lawrence join her, but said nothing. A flock of birds flew over.

'How free they are!' he exclaimed—then closed his eyes hastily, avoiding her scrutiny. 'You've made me love this again; so much as to make the thought of not seeing it again unbearable.'

'You'll see it, possess it,' she assured him, praying she was right, 'and possess me.'

His hand went to her shoulder, he bent to kiss her forehead. 'Thank you for being with me.' He made as if to leave her, and couldn't. Swiftly, he pulled her to him, holding her close.

Katherine spoke at last, forcing her voice to be unemotional. 'We must get ready now, have breakfast. Then we'll be on our way...'

She took a final glance from the window. 'When we return, we'll take the horses out...'

★ ★ ★ ★

All the way into town, in the brougham, Lawrence sat upright, one leg crossed over the other, hand resting on the knee. He stared, unseeingly, out; his lips drawn into a firm line. And he didn't speak once. Several times, Katherine thought to break the silence, but did not.

Lawrence alighted first outside the imposing building, offering his hand as she stepped on to the pavement, then taking her arm. He nodded to George and, still without a word, mounted the steps to the heavy door. Beside him, unnerved as she was by now, Katherine took scant notice of her surroundings, receiving merely a vague impression of forbidding, panelled walls, dark, ugly furniture, sombre-visaged persons.

She was told to sit on an uncomfortable chair aqainst a cold wall, the only wall unpanelled.

'Wait here, I shall only be a moment,' Lawrence ordered, rapidly. He crossed to a door, knocked, had a whispered conversation with the clerk opening it, then vanished.

It was only then Katherine understood what he was about (what he'd most likely intended all along)—sparing her the possible distress of the verdict. He was seeing it through alone, after all, as she'd intended he shouldn't. The faintest of smiles touched her lips; how had she supposed to over-ride his will with her own?

For some time she stared at the heavy-framed portrait on the opposite wall. Some formally-robed dignitary, face grave and inscrutable, eyes narrowed suspiciously. Was Lawrence, at this moment, facing such a countenance?

Why, oh why, hadn't he let her go in with him? She was here to give him some...what? Strength? Maybe he'd find that only in thus sparing her. This, indeed, seemed the harder—sitting and not knowing; only...wondering, thinking, fearing...

A quarter of an hour passed. She crossed to look out on the street. Men and women going about their business. Boys and girls playing, messenger-boys running... All unheeding, uncaring, while here a man's life was suspended—in a void between happiness and...condemnation? Between life and...having life taken from him. Katherine closed her eyes against the threatening tears. Lawrence must not emerge to find her weeping.

Returning to her seat, she removed her gloves, placing them in her lap, and forced her eyes away from that depressing picture. But they only sought the clock, ticking away the minutes inexorably. Would these minutes be Lawrence's last in freedom? Was some unforgiving, unseen force working against him? Or for him—for them both?

How long had he been in there—how much longer? What was happening? She knew nothing of exhumation and what might follow. What were they saying to him, asking him, accusing...?

'Stop this,' she said, firmly, aloud, to

herself. She clasped her hands but finding them cold and clammy, unclasped them and set them, fingertips meeting, at the point of her chin. Nearby, a clock struck the hour, making her jump; she was sitting thus, some while later, when Lawrence emerged. Some way away, not the door he had disappeared through, it afforded the chance to watch him walk towards her. Even from this distance she could see how white his face was, how old he looked, ill too, as though from some debilitating sickness. 'Oh, God,' she thought, 'what is the verdict?' Surely, like this, he hadn't received a satisfactory one.

Unable to endure the suspense, she rushed to him, dropping gloves as she ran.

He laughed. Would she ever hear anything more wonderful?

'Do I still put you to such confusion that you scatter belongings to right and left when I approach?' His voice was mocking, amused, tender. He was free.

Lawrence nodded, reaching her. 'All is well, Kate. They are satisfied. Samantha died, as they stated before, by mis-adventure, with no blame attached to me.'

'Oh, thank heaven, thank heaven!' she cried, hugging him, then looked up, surprised, to find one of the sombre-visaged persons proving human and smiling.

Lawrence bade the onlooker 'Good day', and hustled Katherine outside. He stood motionless, his hand resting on her shoulder, looking up at the sky, down and up the street then across it.

He nodded, approvingly. 'It's good, Kate—all of it.' Then he took her elbow, steering her towards a nearby hotel.

She was surprised to discover it was time for luncheon. They ordered, then found neither could eat. She felt Lawrence's eyes on her while she toyed with the food.

'It's no good, is it?' he asked, smiling wryly.

Katherine shook her head. He paid the bill and they left.

They found George at the coaching inn. A smiling George, vociferous with delight that all had gone well. And still Lawrence said little, Katherine likewise, only pausing now and then to smile at each other.

'I meant to be with you,' she began, once inside the brougham.

'You were, Kate,' Lawrence responded, quietly. 'You've never been closer to me.'

'Thank you, though—for trying to spare me.'

He nodded, but said nothing, then reached for her hand. It lay in his for the rest of the journey.

Nearing Masterton, she noticed his eagerness, sitting forward in the seat, as she had only a few days previously. At the lodge, John and Sarah smiled and waved. And Katherine gave her tears their way then, for they were joyful. Lawrence's fingers caressed her own and, glancing at him, she observed the colour returning to his cheeks. He smiled again.

'I cannot quite believe it yet. That this can't be taken from me. That Rivers can't reappear with threats, that no one on this earth can spoil it.'

He ordered George round to the stables, and Katherine smiled gratefully when the coachman left them. Helping her alight, Lawrence looked long and hard into her eyes, his own serious, though not sad. Her hand, still in his, he raised to his lips, then encircled her with his arm. He kissed her, lingeringly, then buried his face against her neck.

Moving suddenly away, he called Skip, who bounded from Midnight's stall. Lawrence went down on a knee, rolled the dog playfully in the hay, then smiled up at Katherine. 'All is well now, Kate,' he affirmed. 'All is well.'

Swiftly, they saddled their horses. But before mounting, Katherine checked Lawrence's hand on the bridle. 'Won't you tell me now,' she begged. 'Tell me the whole story...'

'But I...' he started protesting, but she shook her head. 'You haven't told me all—not why you didn't, from the first awakening of our love, confide in me. A few words would have clarified everything. Why you didn't immediately tell me you could be charged with Samantha's murder. It wasn't purely because Rivers and Barnabas threatened you, was it?'

She observed his surprise—how, initially, he appeared evasive. Then she heard his deep, shuddering sigh. And yet he said nothing. He half-turned from her.

'And why, Lawrence, keep your poor mother locked away?'

Sharply, he swung round, dark eyes wary. 'When did you...?'

Katherine smiled a little. 'I can't even recall how long I've...been aware of her presence. Her screams terrified me from my first night here.'

'They've stopped now,' he said, partly to

himself, 'she's not nearly so...tormented.'

'Because she's happier about you—about the future?'

Lawrence regarded her quizzically. 'You appear to know a great deal—have you...?'

'Met her?' Katherine nodded, 'Although we have spoken together, introductions scarcely seemed in order—for her.'

'She was ill.'

'Deranged?'

Her word brought a sharp laugh from his taut lips. 'Yes, Kate.'

He awaited her reaction, fearfully. 'Now you know, what do you intend?'

She didn't understand his anxiety. 'Intend?' she shrugged. 'Why?'

'How soon will you be...leaving?' His voice sounded strangled.

'To prepare for our wedding? I thought we were marrying here?'

'Katherine'; placing a hand on her shoulder, Lawrence scrutinized her, 'you have seen that she is not...well, as the rest of us.'

'And how does that affect us? Except that I'll have you know one thing—and you may look amazed, but you can learn now that this Victorian feminine submissiveness holds no appeal for me! When I am mistress here I will have no one banished to far corners of the household.'

Suddenly, Lawrence was laughing, as though a cloud had lifted. 'You are not troubled because she is...as she is?'

'No doubt something happened, distressing her, and she...retreated within herself?'

'To think I was afraid to tell you! Oh, Katherine, what a fool I've been—how I've belittled that enormous heart you have.'

'Tell me now...'

Lawrence sank on to a heap of straw beside Reveller's stall. 'Mother was always very...aware—of atmosphere, of things one couldn't see. If she'd been born in Scotland, they'd have said she had "second sight". She was upset by the injury Barnabas suffered and further disturbed by Father's sudden death; the night of the fire she was demented. I understand she saw the blaze from her room and maybe, with her special perception, sensed that I was trapped. Since, she has needed constant supervision. The doctors advised an institution, but I refused. Here she would stay, if it meant hiring an attendant nurse and keeping her under lock and key. And it meant just that, for ages...'

'But no longer....?'

'Perhaps you're right. We will see, my dear. We'll do as you suggest and have her join the rest of the household.'

'Good. So you were not trying to conceal her from me?'

Lawrence snorted. 'Yes, I was—I had to, Kate, the moment I found myself loving you. You see, she was the second member of the family to suffer mental illness. Barnabas, abetted by Rivers, had almost convinced me...'

'Of what?'

'That insanity was an inherited family weakness...'

'Oh.'

'It isn't, Kate—believe me, it is not. I have seen doctors, specialists in disturbance of the mind, they have all assured me...'

Katherine smiled. 'That you are sane? Oh, Lawrence, I need no proof of that! But you must have suffered agony.'

'Immediately Barnabas saw how, after the fire, Mother's condition deteriorated, he threatened to convince her I'd murdered Samantha. It was still possible to communicate with her. At times she was completely lucid. I could not let her suffer further distress.'

'You paid for his silence.'

Lawrence nodded. 'Not satisfied with that, he and Rivers repeated their assertion that I'd killed Samantha in a fit of madness and then set fire to the place. They...'

'...demanded more money lest they carried the tale to the police?'

'I couldn't risk rumour of that until I'd given my statement—with a lawyer to support it. And found those willing to certify my sanity. Only then, Kate, and because I had to go on living, *for you,* I challenged Barnabas to do his worst.'

'And he did nothing.'

'True, but those days were no less awful—remember my evil temper, the way I could no longer work? The only way to ensure they held nothing over me was by requesting exhumation myself.'

Lawrence rose at that and, mounting, helped Katherine into the saddle. He laughed light-heartedly as they rode out into the sun. He coaxed Reveller to a gallop, so she had to urge Midnight on to keep pace. Round the lake they went, with Skip barking beside the horses.

At the church, when Midnight brought her to his side, Lawrence helped Katherine dismount, then, retaining her hand, silently led her inside. At the back pew he released her hand and dropped to his knees, covering his eyes. Katherine knelt beside him, feeling suddenly shy, but knowing she must be there.

After what seemed an age, Lawrence rose, slowly; he sighed, but not unhappily, '...and thank You,' he murmured, echoing Katherine's emotions.

He led her then to the altar, and turned her to face him.

'Here, my love, I'll promise everything, as soon as it's humanly possible. Until then, know this...it will be so, nothing will prevent it.' He smiled, suddenly, kissing her quickly on the mouth. 'I'm sure the good Lord will see that only as it's meant, a token of my love and good intention. He won't frown, will He, thinking it out of place here?'

Katherine shook her head, smiling as they went outside again.

They rode back, galloping, and then slowed to look all around them. Approaching Masterton Hall, Lawrence flung an arm expansively in a circle, as if to embrace the whole estate. 'I've never loved my home more than at this moment!'

Passing to the east of the house, he reined in his mare, motioning Katherine to stop.

He nodded towards the ruins. 'I think a school-room, don't you, Kate? And perhaps a study for Simon—for when he's older...'

'What a lovely idea—and, maybe, a larger nursery?'

'You spoil me already—give me a son and I shan't know how to thank you!'

'Oh, I'm sure you will,' she responded, her eyes mischievous. 'But then you may find yourself thanking me for a daughter also!'

Lawrence chuckled and flicked Reveller with the reins, making her canter towards the stables.

With Skip frisking at Midnight's heels, Katherine followed more slowly, contemplating this house she loved, and its master, ahead of her. Erect in the saddle, he rode surely—just as, now, he would go through life, with no evil threats in his mind, no inhibitions about his injury, no bitterness about anything.

As though sensing her thoughts, Lawrence sprang from the saddle on reaching the stables. He appeared ten years younger than he had that morning. He waited for Katherine and then crossed to her, his step eager. He took her reins.

'Tell you what...' He was smiling, like

a small boy anticipating a treat. 'Since we neglected luncheon, we'll toast muffins in the music room. Quite alone, as we should be. Then, my Kate—' he made her wait, his dark eyes teasing her—'we've work to do. Plans to draw up for the renovations—you'll have to help.'

He lifted her from Midnight's back, and caught her to him, his eyes still laughing. 'You may feel, my dearest Kate, that you've been here a long time already, that I've worked you hard. Let me warn you, your task is but beginning!' He kissed her lightly, his lips trembling with scarcely suppressed amusement. 'But I promise you laughter as well—and a lot of loving.'

A lot of loving.

Katherine nodded, smiling to herself. That, *he* would have. Right from the start it was all he had been lacking.

This Large Print Book for the Partially sighted, who cannot read normal print, is published under the auspices of

THE ULVERSCROFT FOUNDATION

THE ULVERSCROFT FOUNDATION

. . . we hope that you have enjoyed this Large Print Book. Please think for a moment about those people who have worse eyesight problems than you . . . and are unable to even read or enjoy Large Print, without great difficulty.

You can help them by sending a donation, large or small to:

**The Ulverscroft Foundation,
1, The Green, Bradgate Road,
Anstey, Leicestershire, LE7 7FU,
England.**
or request a copy of our brochure for more details.

The Foundation will use all your help to assist those people who are handicapped by various sight problems and need special attention.

Thank you very much for your help.